THE VACATION LODGE II

Between a rock and a hard place

D.J. WALTERS

First published in Great Britain in 2019 by:

WW

Walters Way Publishing
www.djwalterswriter.com
djwalterswriter@gmail.com

Copyright © 2018 Dionne Jennene Walters
All rights reserved.

PUBLISHER'S NOTE
This is a work of fiction. Names, characters, places and incidents are either the products of the author's imagination or are used fictitiously. Any resemblance to actual people, living or dead; events or locales are entirely coincidental.

Without limiting the rights under the copyright reserved above, no part of this publication may be reproduced, stored in or introduced into a retrieval system, or transmitted in any form, or by any means (electronic, mechanical, photocopying, recording or otherwise), without the prior written permission of both the copyright owner and the above publisher of the book.

The scanning, uploading and distribution of this book via the internet or via any other means without the permission of the publishers is illegal and punishable by law. Please purchase only authorised electronic editions and do not participate in or encourage electronic piracy of copyrighted materials. Your support of the author's rights is appreciated.

While the author has made every effort to provide accurate contact numbers and addresses (including websites and emails) at the time of publication, neither the publisher nor the author assumes any responsibility for errors, or for changes that occur after publication. Furthermore, the publisher does not have any control over and does not assume any responsibility for author or third-party websites or their content.

This book is sold subject to the condition that it shall not, by way of trade or otherwise, be lent, re-sold, hired out or otherwise circulated without the publisher's prior consent in any form of binding or cover other than that in which it is published and without a similar condition including this condition being imposed on the subsequent purchaser.

Catalogue record for the publication data:

ISBN-13: 978-1-9999276-3-9
The Vacation Lodge II by D.J. Walters
Fiction- Romance- Erotica

Manufactured and Printed by Ingram Spark
www.ingramspark.com

THE VACATION LODGE II

Between a rock and a hard place

WALTERS WAY PUBLISHING

OTHER TITLES BY D.J. WALTERS

The Vacation Lodge

For Shay Nichole & Nichole Jade;

~There is no friend like a sister and I've been lucky enough to be blessed with two ~

An unbreakable bond

with undying love

trust

honesty

and

respect

from the

very beginning

to the

very end.

REVIEWS

"Steamy and exciting"
-Pride Magazine-

"Outstanding"
-The Voice News-

"Worthy and deserving of a place in your suitcase."
-Metro News-

"It's refreshing to see an erotic thriller featuring black, mixed race and Asian protagonists"
-Cosmopolitan UK-

"The characters come alive…Be prepared to have your fantasies tantalised!"
-Online Reviewer-

"The Vacation Lodge takes our imagination to wild and wonderful places"
-Online Reviewer-

"I was hooked from the start, constantly wanting to know what happens next."
-Online Reviewer-

"Artistic, memorable and breath-taking!"
-Online Reviewer-

THE VACATION LODGE II

Between a rock and a hard place

~ Chapter 1 ~

Astonished, my eyes gaped 'round as we stood hand in hand before the glistening arches. Flurries of people quickly slipped past us and through the entrance but time stood still as we captured the beauty of it all. Golden gates lined the perimeter of the precious grounds and wrapped around the edges like solid-steel armour. Royally dressed soldiers sat on sturdy elephants. They were adorned with jewellery and fine cloths that complimented their red and golden uniform. Their bearskin hats sat tall on their head as they marked the entrance of the arches. Both soldier's salutes were as strong as their shoulder pads and they commanded the elephants effortlessly. A sovereign trumpet coerced the obedient elephants to stand to attention and sound off in unison. And the glowing bells that decorated the elephant's cloth jingled lightly as their mighty trunks rose into the air. It was eye-catching indeed.

But to us, none of that mattered. We were grateful just to be there, together. His touch felt sexy and secure as his locked fingers gently stroked the back of my hand. And my fingers couldn't help but mirror his movements. I inhaled in pleasure as our eyes met and the sparkle from the towering, golden sign reflected in his gaze. We shared a lingering kiss; one that felt so sweet, I could still taste it long after his lips had left mine.

As we stepped inside, I paused for a moment or two, taking in all of the lights and loops that was *Dazzleville*, the enchanted fairground. Emerald green grass tickled underneath my feet and spread across the expanse of the park grounds. In the distance, I saw a party of people slowly levitating into the air. Then a flood of joyful screams leapt out of their mouths as they rapidly collapsed onto ground level. A stream of hands flew up as they rushed down and around the flashing big wheel. Artlessly, a waft of whoops followed them as their voices tried to catch up to their bodies. And I watched in reverence as they were whipped up then back down on the breath-taking ride. Soothingly, the warm smell of roasting hotdogs garnished my senses as the sizzling burgers splashed against the griddle. It was heavenly. My eyes glowed as I looked up to admire Nelson and his deep dimple; gratified that I was the only woman on his strapping arm. He didn't have to but he chose me and that kept me in awe of him. When his amorous eyes peered down at me, it felt so right and I held onto him proudly as we ventured through.

Beams of light illuminated the floor in varying directions leading us to an array of rides in the funfair. We followed the red path and a wave of merriment swept through the grounds as a rush of people spun past us, seated in their Waltzer cups. The path led us to the Fantasia train ride and Nelson's cheek began to rise as we joined the queue. We waited only for a few moments before the rosy-eyed riders stepped off the train, barely noticing any of us as they passed us by. Some sat for a while, still in astonishment until the conductor had to usher them off. And my heart thumped in anticipation, not knowing what to expect. As soon as the carriage had emptied, the conductor lifted the barriers and we rushed right on. Nelson urged us to the front of the ride and strapped us both in so we were the first port of call. Tentatively, my eyes mapped my surroundings and my heart thumped even harder.

Within moments, we were transported through the wooden doors and into the darkness. For a while, it was silent and only the subtle draft of wind could be heard. Apprehensively, I tried to readjust my eyesight. "Oooooh oh…" Moans and groans started to echo through the tunnel and I expanded my eyelids as I attempted to peer around.
"Aaaah ah… a…" Sounds of pain bounced off the walls and transcended through the black hole. I couldn't see a thing! But the squeaking of the carriage wheels were clear to hear as we hobbled through the dark. Watchfully, I held on to Nelson a bit tighter and somehow, the grip on his arm made me feel a lot safer.

Suddenly, a bright light flashed on a life-sized cage. My head shot 'round. There stood a couple, locked in the cage. Her face curled up, and his, contoured. My head darted to Nelson then back to them. The grief left her mouth as she wrapped her bare body around his equally nude soul. My tongue chased the circumference of my lips. Her thick leg wound around his as his hips gyrated into her and her curly locks brushed her back as she sought his support. His skin was chocolate and glistened underneath the light. Her jaw dilated; his tongue slathering all over her breasts.

"Ooooh oh," Painful pleasure escaped from within her and propelled off the walls. My eyes gaped open in shock and my saliva began to dry. The lights flickered. The circuit shut off and I lost sight of Nelson. Blackness. My breath halted. I could feel him but could no longer see him, again. The carriage quaked as we slowed and I shuffled a little closer to Nelson. I felt a reassuring stroke on my thighs. And though I was pretty sure that we would be fine on the ride, the darkness made it even harder for me to convince myself. The carriage stopped.

There was a bright flash. My blinking doubled. The flicker played tricks on my eyes. Behind a cage, stooped a woman. She grabbed hold of the cage aggressively with a lustful look in her eyes.

Clang!

The lights went out and I immediately tugged at Nelson's thigh. My eyes searched through the black but my attempts were hopeless.

Jerk!

The carriage began to circle around.

"Aaaargh uh…" Her cry bounced through the tunnel and a gulp whipped to my eardrums. The beacon shone and I could see. My pupils adjusted in reprieve. A chiselled, mocha buttocks flexed at eye level right into her round peach and my upper lip began to steam. As he squeezed his cheeks, the sweat dripped down his bare back and seeped through my pores. Her eyes fluttered slowly as he thrust his sturdy piece in and out of her.

"Aaaaaahh ahhh…" Her moans intensified. And when he firmly held onto her bush; urging her head back, they strengthened even further. His pounds were almighty. Warmly, Nelson slid his hand over my thigh as we kept our eyes locked on the couple in the cage and my vagina began to twinge.

Slap. Slap. Slap.

The impact of his thrusting hips off her bountiful bottom was clear to hear as he charged his way into her over and over. Her hands were still wrapped firmly around the bars. Her firm breasts flounced in time with each hit and her nipples hardened as her arch flexed. The more he gripped her body with dominion, the more her juices began flowing, as did mine.

"Oooooooh!" She was gone. An elongated moan caused the beacon to shut off completely, submerging us back into blindness. But this time, I wasn't scared, I was excited. My tongue lustfully moistened my lips.

Taking advantage of the darkness, I loosened my grip on Nelson's arm and began to run my fingertips over his growing crotch. I held my breath and bit my lip intensely before advancing closer for a deep, wet kiss.

Kachoh.
Kachoh.
Kachoh.

The rocking carriage unsteadied my movements as I sought towards Nelson. Before I even had the chance, red lights flickered on over another cage. Enclosed were two women; two shapely women, wearing nothing but stilettos. Nelson's hand rose up my thighs. My walls clenched. He squeezed my meat firmly and my eyes rolled playfully. I knew he loved that shit. Our carriage slowed, then stopped, right in front of them. One sat on a tall table with her legs spread wide whilst the other dripped melting ice-cream all over her bounteous torso.

The tanned female smirked as she watched the cream drip down her breast, then stomach and straight onto her bald vagina. Her clitoris stood erect. She bit her lengthy nails in between her teeth. The standing female, who was slightly bronzer than the seated lady, carefully eyed the movements of the dripping cream. She giggled as she smoothly licked the cone then traced the trail around her tawny breast. She tasted her upstanding nipples; one of which had no ice-cream on it at all. And in the carriage, I could feel Nelson's fingers slipping in between my crotch so I opened my legs a little wider. I smoothed my hands all over his loins and felt his growing piece. Lucratively, my lashes ruffled in delight.

Smash!

She slammed the Ice-cream straight into her vagina then held her own gaping mouth in shock; as if it were an accident. But her playful, puppy dog eyes told a different story as she stared up at the tanned female who still had her legs outstretched. The sitting female stared down at her for a while, severely disappointed and the cowering female gaped back. Cream had splattered all over her. She began to examine the sloppy mess on herself, then she bit her lip. And the cowering lady that kneeled in between her legs began to smile. She licked her lips intensely before daubing her tongue all over the tanned female's erect clitoris. Her head swirled round and round as she devoured all the cream on her soaked vagina.
"Aaaahh ah…" she groaned.

Clang!

It was pitch-black, again. The carriage staggered, then slowed. His finger brushed past my nipple and my eyelids shut slowly, embracing the darkness. The train stopped. As I searched for his penis once more, he raised my hand and stuck my finger deep into his moist mouth.

"Mmmmh…" he moaned and my lip began to curl. From that sound alone, I could tell that he was enjoying himself just as much as I was. He slid a single finger over my underwear, caressing my tip and my own cream started to salivate. My legs started to separate even more and my head arched back as I embodied the sensation of him encircling my nipple and clitoris in unison. My finger slid in and out of his mouth; in time with his rhythm. I could feel his warm breath all over me and I was loving every part of it.

"Aaaahh!" A scream leapt out of my lungs. The red beacon flashed and a pulse almost lurched out of my chest. A sweating woman was staring right into me and her hot breath was dispersing all over my face. Her hands were smeared all over my body and my heart plunged into my stomach.
"Aahhh!" I grabbed hold of her perverted fingers and forced her away from the carriage. My head darted to Nelson and my mouth dropped in disgust. He was still enjoying it; the woman on the other side of the carriage. Instantly, I ripped her eager hands off Nelson's groins and shoved her away from us.

Clang!

The beacon switched off and my palpitations penetrated. I clenched onto Nelson, even tighter than before. But then the wooden doors re-opened and the cart left the tunnel. The ride was over. My eyes squinted for a while as I adjusted to the daylight and my body sat frozen. I was in shock. The conductor began to usher us all off the ride and I looked around at the others on the train as they climbed out. But I couldn't move. I had to sit for a while to digest it all and Nelson smiled to himself as he stepped out. The conductor headed towards us with his palm leading the way and Nelson knew exactly why he was forwarding towards us.

"C'mon." Nelson giggled as he leant his hand towards me and I raised mine towards his. One foot, then the other, I managed to climb out.

"Wow…" It was the only word I could utter as I turned to Nelson. *What a weird and wonderful ride.*

"Come on! Let's keep going!" He exclaimed as the red path flashed underneath our feet again. He clasped my hand enthusiastically as his feet followed the lights. The path dimmed as we reached a mystical looking cabin. Golden tassels dangled underneath a glowing sign which read:

WHAT WILL YOUR FUTURE BRING?

My eyes glistened as I turned to Nelson. It was now me who was eager to dive in. The velvet curtain brushed past us as we stepped inside and the bells jingled above us. But no one was inside, apart from us. The strong fragrance of opium incense floated in the cabin, leaving a winding trail behind. The soothing scent awoke my spirit and relaxed my mind. In the centre of the room, stood a glowing crystal ball on a podium and I just longed to touch it. As I approached the ball, it began to glow intensely; as if it were calling out for me. And my chest rose in the podium's direction. As soon as I'd reached within touching distance, a fear crept all over my skin. *Do I really want to know?* I questioned myself before taking a step closer. Anything could have happened after I'd placed my hands on the ball but I had to mentally prepare myself for that reality.

"So, what are you waiting for?" Nelson quietly questioned me.
"I don't know," I responded. I was so eager to step inside that I wasn't quite sure what I was actually waiting for.
"Go on, touch it," He goaded me. Hesitantly, I raised my hand towards the crystal ball and gently placed my hand on it. It felt warm and welcoming. Then, a rush of energy shot through my body, causing my hairs to stand on end and my head momentarily floated in the clouds.

As I looked down, my mouth gaped open in shock. There I was, in the crystal ball with a beautiful baby in my hand. We looked so in love; the baby and I. My eyes glittered as the mirage of myself rose her nightdress to nurse the meek child and at that point, I knew the baby was mine. As I analysed the mirage with a closer inspection, I could see the mother in me time-watching in a concerning manner. I noticed a silver band on her wedding finger as she anxiously flicked her wristwatch towards her eye-line. My curious eyes rose towards Nelson. He could tell that I wanted him to touch it. I just had to know.

Without a second thought, he placed his hands on the crystal ball and my mirage looked behind her. I could see her calling out but no one came. My face fell as I watched the lonely image and my eyes grew heavy. I couldn't watch. I couldn't stand to see my lonely image stare back at me.

"Look!" Nelson beamed at me and my eyes shot to the glass. There he was; tie loosened, embracing both me and the baby. I knew he had to be the father; and even if he wasn't, I was glad that I could see him in my future. Immediately, I let go of the ball to hold him in my arms and the image disappeared.

And as our embrace lingered, my attention couldn't help but be drawn to the sweet smell of candy floss that swam past my nose. My senses savoured the fragrance. But it was the soothing sound of popping corn that really awakened my appetite and I was compelled to follow my senses. The odour from the warm corn smelled irresistible and I was eager to find the root of the scent. Nelson followed behind and the closer we got, the more my stomach began to flip in excitement.

At the candy stand, there was an abundance of sweet treats to choose from. A jolly man stood behind the till and smiled as we approached him. I, in turn, acknowledged his response as we came to a still. My eyes scoped the tuck shop as I searched for the perfect treat. Multicoloured lollies twisted round lengthy wooden sticks. Juicy, red apples were glazed over with sweet, hard toffee and warm, pocket-sized doughnuts were doused in cinnamon and sugar. My appetite wept.

"What would you like ma'am?" the jolly man asked attentively.

"Can I have a pack of doughnuts and some candy floss on a stick please?" My eyes glistened as I responded.

"And for you sir?" he turned to Nelson.

"I'll take a gob-stopper please." He replied, ever so cordially.

The jolly salesman nodded as he attended to our orders.

My tongue skipped in delight as it wrapped around the cotton candy.

"I take it you are enjoying?" Nelson giggled as he laced his tongue around the gob-stopper.

"Mmm hmm." I giggled back as I took another bite out of the candy floss and my feet began to float.

"Where are you going?" Nelson asked with a concerned look on his face.

"Nowhere without you." I chuckled playfully as I looked down at him and an uncontrollable laugh began to muster out of me.

"No seriously, stop," he called out to me but I had already begun to drift.

"Oh, lighten up Nelson. If you laugh you can join me," I giggled as I glared down at him.

Beep.

A shackle trapped his foot to the ground and he looked up in despair. "Laugh, Nelson and set yourself free!" I called out to him. He forced out a laughter.

Beep.

Another shackle bolted his other foot to the ground and I tried to reach down to him. But I was already too far away and fear launched through my veins. *Shit! What on earth was happening to me?* My feet were in the air and my head was in the clouds. A single tear rolled down his cheek and my heart began to pound. No matter what I did, I just kept rising higher and higher into the sky.

"Don't leave me, Raven." He began to sob silently as he tried to reach out to me but I was just too far gone. I hated seeing him so helpless.

Beep.

The chain cuffed 'round his hand and buried deep into the ground. I began to weep. He was slipping away from me and there was nothing that I could do about it.

"I can't help it, Nelson. I'm sorry." My sobbing volumised as my feet were swept up from underneath me. *I couldn't lose him, again.*

"She's coming back to us," a voice consoled in the atmosphere and I cried out to him.

"Nelson!" I yelped but not a sound left my voice box.

Beep.

He was dust. Black powder sprinkled onto the floor and whipped all over the sky. He'd disappeared and all I could see was an ocean of gloom. I yelped out once more but my attempts were hopeless. It was just too dark. Tears rolled down my face and my heart began to clench.

~ Chapter 2 ~

Wails of struggle seeped out of my voice box as my body laid there paralysed. Sounds of distress haunted me but I couldn't move. I was free in the mind but trapped in the body. My eyes shuffled behind my closed eyelids as I tried to regain control of myself. It was all too much. My neck tightened as the moans persevered through my struggle. My eyes welled up.
"It's okay, Raven. You're safe." A warm hand landed on my forearm. A gasp of breath soared into my lungs as I began to resurface. My lids straggled. The light was blinding. My eyes squinted painfully as they tried to adjust. My limbs weighed a tonne. A smiling woman hovered over me as I began to turn my head on the wilted pillow. My body laid flat and lifeless as I processed my surroundings. The bright sunlight pierced through the white blinds as the wind swayed behind them. The plain room was furnished with only a leather chair and a bedside table. Then there was me; covered in nothing but a thin, white sheet and a knitted throw. An intermittent beeping sounded from behind and penetrated through my ears. My head was pounding.

"You're in *Broadway Hospital*, Raven and I'm your nurse, Bethan. Your seizure had gotten the better of you but I'm glad to see that you've come around." Her brown eyes glowed warmly as she gently assessed me.

"Your body must be exhausted. Sip this," she said as she handed me a plastic cup of water. And I endeavoured to process her words.

"Seizure?" I replied weakly after taking a few sips out of the cup.

"Yes, I believe the stress of the turbulent landing came as a shock to your system and caused your body to seize up. It was the impact from your head injury that initiated your coma," She responded.

"Wow… a coma. How long have I been here?" I feebly asked.

"Just under a week, but you have been kept in good care," she replied. "I would like to encourage you to have something solid to eat to aid the healing process. Have a look at our menu to see what appeals to you most." Bethan handed me the menu before briefly slipping out of the room. Slowly, I readjusted my position to get a better reading view. My how my body ached. It felt as though I had done a full body work out at the gym. But, I had been in bed for however long so I wasn't quite sure why my muscles hankered so much. As I sat up, I mulled over the menu for a while. Much to my surprise, I didn't actually feel that hungry and the bland choices didn't help either. I eyed the options on the afternoon menu as I forced myself to come to a decision; assuming that at least one of the choices would aid my recovery, at the very least. In the end, I settled for the

Spaghetti Bolognese, knowing that the recipe was almost impossible to get wrong.

As I waited for nurse Bethan to return, I briefly scanned the room. A few magazines sat on the bedside table beside a jug of water. A modest bunch of red-stroked lilies sat in a vase of water across the way from me. They decorated the plain room beautifully. Slowly, I turned over to reach for one of the magazines beside me. *GQ* wasn't really my sort of thing so I opted for the copy of *Cosmo*. It was one of my favourite magazines and the sexual columns always aroused my soul. A small smile crept on my face as I skipped straight to the relationship advice column.

"So, have you made your decision?" Bethan asked as she waltzed back into the room.

"Yes. Can I have the Spaghetti Bolognese with the side of boiled veg please?" I politely responded.

"Good choice," her cheeks automatically rose. "Well it's a popular choice, to say the least," she continued.

"It was the only thing that was at least half appealing on the menu, to be honest," I told her and nurse Bethan began to smile, slightly avoiding my negative commentary.

"I see you've found the magazines your husband left here for you." She smirked as she spoke.

Husband? I paused then briefly lifted my questioning eyes from the magazine.

"What do you mean, husband?" I asked her in a concerning tone.

"Sorry, your partner left the magazines here when he dropped you your flowers. Pardon me." She corrected herself but I still hadn't a clue what she was on about. "I just assumed you were married as he has been here every day since," she went on.

"Who?" I asked as I tried to fathom the wild assumptions she was jumping to.

"Your partner, Raven. He has just popped out but mentioned that he will be back soon," she assured me as she left the room. I had no idea what she was talking about but she sounded so convincing, I had to question myself. *Did my head injury give me amnesia too?* I sat and thought for a while as I wondered what the fuck she was on about. *Had Nelson really come to visit me every day since I had been in the hospital?* I knew he wasn't my husband; he wasn't even my partner but my brain needed to make sense of what she was saying somehow. *Were we actually married now?* I looked down at my left hand. Bethan interrupted my thoughts as she barged past the swinging doors wheeling a trolley with a steaming hot bowl of food on the top. She began reciting the foods she had brought to me.

"I have your Spaghetti, your veg and your dessert for afterwards," she told me.

"Thanks." I smiled as I began to tower over my food. I was excited; not only by the food but by the thought of exclusivity. Spaghetti swivelled around my fork and slipped down my mouth and my stomach embraced it in gratefulness. I wasn't sure whether it was because I hadn't eaten anything solid for a few days but the meal was a pleasant surprise. Bolognese sauce whipped onto my lips as I slurped the spaghetti wholeheartedly and the vegetables actually tasted nutritious. And after a few mouthfuls, I was completely stuffed but I was determined to force another forkful or two down me.

"Raven, you're awake!" he beamed as he pushed past the swinging doors and my eyes shot 'round. He was here and he was headed straight toward me. My lids batted at double speed. *Why on earth was he here?* I couldn't get my head around it. No matter how hard I tried, I just couldn't believe my eyes.

~ Chapter 3 ~

Twelve months later

Finally, we were on our way and there was no hiding my excitement! I was actually getting married to a decent guy. A whole me! I stood stunned for a moment or two as I took it all in.

Lilah squeezed my hand impulsively with a beaming look in her eyes as the announcement for boarding sounded through the tannoy.

"C'mon girl! Let's go!" She lurched out of the seat grabbing hold of my hand.

"Alright! Calm down! The plane isn't leaving without us," I fired back as I was launched onto my feet. Lilah was more excited than me. Anyone would have thought that it was her wedding we were about to attend.

"It definitely won't be if I have anything to do with it!" Her head shot to me with a sassy look in her eyes. "There's nothing stopping my girl from getting married!" Lilah barged into me playfully.

My heart skipped a beat at the thought of it; the thought of me walking down the aisle with a fabulous bridesmaid behind me. I only chose one; with all of the kafuffle of going abroad, it didn't make sense to have any more. Plus I had always been a firm believer that too many cooks spoiled the broth. I didn't want too many girls with too many opinions ruining my day so one was enough. And I couldn't think of anyone more fitting than Lilah. She was easy going but the life and soul of the party, so I knew my hen night would be a blast at the very least!

Lilah was my bosom buddy and always had been since our first day at accounting school. Over 10 years had passed since then but I still remember how awkward I felt when I asked to have lunch with her. I had no problems smashing exams and getting qualifications but I found it so daunting to approach people. Luckily, she didn't and we've been inseparable since; well at least in between boyfriends and man friends. Lilah was successful and sexy and had no problems finding guys and relationships. The problem was that she wore her heart on her sleeve and the guys that she fell for were already in relationships. And if they weren't in relationships, they had a whole lot of issues, leaving her in relationshit and me to pick up the pieces. I didn't get it. Lilah had so much going for her. She was a Southwest Asian beauty with olive skin and loose dark curls which waved down the entire length of her back. Wispy baby hairs smoothed over her forehead and into a loose bun which always revealed her oversized hoop earrings. Her high cheekbones upturned her green eyes and deepened the prominence of her dimples. She possessed a seductive hourglass figure, and though her Lopez behind had developed over the years, it was all natural. She dressed well for her shape and whenever we went anywhere, she always caught someone's attention. Not only was she smoking but she was sassy, supportive and smart. And to top it all off, she worked damn hard. But the subordinate guys that she chose were her Achilles heel and she was obsessed with believing that she could change them. She never did so from time to time, her heart was left raw and her friends needed to remind her how awesome she was again. This was one of those times. She had recently broken up with Sean because he lacked the understanding of how to keep his dick in his pants. And unfortunately, on this occasion, his reckless actions had left another female expecting. Getting someone else pregnant was the straw that broke the camel's back for Lilah this time. But it had been more than a few months now so she was on the mend. I could already see her getting back to her old vivacious self. She was single and ready to mingle. Until she met the next one. But I didn't mind. There was no doubt that she had been through it all with me as well. Not all the choices I had made in the last 10 plus years had been sensible ones and she had never passed judgement. That's what I loved about Lilah. No matter how stupid I had been, I could always be honest with her, she could always be honest with me and our respect remained mutual. That's why I didn't even have to bat a lid when I chose her as my bridesmaid.

"Are you excited to see your man, or should I say, husband?" She gleamed as we advanced in the line.

"Fiancé will suffice and of course!" I sassed back.

It had been ages since I had seen him and I longed to be in his guarded arms once more. We had been away from each other for the past fortnight as we prepped ourselves for the wedding and he was obsessed with the idea of purity before marriage. And whilst I admired his traditional ways, I was sure that our reconciliation was long overdue.

"Do you know where he is, roughly?" she asked and I immediately shrugged my shoulders.

"No, the last time I heard from him, he was getting in a Taxi with Seb." I flicked to my phone to see if there had been any more updates; there was none. He was due on our flight and I couldn't wait to see him.

"Well they better not miss the plane!" she retorted.

"No, they're way too organised to do something as foolish as that." I rubbished her comments.

"Good, 'cos I don't need anybody messing up my holiday!" She stuck her tongue out playfully and I raised a cheeky brow in her direction.

As I handed one of the cabin crew members my passport, I gave a brief look back before shuffling on towards the plane entrance. I couldn't see him and my feelings flitted between worried and pissed off. But I knew it was not in his nature to be late so I had to remind myself of that fact as I searched for my seat. Also, there was still time, though my keenness was trying terribly hard to convince me otherwise. I had the pre-wedding jitters and my anxiety was causing my wild thoughts to get the better of me. I tried desperately to grab hold of them. After lunging my hand luggage overhead, I was finally able to get a seat. Lilah sat by the window in front of me so we could still have a good gossip if I felt like a change in conversation without leaving my seat. But the seat beside me was for my husband-to-be and I wasn't compromising that for anyone. Family and friends dispersed over the plane as they all sought comfort in their assigned seats. I truly appreciated the fact that my nearest and dearest had all made the effort to help me celebrate my big day. We were travelling long haul so cosiness was my top priority; that's why I had to travel business class on this occasion. Not only that, but it was going to be *my* wedding so it only made sense to fork out the extra pennies for a taste of luxury.

And as I gazed up from the personal screen, there he was; strolling towards me; my husband-to-be. My heart skipped a beat. It had only been a fortnight but it felt as though I hadn't seen him for a lifetime. I sighed in relief as our eyes met, grateful that he and Seb had made it on time. His hand luggage strapped over his shoulder and sat comfortably on the small of his back. He wore his dark grey tracksuit and it fitted him well. It revealed everything and nothing all at the same time. The track wear outlined his thick chest and glided over his dick print. I could have ripped his clothes off there and then but I was trying to compose myself. His cheek began to rise as he neared me and my vagina began to twinge. It was the first tingle I had felt in the last fortnight and my mini-me delighted in that fact. He looked so manly and he was all mine.

"Hey, Andrew," I breathed as he leant over the seat to embrace me. His firm hug made me feel so secure. Blood raced underneath my skin.

"Hey beautiful, you okay?" he asked.

"I am now," I responded with my hand still firmly placed around his neck. I wasn't ready to let go. "I've missed you." I exhaled and he giggled as he took the seat beside me.

"I bet you did," he toyed with me and his black frames rose. Sebastian slid in beside Lilah.

"What took you guys so long?" I questioned him curiously.

"You know Seb always takes long to get ready and the traffic on the way here was madness," he responded casually.

"Oh, really? For a moment, I thought I was going to get stood up!" I joked although a small part of me somewhat believed my words.

"Now, you know I wouldn't do that," he quickly reassured me. And it was true, he was so reliable that it was hard to believe that he could even miss a bus let alone our wedding.

"Anyway, I'm glad you're here now." I smiled as I glanced into his tawny eyes momentarily and eased into my seat. That was what I loved about Andrew, he always knew how to reassure me and make me feel safe.

It had only been a year since we'd first met but everything felt so right. Everything had fitted into its place so perfectly with us that it was hard to turn down his proposal. Although it wasn't 'love at first sight', Andrew definitely grew on me quite quickly. I admired the effort that he put into getting to know me, despite my countless rejections. From the moment that we first met on our flight back to London from Jamaica, I could see the twinkle in his eye. But I was so caught up in Nelson that I'd failed to recognise the good man that stood beside me. And he'd refused to leave until I said yes. His dedication was undeniable; from his daily visits while I was in the hospital to the lies he told the nurses just to be allowed the rights to see me. It was clear that he was a man with a plan and he was in it for the long haul. I, on the other hand, was simply grateful to have a chaperone to and from my appointments. And though he was clean looking and kind, he just wasn't my type; he didn't get my juices flowing. But he never failed to contact me to see if I was okay. Eventually, I warmed to his caring nature after meeting up for a few friendly dates.

And even though it took over 6 months for me to finally move on and let Andrew in properly, it had been a whirlwind since. And being the traditional man that he was, his high morals encouraged him to do things properly and ask for my hand in marriage as soon as he knew that I would say yes. And I had no reason to say no. Since the first day I had met him, he'd been reliable, attentive and he had more than a few pennies in the bank. He worked for the Jamaican high commission in the U.K. so he was never short of money or holidays; from very early on, he made sure that I knew that.
And though he treated me well, he never spent his money frivolously and always prepared for the future. He looked after himself and encouraged me to do the same. So whilst most people got out of shape when they got into a relationship, I got into it. My body was looking firmer and

sexier than ever before and my wedding dress fitted flawlessly. When he proposed, I knew there was nothing more I could have wished for in a husband and a father for my future children. I was ready to give up work and travel wherever his job would take us.

Not long after he'd arrived, the plane was full to the brim and ready for takeoff. I could see the flight attendants walking up and down the aisles to do their final pre-flight checks. And though I was strapped in and ready to go, I couldn't help but notice a slight tightening in my chest as it all dawned on me. Flying always made me feel somewhat anxious but this felt kind of different.

"So, are you ready for this then?" I asked Andrew as I sat back.

"For what?" he chuckled as he glanced over to me. My eyes rolled a tad.

"Everything. The flight, the wedding, the marriage?" I asked nervously. His head rose from his *GQ* mag in just enough time to slide his glasses back up his nose. He chortled briefly before pecking me on the cheek.

"Of course. I wouldn't have it any other way." He smirked before returning to his magazine and I let out the deep breath that I'd been harbouring in my lungs.

* * *

The flight was in full swing and we were on our way to *Montego Bay*. A slight shudder unsettled me momentarily as we plighted through a small spot of turbulence. A chill passed under my skin. The thought of turbulence made me feel fairly anxious after my previous endurance of cabin decompression but I had to get over it. It happened every time I flew so I knew there was no avoiding it. And prior to flying, I had thought of a mass of distraction techniques to help me cope. As I turned to Andrew, I could see that he was getting stuck into one of the in-flight movies but I needed him more.

"Are you enjoying that?" I asked as I snuggled my head underneath his armpit and onto his chest.

"Yeah, it's actually quite a good film you know, but I don't think it's your sort of thing." He spoke to me although his eyes were fixed on the screen in front of him.

"How do you know?" I gazed up at him from below with a blithe grin on my face.

"You're not really the action type of girl now are you?" he joshed.

"Erm, I'll have you know, I love a bit of action," I said as I stroked his inner thigh. His lip rose on one side of his face.

"You are something else you know," he told me as he planted his hand on top of mine, moderately restricting my movements.

"Draw that curtain around you and I'll show you the type of action I like," I whispered as I reached up to kiss his neck.

"Raven, you know we shouldn't." He smiled as he tried to resist my temptations.

"Why not?" I asked as I rubbed my lips underneath his jaw.

"I haven't got any condoms on me," he turned to me and my eyeballs spun back fleetingly. His obsession with purity almost killed his spontaneity and his ability to let loose.

"Yes, but I do," I told him as I smoothed my hand over his print. He was adamant that our bodies should be worshipped like a temple and condoms were the only method of contraception that he actually believed in. "I even have this." I pulled out his play blindfold from my back pocket and his smile advanced across his face.

"I can't believe you brought that." He chuckled as he removed his headphones from his ears.

"I know what my man likes," I voiced as I squeezed his piece gently. "Come, let me show you just how much I missed you." I lifted the armrest and he began to recline

As I looked around, I could see the other passengers engrossed in movies and sleep. But I was engrossed in getting this anxiety out of my mind. I reached over him to fully draw our personal curtain.

"Now that's more like it," I whispered as I placed the black velvet blindfolds right over his eyes. I sewed tender kisses all over his neck before biting him playfully. He snickered in enjoyment.

"Mmm, you taste good," I told him before grabbing the skin on his neck in between my teeth and sucking it ruthlessly. My unyielding tongue rubbed until I could feel the taste of his blood between my grip.

"Take it easy, Raven," he spoke discreetly; I could tell that he didn't want to grab the attention of anyone on the other side of our closed curtain.

"Hmm, you want it easy do you?" I whispered into his ear and his tongue savoured his bottom lip. I reached into my pocket once more to retrieve the flavoured condom I had sitting in there. I watched his grin spread even broader as he heard me rip open the packet with my bare teeth. His print began to grow underneath his tracksuit bottoms.

"Oooh, look at you," I said as I smoothed my hand over his crotch once more. "I think someone wants to come out and say hello," I spoke in a low voice as I reached for his penis underneath his pants. My vagina smiled at the sight of his robust snake. His fleshy bell looked delicious and I couldn't wait to taste him deeply in my mouth. I held the condom in my teeth as I lowered my head onto his stiff cock. My warm lips clasped firmly as I smoothed the chocolate rubber over his caramel chopper. My hands followed behind, pressing the sheath down to his groin.

"Aaaaahh," he exhaled softly after my first full taste of chocolate. My head retreated as I looked up to admire the pleasure on his face. His jaw dilated. Slowly, I swirled my tongue down and around his shaft. The taste was so damn good.

"Mmmm," I moaned as I savoured his piece. I inhaled intensely as I relished the flavour of his groins. My walls began to clench. Sensually, I worked kisses all the way up to his tip and consumed his entire length into the depths of my mouth. His hammerhead stroked the back of my tonsils and I heard his breath intensify. I knew he liked it, so I retreated, then repeated. Again, I buried his shaft deep into my mouth, stroking one solid vein with my tongue as I rose up then down, up then down. He adjusted his blindfold to re-cover his clammy cheeks; he loved the mystery of it all. For a while, my swirling tongue lingered on his glans and his hips began to gyrate. He slid down on his seat and I submerged his tool back into me. His breath warmed the back of my neck and I began to salivate. I could feel his dick stroking every inch of my gums and my vagina flustered in excitement. More and more, I wanted to feel his penis inside of my other cavity; but I knew we couldn't. Saliva dripped down my fingers as they followed my lips down and up the length of him. Blinded, his head rolled aimlessly against the back of his seat. I could feel him swelling inside of me and it sent sexual sparks to my box. It only encouraged me to suck him even harder. Back and forth, back and forth my tongue laced over his bell as my grip gently twisted around and down him. My head guided my hands as I rocked over his cock again and again.

"Aaahhhh," he breathed quietly as he inflated inside of my mouth. His hand gripped onto the chair handle. I began to smile. I knew he was coming. Without hesitation, I launched his penis deeper inside of my salivating hole. I swallowed him over and over as he hit the back of my tonsils. He began to pulsate. My hands followed as I sucked him relentlessly, up and down, up and down, up and down until his pleasure points could not cope any longer. His muscles tensed. I took charge of his dick. His juices shot to the tip of the dom. He tried to control his spasm as he sat in the seat and I held him with pride. As he relaxed into his climax, I continued. I continued caressing my tongue all over his still-firm penis, savouring every inch. My kisses didn't stop until his precious piece retreated. That was my man. That was my husband-to-be.

~ Chapter 4 ~

It had been a long flight and tiredness crept all over me as we hobbled through the roads. Flying long haul was never fun but always worth it when we actually arrived. The heat felt mild, which was a slight relief, though the cramped bus kept us all uncomfortably snug. Just as we'd reached the great stone wall entrance to *The Regal Hotel*, the sun had started to set. The clouds were laced with bronze as the sinking rays clutched on to the skyline. And the spotlights gleamed from the gold embossed letters as we drove past the vast welcome sign. Flourishing palm trees rose from the Venetian pebbles and led us all the way along the path.

We passed an illuminated waterfall, central to the hotel roundabout. Multi-coloured lights shone out of the faucets causing the water to intermittently glow like a rainbow. It was a warm welcome indeed and within moments, the tiredness had passed over me. Our transport parked just outside two stone pillars that defined the walkway to the front desk. Infectiously, the enthusiasm of the hotel staff increased my vitality and made me feel perfectly at home.

"Welcome to *The Regal*. Please allow me to assist," the eager bell boy told us as we stepped out of our transfer.

"Thank you," I uttered to the attentive bellboy as he took charge of my suitcase.

"Wow! I can tell that I'm about to enjoy myself!" Lilah beamed as she scoped the view. A marble floor that was woven with gold stretched underneath our feet and out towards the main pool area. Smooth reggae penetrated through the foyer from outside and blessed our eardrums. My head began to sway and so did Lilah's. People gathered on the plump sofas as they relaxed to the Jamaican vibes. The walls were decorated with fine African art and flame like lamps flickered between each piece. The ceilings and desks were furnished with deep mahogany, creating the most calming ambience. A single white lily sat in each tall vase on top of the desks, almost lighting up the walkway. And another member of staff strolled towards us with a tray filled with welcome drinks and wipes.

"Welcome home," she said as she handed each one of us a drink. It was a mocktail. Red, gold and green juice layered the short glass, one on top of the other like the Ethiopian flag. It was a beautiful *Bob Marley*. I exchanged a warm smile with her before accepting the glass. The long journey had dehydrated my waters and they were in desperate need of replacement. I ogled it briefly before chugging it back. Within moments, she had addressed the whole group and I could see the pleasure passing through them all as we relaxed into our new environment. Though this was our first time staying in this hotel, it felt so familiar and the staff seemed to welcome us with open arms.

Lilah waited by the bar as I signed us into our suite. It felt quite strange sleeping separate from my fiancé but he was so wrapped up in traditions. Andrew insisted that we stay in separate hotel rooms until we were wed so Lilah bunked with me. We had booked the Caribbean regal suite for the week so there was plenty of space for us to unwind together and apart. Luckily, Andrew's room was adjacent to ours, so he wasn't too far away from me if I needed some extra warmth in the night. The guys had forked out a bit more than us, for the extra space I assumed, so their room was complete with a full-sized dining area. The floor-to-ceiling windows cast over the Caribbean Sea, creating an outstanding view. And to top it all off, their room had two bathrooms, the master one inclusive of an en-suite Jacuzzi. It was luxury at its finest; a fully stocked bachelor's pad. Lilah begged them to swap for a night but Seb wasn't having any of it; I could tell that he wanted to get his money's worth. But I didn't mind. Our room wasn't standard at all. Our room had almost everything they had, minus the Jacuzzi and the unnecessary space.

* * *

After we had settled into the room, we headed down to the bar for some drinks and some late evening entertainment. On the stage, were two enthusiastic dancers, encouraging the crowd to take part in their ventures. We sought to the bar to get a good view of the stage and Lilah had strategically dragged us towards the hottest member of bar staff that she could find. Behind the adult-only bar, stood a towering, tenacious man with honey coloured skin. And I knew that was the guy Lilah had her eye on; he fitted perfectly into her type. His dark curls were neatly scraped into a man bun, accentuating his well-groomed facial hair. And his thick, black eyebrows matched the strength of his beard, drawing attention to his deep, hazel eyes. Lilah was hypnotised. An African-inspired tattoo crept from underneath his collar and danced around his neck. Though I could see that he was busy serving another couple, I knew that there was no doubt in Lilah's mind that she would be next. His cheek rose on one side of his face as he saw us approach the stools. Lilah squeezed my hand tightly as we sat down. I could tell her femininity was tingling just as much as the twiddle in her toes.

I sat for a while scoping the menu whilst Lilah scoped the vision in front of her.
"Good evening ladies. How may I be of assistance?" He finally approached us and Lilah's hand couldn't help but clench onto my thigh.
"I was wondering whether you could help actually. We usually order cocktails but we were looking to try something new. What would you recommend?" Lilah spoke for us with a helpless glint in her eyes.
"Well, there's nothing wrong with a good old cocktail but in here in *The Regal*, we always like to come with something fresh. Have you ever tried the Jamaican Storm?" he asked.

"No, but I definitely wouldn't say no to one." Lilah's tongue brushed her inner cheek as she shared a wink with me. My nostrils flared. I knew he was on her radar and her flirtatious charm had already begun to surface.

"Well, in this hotel we serve the Royal Jamaican Storm." His chest rose with pride as he spoke.

"What's the difference?" I asked out of curiosity.

"Well, it has all the pleasures of a Jamaican Storm with the extra, royal treatment," he told me as he eyed Lilah up then down. I stared into him for a moment, somewhat confused. His answer had told me nothing at all.

"To be honest, I don't think I need any more convincing, we'll try two of those to start with and then you can surprise us next." Lilah stuck her tongue out playfully and the honey-toned man began to laugh as he started working up a storm.

"Oh my goodness Lilah, look at that arm work," I whispered as he shook the juices in the glass.

"I know, girl. I already spotted that, trust me." Lilah peacocked as she belittled my late reactions. His thick forearms were home to two tatted sleeves which worked their way all the way up his elbows at the very least. His arms were woven with ancestry and bold tribal marks underneath his partly-rolled, white sleeves. His biceps bulged as he rocked the cups right over his head and I could tell that Lilah was impressed.

"You definitely need to get his number," I told her as we sat, patiently waiting.

"Ray, you know I'm not leaving here without some form of contact," she voiced confidently and I had no reason to doubt her words.

"Two Royal Jamaican Storms for two royal ladies." He smiled as he slid our drinks over to us on the elevated bar.

"Thanks," we said in unison as we raised our glasses.

"To a royal wedding too!" Lilah added as she clinked my glass.

"A wedding? Which one of you beautiful ladies is jumping the broom?" The barman asked, fairly intrigued.

"Who do you think?" Lilah shot back in his direction. He eyed us for a moment or two.

"Hmm…Probably you," he said as he pointed towards me and Lilah gasped in shock. "No disrespect, but you look like you're not quite ready to settle down yet; like you still have a little more fun left in you," he winked at Lilah. My jaw dropped. I didn't know whether to take his comment as a compliment or a criticism but Lilah seemed pretty pleased.

"That sounds about right," Lilah giggled.

"I'll have you know, I have plenty of fun left in me; I'm just saving it for my husband." I nudged Lilah as I spoke.

"I know, I'm just playing with you," Lilah jived.

"Well, congratulations to the future, Mrs?" he paused, waiting for me to fill in the gap.

"Martin, Raven Martin." My chest warmed as I grew accustomed to my future surname.

"And?" He turned to Lilah.

"Lilah, MISS Lilah Malik." She leaned into him as she emphasised her title.

"Oh wow. Your name is almost as beautiful as your smile." He eyed her once more. "Well ladies, my name is Akeem and it's been a pleasure meeting you two tonight," he continued.

"So Miss Coolie girl, do you come here often?" Akeem turned to Lilah and my intrigued brow rose.

"No, this is my first time actually. Ray's been to Jamaica before but I haven't." She nudged into me.

"Oh, but don't you have family over here?" He questioned her and Lilah began to laugh.

"Me? No, my family are from Pakistan." She giggled as she spoke.

"What? No way. I really thought you were an island girl," He voiced, stunned.

"She wished!" I added.

"The way you move and your attitude; you could really pass for a Jamaican girl," he explained as he eyed her, still shocked.

"Nah. I'm not Jamaican but I wouldn't mind some Jamaican in me!" she joked and I laughed along with her.

"I have family over here and so does my fiancé but we don't really know them." I cleared up his misconception.

"Oh right. So where is Mr Martin then?"

"Oh, the last I heard, he was playing pool at the sports bar." My chin rose in his direction. "He's not really a fan of staged entertainment," I mentioned, air quoting the phrase.

"Neither am I to be honest, but the guests seem to like it," he agreed with Andrew in his absence.

"So what do you do for fun then?" Lilah eagerly asked.

"Well when I'm not training, I love to dance and hold a vibe; usually at *The Tabernacle*."

"So you think you've got moves then do you?" Lilah toyed with him.

"Well, it's not just me who thinks it. You should come down to *The Tabernacle* before you leave. I could probably show you, girls, a thing or two." He bit his lip playfully.

"Yeah, I wouldn't mind that. What do you think, Ray?" Lilah asked casually as she pinched me out of Akeem's sight. I knew there was only one way that she wanted me to respond.

"Yeah, sure. Why not?" I smiled in agreement as I sipped my Royal Jamaican Storm.

~ Chapter 5 ~

It was the eve of our first full day in *The Regal* and I could tell that everyone had settled into our new environment by the nonchalant look on their faces. Our bright clothes glowed in the evening sky as we consumed ourselves in conversation. The entire group of us stretched along an elongated table with Andrew and me in the centre. Though we were outside, the sunset heat kept us warm as we dined in laughter underneath the cream gazebo. The fragrance from the smoking hot chicken drifted from the BBQ and across our table as we awaited our service. The table had been beautifully set for our courses yet we had indulged in none. I didn't mind though as it was such a blessing to be in the company of all my favourite people and I could just taste the excitement in the air.

Ding.
Ding.
Ding.

Sebastian clinked his spoon against his glass of white wine as he stood in a bid to gather everybody's attention. A wave of hush rippled through the table as our eyes were drawn to him.

"Evening all," he started off. "Well, I never thought I'd see the day…" Sebastian smirked as he turned to Andrew. "My boy is about to get married." He chuckled as he placed a firm hand on his shoulder. My cheeks began to glow as I registered his words. "Rest in Peace," he jived and our party laughed along with him. Seb was always full of jokes. "No but seriously, when Andrew told me that he was thinking of proposing to Raven, I actually remember checking his head to see if he was feeling okay. Andrew, the career-driven traveller, was ready to settle down. I was actually stunned for a moment or two. But I knew that any woman that could convince Andrew to settle down, had to be a keeper. Wow… Excuse me, if I'm fumbling for words. This is my first best man speech and hopefully my last." He chortled. "He is the first out of all us to get married but that doesn't surprise me. Whenever Andrew has his mind set on something, he goes in; all guns blazing. And that's how it's been since he met the absolutely stunning, Raven. Since day one, he has had nothing but admirable words to say about her. And after meeting her, I could see why."

My insides began to melt as he spoke towards me. "You are a compliment to him and I'm grateful that you both asked me to share such a memorable event with you. But when Andrew asked me to be his Best man, I felt both honoured and insulted. Honoured that he thought of me first but insulted that he would let a woman come between us!" He shook his head disdainfully as he turned to Andrew. "He had clearly forgotten the code; bros before hoes Drew!" Andrew and I giggled and I leaned into him endearingly. "No, but Andrew has been my wingman for too long for me to turn down an opportunity like this; to watch him walk down the aisle. Raven is a lucky girl because unlike most, Andrew is genuinely a protective guy. He has always looked out for me; he's one of my best friends. He's always been there to stroke me in the back of a taxi when I was absolutely hammered. And usually for me to roll out the other side and disappear into the darkness!" Seb's eyebrow rose cynically in Andrew's direction. "Yeah, thanks for that Drew!" he joshed. "But all jokes aside, he's the only one that has been able to put up with me throughout the years and it hasn't gone unnoted." Seb paused as he took a moment to nod gratefully in Andrew's direction. "So I'd like everyone to raise their glass in honour of both Andrew and Raven to congratulate them ahead of their union." My heart smiled as they all raised their glasses and I couldn't help but kiss Andrew gratefully in front of our family and friends.

"Thank you, Sebastian and thank you all for coming all this way to help Raven and I celebrate our wedding." Andrew rose to address our guests. "The past year hasn't been easy but I'm sure the future will be worth it. From the moment that I met Raven, I knew she was the one I wanted to marry, despite her countless rejections. Courting Raven wasn't straightforward, but being the persistent man I am, I eventually wore her down." He turned to me and I began to blush brown. "I know it has been a rush to get you all out here but once my mind was made up, I had to seal the deal as soon as possible. And let's face it, it's hard to say no to a cheeky holiday!" Andrew chuckled with our guests before looking over to the BBQ. "I don't want to keep you long as it looks like our food is on our way but I wanted to raise a glass to the future Mrs Martin. May our years be as impulsive as the last." He clinked glasses with me and I shared a longing smile with him. It was those precious moments that made me excited for our big day to arrive.

Only minutes after Andrew had sat back down next to me, the smartly dressed waiters began to flood to our table. Their filled trays floated above their white gloves as they decorated our table with an array of BBQ delights. Grilled swordfish; skewered prawns; corn on the cob; baby back ribs and honey-glazed chicken lined the centre of the table. My stomach skipped at the sight of the feast. We were all accompanied with a number of Caribbean sides to complement our dishes. Small bowls of coleslaw, macaroni cheese and fried plantain wrapped around our main plate and I couldn't wait to get stuck in.

* * *

After loading my belly with more than a plateful of delicacies, I was completely stuffed.
"Oh my goodness, that food was amazing!" Lilah blurted out. "I hope that I don't look too bloated. I don't want Akeem thinking I'm pregnant or anything." She turned to me.

"Don't be silly Lilah, your belly is as flat as a pancake!" I dismissed her exaggerative comments.

"Are you sure? We're meeting up when he finishes his shift later. I don't want to put him off." She double checked for reassurance.

"Lilah, you look fine, honestly. And you kept it very quiet that you guys were meeting up. Why didn't you tell me?" I asked out of curiosity.

"Oh, I knew you already had a lot on your plate with your wedding rehearsal and everything. I didn't want to make tonight all about me," she replied.

"Oh please, we can both shine together and light up this place! Plus, you know that I always want to keep up to date with all the gossip! What are you guys going to do?" I eagerly asked.

"We're just meeting up for a chat and drinks. We'll most probably just stay on the complex but you never know what might happen so don't wait up for me girl!" Lilah pouted with a mischievous look in her eyes.

"Don't worry, I won't!" I said as the bulb behind my eyelids brightened. "Just be safe," I added, knowing how wild she could get at times.

"Girl, you know I always carry protection." Lilah stuck her tongue out in good-humour and I couldn't stop my eyes from rolling.

"No Lilah, I meant to look after yourself!" My lids narrowed as I focused in on her.

"Of course, I will. I'll be fine," she assured me. And as much as I hoped that she would be safe on her own, I was excited to have our room to myself; even if it was just for a few hours.

I peered over to Andrew, who I could see was heavily involved in conversation with his friends. And although I didn't want to interrupt, I couldn't contain the news for a moment longer.

"Drew," I tapped him on the thigh. "Why don't you come over to my room after we've finished with all this? Lilah's out for a couple hours and I've got the suite to myself." I used my seductive voice as I bit my bottom lip.
"Yeah that's cool," he replied after a moment.
"We haven't really spent much one on one time together yet. It's so different going away with everyone."
"Yeah, that's true. Although we are meant to be containing ourselves." His eyes squinted playfully.
"I know babe but I'm sure a teeny nightcap won't hurt," I whispered as I gently clutched his leg underneath the table. His black frames rose on his face.
"Nope, I don't see why it would." He grinned at me from the side of his mouth and my kitty automatically began to purr.

~ Chapter 6 ~

It had been an exhausting evening, more mentally than anything, but I was determined to spend some quality time with my fiancé. Though quite a few of our party still lingered by the dining table, I had slipped up to my suite fairly early to freshen up. Immediately, I stepped out of my clothes and into the shower in a pursuit to revive every inch of me. The shower was set to cold but warmed up within moments of me turning it on. My head tilted back as the spears of water bounced off me and struck the tiles underneath my feet. My nipples firmed at the intense sensation of water rushing past my bosoms and I stood there for a while, appreciating the moment; capturing the water in between my hands. I reached for the shower gel and gently began squeezing it onto my exfoliating body puff. With every swipe, I was fixed on washing the evening away so that I could welcome the night; a night alone with my man.

Andrew had agreed to come over at 9 so I wanted to make sure that everything was perfect. After I had towel dried, I reached for the coconut oil to lubricate my body. No part was left untouched and my skin felt baby smooth. Blood rushed to my nerve endings as my fingers ran all over me. Even, I felt a little turned on by the feel of my thick legs underneath my fingertips. My cheeks were filled with radiance as I began to anticipate how his skin would feel against mine; like a velvet blanket spreading effortlessly over a bare bed. My toes began to tinker.

I headed to the drawers in search of the perfect lingerie for the night. I knew exactly what piece I wanted to wear. Effortlessly, my legs slipped through the black, laced underwear as the all-in-one straps stretched over my breasts and hooked around my neck. As I eyed my reflection in the mirror, I couldn't help but graze my teeth over my bottom lip. The straps had lifted my bust to peak position and the shadow of my areolas peered through the lace. I flirted with my reflection as I placed my foot on the table, revealing my crotch-less briefs. My walls clasped in excitement but I had to contain myself.

I covered up with a silk gown that barely covered my assets and sought to the main room. I dimmed the suite lights and decorated the room with aromatic candles to create a more relaxing ambience as I sat on the sofa and waited. I simply couldn't wait for him to knock on that door. I was ready for him to come in.

Pleasure filled my ears as the red wine launched up the sides of the glasses. I'd poured enough for two as I eagerly expected his arrival. It was almost 9 so I knew that Andrew would be at the door soon.

Knock.
Knock.
Knock.

A bolt of electrocution raced to my stomach as I held the wine in mid-air. The glass didn't even have a chance to grace my lips but that was Andrew; always ahead of time. I took a moment to compose myself before uncrossing my eager legs and heading to the door.

Knock.
KNOCK.

"I'm coming," I hollered masking the panic in my voice. I didn't understand why my emotions were starting to race out of control. Although I had just spent the evening with him, this would've been our first time alone with each other in a fortnight and it felt fresh.
"Hey," I breathed smoothly as I opened the door.
"You alright?" He confirmed with an endearing smirk emerging on his face.
"All the better for seeing you," I affirmed as I closed the door behind him and he began to chuckle.
"I bet you are!" he muttered surreptitiously as he scoped the room. "What's all this?" he questioned, gesturing to my thoughtful decorations.
"Oh, I just wanted to set the mood," I mentioned coyly as I raised a glass in his direction. A short breath huffed from out of his nostrils as he accepted my offering. We clinked glasses.

"Is that right?" His eyebrow rose. "And what sort of mood was that?" he asked inquisitively. I sipped on my glass of deep, red wine and he mirrored my movements.

"Well, we haven't spent quality time together for quite a while now so I wanted to make it special." My gaze lowered as I rubbed the glass along my lip line. I could feel him gaging my intentions. "I just wanted to show you how much I missed you," I went on as I artfully ran my fingers down my silk gown revealing a subtle snippet of my nighttime attire. Without thinking, his glass raced to his mouth as he attempted to wet his appetite. His bronze eyes began to shine and my heart turned to molten. Automatically, my lids began to close as I leaned into his neck to inhale his scent; deep and musky. "You smell gorgeous," I whispered as my lips brushed his earlobe. My assets were cocked high in the air.

"Thanks," he uttered as he tried to mask his flattered expression. He gulped down a couple more mouthfuls of wine. I eyed him briefly.

"Why are you so stiff?" I toyed with him. "Come, let me help you loosen up," I said as I sketched my finger over his chest.

"Now, now, don't you know good things come to those who wait?" he teased and my eyes almost naturally wound back in my head.

"I prefer to believe that good things come to those who work their behinds off, but I suppose that's a matter of opinion."

Slowly, I released the glass from his hands and placed it on the table. His hard to get act was making me want him even more. "I want to help you relieve that tension." My fingers delicately clawed the back of his head. "A little massage, that's all." I softened my gaze as my nose grazed against his. His frames began to steam up as he pondered on my proposition.

"Don't worry, you won't be needing these," I mentioned as I lifted his spectacles away from his eyes. I placed them on the table and I could see a glow igniting inside of him. "And you won't be needing this." I went on as I reached for the lining of his top. Without hesitation, he had also reached down to assist me and my eyes were blessed, once again, with his chiselled, brown chest. Air rushed into my lungs. My tongue couldn't help but drape around my lips as his pectorals flexed, finely revealing his almost camouflaged nipples. My how I'd missed that view.

"Come with me," I gently commanded as I took his hand and lured him in the direction of the bedroom. The sensual scent from the candles followed us in. His eyes scaled the room as he adjusted to his new environment. He seemed silently impressed by the order I was able to maintain so far in our short stay. I stopped; my eyes briefly assessing him. "I want to do this properly…" I reached for his buckle as I proceeded in taking off his entire bottom half. A smooth inhale blessed my nostrils as I was faced with his bare body, once more. He sought to the bed and I couldn't take my eyes off him, nor did I want to. His perfect peach protruded out of the sheets as he laid face down on the bed. Little by little, I lowered them before straddling his behind.

A loose lump of coconut oil dribbled through my fingers as it adjusted from the temperature of the room to my body. And my body rejoiced in delight. I couldn't wait to get my hands on him. And with my first suave touch on his back, his eyelids slowly slid together. His back was tense like he was carrying a weight on his shoulders. And automatically, I felt guilty for not being there for him recently. The guilt guided my fingers as I began to knead deep circles into his neck then his shoulders. And as I continued, his muscles began to relax and the strokes got easier. With every knead, I could feel the tension oozing out of his body. Loosely, his muscles began to flow through his torso as they started to follow the wave of my fingertips. I could see he was starting to enjoy it. And the more pleasure crept over his body, the easier it felt for the guilt to alleviate from mine. As I kept going, my soul craved more of him. Gently, I pulled on the strings of my silk gown for a bit of extra breathing space. Then, small circles expanded as I endeavoured to caress his entire frame. Smoothly, my hands ran down the entire distance of his arm to the tips of his fingers and back again. And with every silky movement, I could see his body sinking into the bed.

"Mmmmhhh," he moaned as I fingered his pressure points and I couldn't help but smile. My nightgown dropped to my elbows, revealing a little more of my hand-picked attire. Slowly, I levered my hands around his torso but the dropping gown stunted my room for movement. One arm, then two; the silk gown slipped to the floor. My nipples exhaled through the lace of my halter-neck straps. *That felt much better.* And as I reached forward once more, I began to plant tender kisses on his back with my fingers following the trail.

My hole expanded in decadence each time my back arched to stretch along his body. Up and down, my warm lips traced him casually, in between each stroke. His toffee skin shined as the candlelight reflected off his toned back and I wanted nothing more than to taste him. Oil ran past my lips and slid past my tongue as I attempted to sample his body. And as I continued, my solid nipples couldn't help but graze the entire length of his back. But he tasted delicious and confectionary, just like toffee. I bit my lip. The more I explored, the more pleasure I received from giving it to him. Rhythmically, my body rocked as my hands worked their way up and down his deltoids. And as I swayed, my pendulum naturally rubbed on his behind through my crotch-less briefs. Back and forth; back and forth. The massage was giving me more pleasure than I had previously expected.

"Turn around," I hummed; my coily bush brushed past his neck. His eyes unsealed briefly. "I want to feel your chest between my hands…" I went on and his cheeks began to rise. Leg high in the air, I gave him more than enough space to reposition himself. His eyes extended as my leg lowered.

"I see you've dressed for the occasion." He smirked as he got comfortable on his back and my eyes lit up.

"I could say the same about yourself." My tongue brushed my inner cheek as my eyes slit downwards. His cock was steadfast and that sent signals to my snake pit. Shrewdly, I sat over his groin, pressing his firm penis down to his stomach and immediately I sought for the tub once more. Oil dripped and slipped past his erect and almost disguised nipples as they blended into the brownness of his chest. He began to tense as the oil tickled his torso and ran down into the distance. I caught it in the palm of my hands before it dripped onto the bed and smoothed it up and around the shape of his pecs.

"Aaaahhh," Andrew let out a sigh of relief as my hands took firm control of him. His knuckles buried deep into the bed as I worked my way through one, then another; limp and lifeless. I loved the control.

Steadily, my palms brushed past his stomach and into his neck. His head rocked back. Grease slipped through my fingers as his skin slid into position. Over and over, my fingers reached up and down the length of his chest and my hips swayed. Blood swelled at the tip of my ladyness. With every stretch, my plump clitoris swung over his penis and my lips began to moisten. Small waves of joy pulsated through me as my fingers searched and searched his torso. The more I searched, the more I took pleasure in my expedition. As I continued to glide my hands up and down his chiselled chest, my lady lips started to sweat even more and my walls relaxed. The craving for fullness urged inside me and I longed for his piece to fill that gap.

"How about a happy ending?" I flirted as I leaned into his stomach. His chest filled with air; his heart torn.

"Raven, there's only a few more days left now," he uttered, after a moment of thought.

"I know but I want you so ba-"

Knock.
Knock.
Knock.

There was a pause.

"Who's that?" Andrew questioned as his body began to stiffen.

"I have no idea and I have no intentions of finding out. All I need right now is you inside o-"

"Raven?" A muffled voice called from behind the door. "It's Lilah. I forgot my key!"

"Fuck." I breathed as my eyes spun back in my forehead. I knew that I couldn't leave her out there.

"Uh! I'm coming!" I grunted as I climbed off Andrew.

"Oh, thank goodness! I'm dying for a pee!" I heard the relief in her voice. As I headed to the door, I could see Drew desperately trying to cover his decency. And at that point I knew, my luck was out.

~ Chapter 7 ~

It had been an eventful day by the poolside. The morning sun had quickly crossed the sky and the twilight hours were now upon us. And whilst we had been in and out of the water, Lilah and I were both keen to freshen up; though Lilah was keener than I was to some extent. So as soon as we got to our suite, she monopolised the bathroom and had been getting ready since. It was only after Lilah had rid her body of every last inch of hair that I was able to use the bathroom and by that time, the sun had disappeared. And though the night had swiftly crept up on us, Lilah was still desperate to paint the town red.

"Yessss!" Lilah sang along as she waved her finger high, in time to the music that blazed out of her portable speakers. Her white towel still wrapped 'round her though she had finished showering more than half an hour beforehand. I had just come out of the shower and she still looked the same as when I went in; hair tied, slowly sipping on her glass of prosecco. As I took my towel off and placed my silk gown on, I could see her searching for the flawless outfit that she was going to wear that night. And she sang her heart out in between searching. But it didn't surprise me though; that was the way she got ready, every day. Playfully, I rolled my eyes at her as I proceeded on opening the balcony doors for some fresh air.

"How about this?" she asked as she pressed an all-black, halter neck flared dress to her shoulders.

"Nah, too showy," I told her after a moment of analyzation. She turned to the mirror, confirming whether my thoughts held any weight. After a second look, she sighed in agreement. It looked more like a salsa dress but we were only going to a bar. Her shoulders dropped as she returned to her suitcase to find another flawless look. I could tell that she was overthinking her choices. I already knew what I was going to wear and I didn't need anyone's supporting opinion to help make up my mind. We were only going to a bar and I was only going to keep her company. Though I knew that it didn't just feel like any bar to Lilah. We were meeting Akeem at *The Tabernacle* so I knew that she wanted to make an impression.

"Yes! That has to be the one!" I exclaimed as my eyes caught Lilah in her silhouette-hugging body-con. Her black, sleeveless dress slipped over her shoulders and on to her figure. I watched as she twirled in the mirror. The fitting material pulled over her bottom half and split at her cleavage, forming two square panels just over the meat of her bosoms. Spaghetti straps crossed over her fleshy chest and zig-zagged over her back. It was simple yet effective.

"I don't look too bad if I do say so myself." She smirked as she flirted with her reflection in the mirror.

"No, you look good. Akeem will love it," I said as I pulled my wine dress over my legs and onto my shoulders. "Can you zip me up please?" I asked as I struggled to reach the zipper at the back. Whilst I knew that my choker dress fitted me well, it was always a two-man job.

"And you never know, he might get his first kiss tonight, if he plays his cards right!" Lilah boasted as she pulled the back material together to ease the zip up to my neck. And my eyes dropped to the ground.

"Well at least one of us will be getting some tonight," I murmured.

"Girl!"

"I was so close last night until you came in!" I shook my head in comical disappointment though I was more annoyed than I let on.

"I know. I'm so sorry!" Lilah reached forward to embrace me from behind. "Don't worry, you are going to get it too! Trust me!"

"I hope so! It's been too long," I told her as I poured my own glass of prosecco.

"I know its crazy out here with all these people and everything going on but you just have to make it happen. By any means necessary!" Lilah insisted as she raised her glass towards mine and my cheeks lit up.

"Yes! By any means!" I echoed, clinking glasses with her. And the feel of the bubbles at the back of my throat automatically raised my spirits.

***

A crowded queue formed outside of *The Tabernacle* that stretched way past the club; with ladies in large groups dressed up to the nines. Most of them were merry but some were boisterous and that heightened my senses. There were only two of us and Akeem hadn't arrived yet. Groups of girls gathered behind smartphones as they snapped their early memories of the night. A strong whiff of perfume came from the group in front of us as they flashed their locks behind. I could tell that they were out on the prowl by the power of their scent. The bass from the bar was clear to hear way into the street and the crowd danced along to the tunes as we held our spot outside. A well-padded security guard marched up and down the line commanding the preparation of our I.D.

"No I.D. No Entry," he bellowed as he trooped past the crowd.

It didn't take long for us to reach the front and a huge, stern-looking woman towered over us. Her words were minimal but her actions spoke for a thousand. She held her hand out as she eyed us up and down and I immediately handed my I.D. over. Lilah followed suit. Nervously, I licked my lips as the security guard's eyes flitted from the I.D. to us and back again. It was almost as if I had something to hide but I didn't. I hated intimidating situations like this but Lilah was a social butterfly. She smiled confidently at her to lighten the mood and a crack of a smile started to appear on the guard's face. Within moments she had nodded in acceptance and opened the barriers for us. Lilah clutched onto my hand as we hobbled into the darkness.

As soon as we stepped in, our ears were consumed with the boom that penetrated past *The Tabernacle* doors. A luminous light shone on all of us, making our eyes and teeth glow in the dark. And the bothersome bits of fluff that were hardly noticeable in normal light, were clear to see under the ultraviolet rays. The windows were entwined with stained glass and images of a holy nature. It was rather ironic as the stained glass rose above the above the bar staff and sat alongside the filled bottles of liquor. I chuckled to myself as I processed the image that stood before me. Groups of people started to circulate by the bar to get their orders in and we were keen to join them. Two rounds of shots and a cocktail was sure to get us in the mood.

"How do I look?" Insecurely, Lilah turned to me, fixing her almost faultless hair do.
"Girl, you look fine. Akeem's going to love you," I reassured her as I sipped on my Caribbean Storm; it had quickly become a favourite of mine.
"Are you sure?" she double checked as she pulled out her red lipstick to top up her top-up.
"Yes, where is he?" I asked as I scanned the bar curiously. The bar was filling up and he was nowhere to be seen.
"I have no idea but he better show up soon!" Lilah retorted sassily.

The lights dimmed as we walked through the crowds and shone on one particular spot. A long cross shape penetrated through the middle and rose to chest level. The people gathered around and the music lowered. The level of light made it almost impossible to search for Akeem so we joined the crowds whilst we waited for him to show up.

Zzzzuuuuummm

A machine violently revved behind the stage and our ears tuned in.

Zzzz
Zzzz
Zzzzuuuuummm

Three men in welding helmets stood firm at the beginning of the stage; their leg stance wide, shoulder to shoulder.

Zzzzuuuuummm

Bright metallic sparks flew from their crotch as they coerced a pole into their grinder. The crowd roared. My eyes were fixed on them; unsure of how to feel. Their heads slowly scaled the stage.
Then, the men marched forward, each one taking possession of a length of the stage at the tips of the cross. My breath paused. The men and their grinders were only metres above us.

Clang!

The lights blacked out and a slow, sexy sound blasted into the venue. The crowd cheered, seething in anticipation. In unison, the men shoved their metal poles into the grinder and the flashing spikes avalanched over our heads. But this time, it was in rhythm. With every beat, their hips thrust and the pole ground into the machine.

Flash flash.
Flash flash.

Sparks flew off into the distance and the audience went wild. Their muscles tensed as they controlled the machinery and rhythmically marched through the stage until they had switched positions. Knees bent. Hips flexed. The pole sat comfortably between their legs.

Flash flash.
Flash flash.

The grinder roared and the crowd looked on in awe. There was something sexy about these men. They made the art of welding look appetising.

Before the slow jam had even finished, the men marched off the stage. They had worked the crowd into a frenzy then disappeared. *What an awesome start.* The ends of my lips pressed down the sides of my mouth, impressed by the opening act. Within moments, the song had switched and the base infiltrated through my chest. When the lights rose, only one welder sat on the stage. On a chair, shoulders slouched and legs open. His solid arms bulged through sleeves and sweat leaked through his shirt. As he sat, his crotch popped into the air in time with the beat.

Boom, boom.
Boom boom boom.

The girls screamed and I couldn't help but lick my lips. But I could see Lilah was distracted. Every minute or two her head peered round in the hope that she would see Akeem. But he still hadn't arrived. Thank goodness for the entertainment. Slowly the welder rose to his feet, popping and locking his way all the way to the top. The outline of his abdominals branded their way through the shirt and were clear to see as he worked his way 'round. His fingers guided his feet as they shuffled across the stage and the crowd went berserk.

I turned to Lilah, she looked distant and clearly wasn't enjoying the show as much as I was. But as I looked 'round, I caught a glimpse of him. It looked just like him.

"Hold on." I elbowed Lilah, "Isn't that Akeem?" I questioned her for confirmation. Her eyes darted through the crowds. She had seen him more than I had so I assumed that she would be the expert. I could see a glint in her eyes as her levels of hope rose.
"Where?" she eagerly asked. I grabbed her head to guide her eyes.

"There!" I said as I moved her head to optimum position.

"Oh… my…" Her head froze, "It… is," The pulse strengthened in her temporal lobe. *I knew my eyes hadn't deceived me.*

When Akeem said he was a dancer, I never once thought that he meant this. Lilah's focus had now fixed onto the stage and hadn't moved since the moment Akeem had lifted his welding helmet and revealed himself. And we both stood there, stunned. His hips rolled smoothly and with purpose; as if he were trying to tell us a dark and twisted tale. And the girls went wild for his sensual moves.

It didn't take long for her to capture Akeem's attention. His hazel eyes winked the moment he had spotted her and I could almost feel the hysteria leaping through her veins. In fact, I was charged too. Sweat dripped from his forehead as he removed the helmet clean off his head and the crowd cheered as he flashed his curls. He rose from the seat and slipped off his belt.

Whip!

His hips flicked sexually as he pulled his belt taught. *Wow.* I wasn't usually attracted to guys like Akeem but he looked smoking. His glistening, golden biceps flexed hard as he ripped his shirt off. Thrilled, Lilah squeezed my hand tight. He dropped to his knees and eyed the crowd in his gorilla stance. His hazel eyes pierced us all and the crowd followed his movements. Instantly, he began grinding the floor with conviction and my blinking doubled.

He was fucking the floor like it was the sexiest piece of booty he had received in his life and my lips began to dry. His knees gracefully caressed the stage as his firm peach rose up then fell down. Screams of merriment possessed my ears as dollars floated on to the stage. The more his hips curled, the more his waistline was filled with dollars as the audience lapped it all up.

Erotically, he crawled to end of the stage with his hips still winding and he held his hand out. A flock of girls leaned forward but there was only one hand that he was reaching for. My chest began to tighten and Lilah's body played stiff.
"Go on!" I urged as I elbowed her forward and she reluctantly rose her hand. Step by step, she climbed onto the stage and followed Akeem to the abandoned chair planted in central view. Whilst the crowd cheered her on, I squealed internally. Part of me was excited whilst the other part frantically wondered what he was about to do to her.

His waist snaked 'round as he spun to the ground and he separated her legs. Within seconds his head swum from her crotch to her chest and her cheeks puffed high. Effortlessly, he grabbed hold of her shoulders as he climbed onto the chair and began winding his groins in her face. Naturally, Lilah's tongue leapt out of her mouth but it was too late, he had already jumped off. Akeem faced the crowd as he ripped his bottoms off to reveal his ever-so-snug thongs. The screams volumised as his v-line thrust and his honey dipped behind shined. He certainly hadn't packed lightly.

Casually, he rolled back and landed with his piece in her crotch. And Lilah couldn't resist grabbing his buttocks as it slowly rotated like a piece of rotisserie meat. I burst out in laughter. I could tell that she was making up for lost time. Smoothly, he spun 'round on her lap until his chest was facing hers and lured her head into his gyrating parcel; Lilah happily followed his lead. Her head grazed against his bare chest as he gently took charge of her. I inhaled intensely, imagining the scent that dressed his lean body. After rising to his feet once more, he lurched forward and grabbed the meat on her legs. Suddenly, she was in the air and had no option but to wrap herself around his thighs. Then he lowered her until her hair brushed the floor below her. Slowly, he began grinding his waist into her crotch as her head tilted backwards and the grin on her face expanded. And I couldn't help but visualise myself being thrown around the bedroom with such effortless dominion.

Pump!

He shoved his package into her mailbox before whipping her back up. My heart stopped for a minute as I watched. Akeem's hips had bounced her into the air and her dark locks clapped against her back. Her arms wrapped around his neck a little tighter. He gave her a kiss on the cheek before lowering her to the floor and the crowd cheered violently. I could tell that they loved it just as much as she did; in fact, I did too.

"Oh my goodness. That was amazing!" Lilah breathed as she rushed back to embrace me, still flushed from it all.

"I know. You two were on fire!" I added as I grabbed hold of her, delighted. In an odd way, I was quite proud of how brave she had been to even go on stage in the first place; with everybody watching her.

"That was the craziest experience I've ever had, hands down!" she exclaimed as her eyes followed her thoughts, almost as though she was reliving every moment of it again in her head.

"Well, at least you don't have to worry about where Akeem is anymore!" I was almost as enthused as she was.

"Yeah. He said that he's going to come and find us once he has freshened up!" Lilah spoke with an inerasable smile on her face.

"Oooh!" I squealed in excitement.

"Though, after that dance, I wouldn't mind getting him dirty all over again!" Lilah laughed like a hyena and contagiously I couldn't help but join in with her.

***

After we had started to come to terms with Lilah's ordeal, we headed to the bar for another round. Being on stage had caused her to break out in a sweat and watching her on it was thirsty work too. Whilst she opted for something stronger in taste, I chose the same cocktail. And within moments, we had drained our glasses so we ordered another couple of drinks to sip. Soon after, the lights dimmed once more and the crowds gathered by the cross; the next act was about to grace the stage. And as soon as the music boomed through the venue, a masked man appeared, topless and wearing black, loose bottoms. The crowd stood still. For a moment, his vendetta mask eyed the audience as he followed the direction of the pole in his hands. My chest froze, feeling moderately on edge by his menacing stare. Then, the ends of his stick lit up in flames and the crowd applauded. The two balls of fire blazed as he spun the burning stick high in the air and his chocolate biceps flexed. His hips wound in time with his stick and great balls of fire illuminated the tone in his abdominals. Naturally, my lips wept. The pole flicked across his arm then his back and right over the other side and the light was dazzling. Waves of flames circled in the air as his waist figured eight and the screams volumised. Then he flipped back with his glowing pole still in his hand and the hollers boomed. Once then twice, he tumbled in the air, showing great control over the flame and our eyes were fixed. His lean muscles flexed as his foot levitated into the air and the stick grazed his mouth.

Woof!

A ferocious flame exploded from his breath and his capoeira skills shone.
"Whoooh!" I screamed as he stood to his feet, captivated by his act. Then he lifted his mask to put out the flame and I firmly clutched on to Lilah. "Oh my fucking days," I said as my force restricted the blood circulation in her hand. As he leaned back, his mouth broadened and he slowly lowered the flame in. I couldn't believe my eyes.

"That's fucking Nelson!" I breathed and Lilah couldn't believe her ears. The fire went out and the rhythm and bass slowed.

"What the hell is he doing here?" Lilah snapped in disbelief and I hardly had the words for her. My eyes followed him, astonished as he dropped the burnt-out stick to the ground along with his mask. "He does look hot though," Lilah added as her teeth caught her bottom lip but I was still too stunned to respond.

The hollers jeered as he snaked his chocolate body 'round and reached his hand into the crowd. My breathing halted. The wired lady couldn't help but grab her mouth like a giddy child as she was ushered on to stage and within moments of running rings around her, she was down on the floor. Nelson turned to the audience and whipped off his bottoms, revealing his solid behind. And the dollars floated onto the stage like the first leaves of autumn. His bulging underwear was clear for everyone to see. "Girl," Lilah gripped my arm in shock and my heart winced lightly. And although I found it hard to admit, his firm back did look appetising as he mounted the gagging female, lying on the floor. Forwards and back his trunk slid over her face and she lapped it all up.

In a flash, Nelson had picked up his stage volunteer and his face was now in her lap as he held her upside-down. The cheers blared as he wound his head and his waist into her. And the more the excitement intensified, the more notes fell to the stage floor. There was no doubt that the crowds were fantasising but a strong heat couldn't help but race inside of me. I watched as he turned her around and pushed her on all fours like a rag doll. And a slight flush of jealousy steamed through my system. *What was wrong with me?* I questioned as I reminded myself that I had moved on and was about to wed my fiancé. And even though I had no intentions of ever getting back with him, I found the image of him grinding his piece into another woman's behind somewhat unsettling. His groin rippled onto the girl's jeans and his smooth chest flexed. A cold sweat coursed through my skin. He'd worked his way all over and the crowds were loving every minute of it; even Lilah couldn't contain her excitement. And after what felt like a lifetime, he finally lifted the flustered woman to a standing position and placed a small kiss on her hand. Whoops and cheers deafened the room.

"Nelson's moves are fire, Ray. Now I see what all your fuss was about," Lilah accoladed as his danced closed and the audience hollered on.

"Mmm," I managed to utter as I processed it all. The applause filtered through me like a wave of white noise. I still couldn't believe that Nelson was a stripper. The thought of it alone caused an acid reflux in my system and the images before my eyes made it even stronger. My lids shut tightly as I tried to erase it all from my head. But as my eyes reopened, his gaze caught mine and I froze. My emotions had been numbed. I couldn't even bring myself to exchange a polite smile with him. In fact, I was so lost in my thoughts that all I could do was glare.

"So did you enjoy that little dance then?" Akeem breathed as he crept up to Lilah from behind and her cheeks began to glow.

"Well, it wasn't too shabby." She flirted as she turned to face him but my feet felt stuck. I was still in shock from it all.

"Too shabby? Couldn't you hear those screams? All those females wanted to be you." He eyed her as he grabbed on to her waist and her face flushed. I swished the straw around my glass as I tried to bring myself back to the moment; though the blast from the past had caused a slight jolt in my system.

"Well, it's a shame there's only one me," she toyed and my eyes began to roll. And as they joked and laughed, Akeem looked captured and it didn't surprise me. Lilah's game face was always on point and she knew how to get what she wanted. And whilst they chatted the night away, I sipped my drink quietly; still lost for words. And the more they talked, the more apparent it became that I was the spare part so I slipped off to grab a seat by the bar. But as I sat down, I saw him once again. I saw Nelson through the crowds and he was heading straight towards me. Almost instinctively, my hands began to clam up.

~ Chapter 8 ~

"Hey Raven, long time," Nelson beamed as he leaned into me for a faire la bise. And though blood was racing through my veins, I attempted to switch on my calm and collected mannerisms.

"I know, how have you been?" I asked with just as much enthusiasm, using a tone of voice that was so high, I was sure that dogs could've picked up on my frequency.

"I've been good. I've just been doing my thing-"

"Yes, I can see that! You're a stripper now!" I interrupted his flow, not as collected as I had previously thought.

"Well, I prefer the term dancer, but that's a matter of opinion," he muttered as his eyes coyly shuffled to the ground.

"Yes, a dancer that takes their off clothes for money. But who am I to judge? I can't knock the hustle!" I laughed before sipping my fifth dose of cocktail for the night. Though I had been drinking all night, somehow my mouth had suddenly begun to dry up. Silently, Nelson smirked as I slurped then eyed me for a moment before he spoke once again.

"So how did you get all the way to Jamaica without letting me know?" he curiously asked as he sat on the stool beside me. My eyelids sharpened.

"I know, things have been so busy. I barely had the time to keep up with everyone. You know how it gets sometimes," I said guiltily as I swivelled the orange slice around my glass; not quite sure of how to share the news with him.

"Yes, I hear you. That's how life is, I suppose." His lip curled solemnly as he spoke. "I won't lie to you though, you look beautiful. Even more beautiful than the last time I saw you." He smiled weakly and blood raced to my cheeks.

"Thanks." I giggled awkwardly, not quite sure of how to appropriately respond to his comment. Though his words made me considerably warm, I knew that it wasn't right for my heart to melt in my current circumstances.

"So are you here alone or..." he asked and my chest seized up. And as hard as it was to admit out loud, I knew that I certainly wasn't alone anymore. But that was none of his business; my self-convincing process had already begun.

"No, my friend's over there with one of the other dancers, Akeem, so I thought I'd give them some space." I gestured to where they stood as I spoke before slurping my almost drained glass.

"Oh yes, Akeem! Weren't that the girl that he brought on stage tonight?" he asked for confirmation and my nostrils couldn't help but flare.

"Yes. That's why she's probably so wrapped up on him now!" I exclaimed as I rolled my eyes jovially.

"And you're left here alone." Nelson pouted his bottom lip mockingly. And though I knew that it wasn't entirely the case, cowardly I allowed him to believe his assumptions. I didn't know how to break it to him. "It's cool though. I don't mind keeping you company," he went on as he reached for my thigh and my legs stiffened sharply.

"You are funny." A chuckle leapt out of my mouth before I even had the chance to think. Casually, I removed his hand from me and his brows crossed me, rather puzzled. I giggled softly once more. Unfortunately, things were different now and I knew it but the reality of it all was so awkward to admit. It just seemed much easier to avoid the whole situation altogether.

"So how's Mara?" I questioned curiously. Whilst part of me had asked to move our conversation on swiftly, another part of me was intrigued to know how and if they were still together.

He shrugged his shoulders nonchalantly and my chin raised towards him, "Mara's Mara," he mentioned. My eyes narrowed as I tried to decipher his basic yet baffling response. "She does her thing and she lets me do mine so our relationship is what it is," he told me casually. And though I smiled externally, a small part of me slightly burned inside. I just couldn't get my head around their situation but I had to remind myself that it had nothing to do with me anymore.

"Well, I can see that Mr Vendetta," I bantered back and he burst out in a laughter that revealed the enjoyment that he received from his alter ego.

"What can I say? There's just something about being on stage that just makes me feel alive. Plus, there's no harm in a bit of fun." His cheeks warmed as he spoke, almost as though the performance was his escape. I eyed him briefly as I placed my drink on the table.

"Yes. As long as no one gets hurt." My eyebrow snarly rose.

"Trust me, no one is going to get hurt." Nelson shook his head as he spoke. And whilst I could sense the embarrassment that he felt from our previous encounter, I knew that there was no point in trudging over old ground. It wouldn't have done any of us any good. "So how about you? How's your love life? I know someone must've swept you off your feet by now?" His eyebrow haunted me and my chin coyly tucked into my chest. I knew it was time.

"Well yes, I suppose." I blushed as I spoke. "That's why I'm here." I paused for a moment as I tried to gather my thoughts and Nelson briefly scanned the venue.

"Oh, I didn't realise there were more of you at *The Tabernacle.*"

"No, there's not," I confirmed and Nelson's stiffening shoulders began to relax. I took a deep breath before I continued, "But I came to Jamaica with my fiancé… to get married," I told him though I felt somewhat embarrassed.

"What? You're kidding me right?" he questioned me, stunned. I shook my head bashfully as my engagement ring shone underneath the club lights. It was the first time I'd felt ashamed about my marriage and I knew exactly why. It hadn't even been a year and I had already moved on. But as hard as it was, I knew that I couldn't deny my husband-to-be. He stared at me for a while, smiling as his eyes flicked from my cowering face to my ring and back again.

"Well… I suppose congratulations are in order," Nelson mentioned as he beckoned the bar staff over for a refill and she swiftly filled us up. "To Marriage," he toasted as we rose our glasses, "though, it should have been me." He winked as he sipped on his drink and my chest automatically flushed. My lashes blinked firmly as I dragged my mind back to reality. *If it was meant to be him, it would have been him*, I had to remind myself as the liquor whipped to the back of my throat.

***

One too many drinks had me stumbling back to the hotel in a more than vulnerable mood. I was confused. Whilst I had a great night in so many ways, seeing Nelson grind on stage had fucked with my head and that talk with him had messed with me even more. I couldn't understand it. It wasn't so much what he had said that had me thinking twice but more the actual presence of him; being face-to-face with him again. It had been months since we had last spoken but that one conversation with him had me questioning myself and my decisions. *Was I actually going to do this?* My feet felt light but my head felt heavy and I was in desperate need of reassurance. I needed Andrew. I needed him to remind me why he was the one for me.

I plonked myself into the lounge chair by the balcony with a tall bottle of water as I attempted to clear my head. And the railings were the only thing that kept me safe as the nightlife thrived below me. My feet swung loosely from the chair and my head reclined whilst I tried to make sense of my thoughts. Sprinkles of stars glistened in the night sky and the moon shone brightly. And whilst the rooftop was deserted, the warm air kept me company as I waited for him to arrive.

"Are you alright?" Andrew asked as he leaned into me and I managed to nod my head. He looked gorgeous in his loose shorts and his dick print encouraged the weak smile to strengthen on my face. "How was your night?" he asked as he sat down and a solemn darkness thickened inside of me.

"It was good… but it would have been better if you were there." My guilt led my words and he began to chuckle. "I didn't realise it was a strip club and I'm still in shock that Akeem is actually a strip dancer," I said and his eyes enlarged.

"Wow… so there must have been plenty of dicks flying around the place," he joked and my thoughts trailed off.

"Yeah, but all I wanted was you," I said as I ran my finger across Andrew's cheek and his dimple deepened. The stars reflected in his eyes and the heat raced through my body.

"I'm sure you were fine," Andrew chuckled as he looked into my eyes. And when I looked deeper, I saw my hopeless reflection staring right back at me. I wasn't fine; especially after my encounter with Nelson. I needed more.

"I am now," I whispered before leaning in and my eyes began to close. A strong vibration erupted underneath my cheeks as my nose brushed against his and our lips connected. As we kissed, a warmth of delight rushed through me. I felt loved. I felt safe. And almost automatically, my hands scaled the back of his head to urge him closer to me; his head responded accordingly. A wave of emotions volumised inside of me as my tongue caressed his. It was what I craved and what I was missing. But whilst our tongues collided and my eyes fused, the vision of Nelson's ebony eyes cultivated in my mind, then his smile. *Fuck. What was wrong with me?* I questioned my thoughts as I cursed the image out of my mind. I was with Andrew and that was what I wanted; my lids squeezed briefly as I reminded myself of that. And I continued my pursuit to woo him.

Casually, I persuaded his hands onto my thighs, then my assets. My teeth grazed the skin of his neck as my mouth inhaled him deeper and deeper. I hoovered over his neck like a vampire on heat and his Adam's apple began to protrude. The more I sucked his skin, the more I could feel his blood surfacing to the top. His hands gripped my meat and my hole amplified as he gently took charge of my behind. I began to smirk to myself. I knew he was loving it and that made me want him even more. My leg slid on top of his lap. His feet relaxed on to the seat as he adjusted to my weight and his legs began to spread. I paused for a moment to admire his beauty and I began to clam up. *That was it. That was the adorable look that he gave me when I first decided I was going to give him a chance.* My chest warmed.

Effortlessly, I peeled off his black frames and placed them on the table beside us. My hand then gripped him tightly. I exhaled in gratefulness as my cleavage rubbed against his body heat and he clutched on to my meat. I eased his nose through my bust like a magnetic stripe and my hairs stood on end. I couldn't help but radiate as he ran his firm fingers over my back and I cupped him like a koala bear. I began winding my hips on top of his lap as my fingers caressed his low fade. And as my hips persevered, so did my dress up my thighs revealing the base of my cheeks.

But I didn't care. I didn't care that we were outside and I didn't care about the possibility of any passers-by. He was my fiancé and I was going to do whatever I wanted with him. I lifted his head to towards mine to swallow the taste of his lips as I ground my pelvis on top of his. And I felt him swell. As his piece solidified, the feel of his dick against my clitoris became ever so prominent. Blood rushed to the tip of my vagina as I rocked back and forth on his cock. His teeth gently bit my breast. My chest clenched. My lids shut tight as I tried to squeeze Nelson's bright, pearly whites out of my mind and his deep dimple.

I needed more of Andrew. I needed him to convince me that I was his and he was mine.
"I want your dick," My breath trailed over his earlobe and he began to chortle.
"I bet you do," he toyed with my emotions.
"Yes, I do. I need you right now on this rooftop." I stressed as I continued to rock over his crotch.
"There are only a few more days left now, you've been doing so well…" he tried to convince me but I wasn't buying any of it.

"Fuck your few days. We've waited long enough," I asserted myself. "Look how hard you are." I flirted my hips and my lips slipped through my thongs. "I know you're ready to blow..." I bit my lip as I continued just on the tip. His head tilted back and his chest inflated deeply. He was stuck; between his morals and his urge to fuck. I stepped off him and dropped to the floor before sliding down his shorts with little resistance from him.

"You'll be my wife soon and we can do this all you want..." He told me as he let out the breath that had been building in his lungs. I crept to his dick.

"I'll be your wife soon so I will do what I want, when I want," I affirmed as I slid the condom onto his penis. My tongue laced the back of his shaft.

"Aaah…" he exhaled as I caressed his nerve endings; his cock was now swollen with pride. And my heart sunk as I watched him. His eyes rolled back as he received all the pleasure, yet, *I had to wait*... I collapsed internally.

"Hmm...That's it. That's all you're getting..." I uttered as I rose to my feet; my dress still halfway up my behind. My arms rested on the ledge as I looked down at the life below. The cars lit up the street and the people scattered like ants. And as I looked back, Andrew's dazed eyes attempted to focus on me. His blood had drained from his thought patterns and plunged straight up to his production. He was steadfast and I was ready. But I couldn't keep begging him for this. My head turned back as I thought. The town was thriving underneath my feet and I felt empty inside.

"Ahhhh," I breathed as a shot of lust erupted inside of me. My eyes watered as I watched the people below and he struck me again.

"Aaah," I moaned as he drove into me deeper and my lip began to curl. Andrew had hit my sweet spot and my legs felt weak.

"Is this what you want?" he asked as he hammered into me again and my mouth disconnected. His fuck was so intense that I was lost for words. So he continued over and over. His dick pounded harder and harder and I held onto the ledge for balance. I began to glow inside. There was something thrilling about watching the passers-by on the ground below as Andrew relentlessly blew my back out. Small bursts of pleasure gushed through my system as his hips smashed into my cheeks.

"Is this what you want?" he asked again but for some reason, I couldn't find the words to speak. My head nodded weakly as he shoved his way into me. And as soon as I had responded, he drove into me harder and faster and my head began to rock. Over and over, he thrust in and out, in and out and my eyes glazed over. Pleasure mixed with pain as his thick dick rubbed my walls then hit me hard.

"Arghhh." My eyes winced as he rooted into the depths of me again and again. A bolt of nausea swarmed into my stomach and his hips responded in delight. The sound of my moans gave him fuel and drove him wild. But the more his meat submerged into my tunnel, the more he chafed my insides. I was torn; torn between the need for connection and the need for relief. His grunts steered my conscience. I wanted him to feel just as good as I wanted to feel complete.

I held my breath as he impelled into me and he began to swell. *Ouch...* The feel of his shaft burned right through me and my pussy responded with contraction. His breathing intensified as my walls rubbed raw and yelps of aches left my mouth. My head and my heart were out of sync. And even though I had not reached my peak, my body yearned for it all to end. But my vagina was swelling, goading him to pick up the pace. His strokes sped up as did my heart. Blood gushed out of my organs at quadruple rates as he pounded his way to ecstasy. My teeth clasped the air through my lips as I tried to breathe through the pain. Saliva rippled on my tongue as the air swept past my throat.

"Aaahh…" he whispered as his piece pulsated inside of me. And a small wave of joy passed underneath my skin, briefly alleviating my agony. His burn had already started to set my walls on fire but his powerful pulse struck me harder. I knew he was about to blow. He clutched onto my waist as he began to reach his climax.

Pulse.
Pulse.
Pulse.

He released his load. "Daaammnn…" he respired as he crumbled inside of me. And though I hadn't even begun to scratch the surface of his heights of excitement, my eyes wound back in relief. *Thank fuck it was over.*

~ Chapter 9 ~

That night as I crawled into bed, I could feel his mark. He had burned a gaping hole inside of me and I felt raw. Even the eco-friendly temperature from the shower wasn't able to cool down the heat that thrived between my legs. I felt bruised. I wanted nothing more than to numb the sting that bounced off my insides. And though I knew that I had caused the pain, I couldn't help but feel used and raped of my dignity, by my own fiancé. But I'd had consensual sex and in fact, I had encouraged it, so I had only myself to blame. My eyes shut tight as I tried to breathe through it all; head tucked under the sheets and curled into a foetal ball. The fire scorched through me.

The more I laid there, the more the heat from my breath acclimatised to my body temperature and relaxed my thoughts. And a quiet vibration crept all over me. The longer I wrapped myself up, the heavier my eyelids became and the easier it was to remove myself from the pain. I fell deeper and deeper into sleep. Behind me, I heard the muffles of mumbling conversation but my body refused to succumb to full consciousness. My body embraced the vibration. A faint cry of whimpering hovered behind my back whilst another voice spoke more assertively. At first, it was unclear, but the more they spoke the easier it was to understand their words.

"Let me show you," the voice spoke calmly and quietly. I felt a smooth kiss on my shoulder and my hazed eyes opened. The curtains were drawn and the lamp had given the room a violet hue. Another smooth kiss ran across my shoulder blades and my lungs filled with breath as I embodied the feel. My blinking slowed as I rolled on to my back and my cheeks grew warm. My eyes met with Andrew as he sat on the stool by the end of the bed with an unsettled look on his face. I smiled weakly at him but his expression was fixed and he said nothing. His glasses were still partially steamed.
"Are you okay?" I asked, quite concerned and he stared right back at me.

"Its fine," I felt a cold hand on my shoulder and my breath clenched sharply.
"Nelson? What the hell are you doing here?" I whispered in utter disbelief.
"Don't worry. He knows I'm here," he spoke quietly as his head pointed in Andrew's direction. "There's no way I could allow him to have you without showing him how to treat you first. Just relax." His voice soothed my ears as he took charge of my body and Andrew's eyes followed his every movement.

He reached into his deep, black leather bag and shuffled around for a moment or two. Then his eyes lit up as he found what he was looking for. One by one, he took my hands and wrapped them in a silk ribbon that stretched from my buckled wrists to each bedpost. My bare chest automatically levitated as he tied me tight. Then he took my legs and strapped a buckle around each one. He spread them wide as he attached another ribbon from my ankles to the ends of bed; Andrew's eyes in full view of my bald eagle. My nipples hardened as my limbs stretched as wide as Da Vinci's *Vitruvian Man*; quietly anticipating Nelson's next move.

Stealthily, he reached his hands into his bag once more and pulled out a black leather tassel. My body pulled taught.
"Relax, you know I would never do anything to hurt you," he whispered as he sensed my dis-ease. "Unless of course, you asked." He smirked and I began to giggle as I gazed into his transfixing eyes. My hairs stood on end as he ran the tassel right through the centre of my torso. My toes curled in delight as the tassels trickled from the edge of my pelvis and over the circumference of my areola. Smoothly, he worked the tassel around me, teasing me and heightening my senses. My goosebumps chased his every touch.
He paused. I waited.

Oooo...

My abdominals tensed as he gave me a playful whip before tracing the tassel over the expanse of my body. Then he stopped. Gently, my teeth scraped over my lip as Andrew's teeth scraped over his fingers. I knew he was watching but I still longed for Nelson's touch once more.

Leisurely, Nelson peeled his top from over his shoulders and my mouth began to water. Muscles that I never even knew existed were defined on his smoothed chest of cocoa and that made me weak at the knees. His eyes fixed on me as he delved deeper into his bag full of tricks, he reached for something else. And I couldn't wait to see what he had in store for me. My eyes glistened as they set on what he'd found and my fingers squirmed eagerly.

Drip by drop, oil dribbled in between my breasts and my back arched in delight. Each drop sent sexual shots to my open crotch and willingly, the space between my open legs expanded. His palms ran like silk all over me as he endeavoured to chase the droplets around my chest. A purple hue illuminated on my skin as the gloss wrapped over my silhouette. My lids began to close. Sensually, his fingers enticed me as they slipped past my breast and around the circumference. Round and round, he encircled my chest and my breathing grew deep. A tingling sensation followed his every move and my heart began to pound. With every feel of him through the centre of my chest and around my ribs, my yearn for him grew stronger and I longed for him to take it further. Gradually, his slick fingers expanded over the meat of my breast and retracted at the tip. My nipples stood to attention. Each time his hands grabbed hold of my bosoms, he clutched onto an extra piece of my soul and my head began to drift.

Then his hands progressed down my stomach and slid back up. One after the other, his hands paced down and up my torso, reaching closer and closer to my pelvic line every time and my lungs began to float. The more his fingers scraped over my pelvis, the more blood swelled in my berry. My tongue whipped over my lip as I craved for him to play with what was between my spread legs. Then, his hands slipped over the meat in my thighs and my cheeks began to glow. Firmly, he caressed them, slowly working his way up and over my pelvis. He lingered nearby. My vagina tingled eagerly.

Little by little, he stroked my outer vagina and my lips grew plump. One rogue finger ran over the crease at the top of my lady lips as he clasped my vulnerability and my passage began to moisten. But he wouldn't touch my clitoris and that was how he took possession of my appetite. My hips raised as I longed for his touch to go deeper and my legs began to squirm. Up and down, his hand clawed the outside of my crotch and each time, a rush of energy raced to my sex. I wanted nothing more than for him to stroke my tip but his fingers played with my emotions. Slowly, my hands reach for his...

For fuck sake. The buckle and ribbons laughed at my futile attempts to guide him. My eyes resurfaced. As I looked in his direction, I could see a growing smirk on his face. He knew what he was doing and it was driving me wild.

His head glanced over at Andrew before it lowered on my swollen pussy. He dropped a sweet kiss on my privacy and sparks automatically flew. I was floating on cloud nine and had just had my first real taste of paradise. Round and round, his head began to twist and my shackled legs relaxed. A thrilling breath of desire captured my heart each time his head spun. It was exactly what I wanted; what I needed and it felt like utter bliss. The feel of his swift tongue melted my insides and indulged my mind. I lapped it all up as his tongue lapped me. I hadn't felt this good in a long while and I didn't even want to imagine it ending.

"Mmmm…" I breathed as his tongue drew back my hood. His strength was undeniable and he definitely knew his way around a woman's body. "Don't stop…" I urged as he persisted on rubbing his tongue over my pleasure point again and again. His tongue thrived and I took great gratification from him having his wicked way with the strapped up version of me. The more his tongue lapped over my dribbling vagina, the more my head began to float.

"Don't stop…" I reminded him as my sensuality heightened. I longed to grab hold of him but my hands were trapped by his buckle and ribbon. The same vibration that filled my vagina with joy began to spread further and further underneath my skin. Air filled my lungs as my eyes began to water. More and more, the desire expanded like a pleasurable pandemic and consumed every piece of me. The feel of his warm mouth over my privacy felt more than incredible and I was about to explode.

"Mmmm…Nelson…" I groaned as pulses of ecstasy shot through my veins. The strings pulled taught on the bedpost; my limbs spasming out of control. But he held on to my hips tightly as he carried me through my state of ecstasy. And his kisses felt good. Each kiss soothed my sweetness and relaxed my mind until my body came to a still; legs still spread. I was in a trance but I longed for his cock to complete me.

"I need your dick…" I told him as his head retreated away from me. A shot of breath burst through his nostrils.

"I know you do," he whispered as he gazed into my eyes, "and that's why I'm here," he said as he loosened the ties around my ankles and my legs broke free. "I know what makes you feel good and I will always be here to assist," he added as he loosened the ribbons from my spread arms and tied my wrists together. Within moments, he had flipped me over and lifted my buns into the air. My head bowed down. My vagina wept as it magnified and longed to be filled.

"Mmmmhhh…" A smooth stroke triggered a lustful wave through my entire core. I couldn't help but jolt forward as his cheeks squeezed tight. He took his time; thrusting hard but steady and my walls welcomed every feel. Every firm impulsion against my behind shot straight through my nerves, sending mini explosions to my mind. A breath huffed out of my lungs every time and my insides glowed in pleasure. Then he stopped. He withdrew his meat from my dripping vagina as he began to caress my back with his tongue. My eyes wound back thirstily. His lips were juicy and bounced off each space like a trampoline in slow motion. My trapped hands clawed at the bed as I longed to stroke him and the sheets bound in my fists.

"Aaaahh," I exhaled as he re-entered me and a warm glow rushed through me. His absence was missed and my g-spot had swelled in search for the next stroke of paradise. *Mmmmn...* My lips moistened as my tongue traced around the circumference. He struck me with pride. A balloon of bliss was filling inside of me and my cheeks began to stiffen. Small waves of emotion filtered through my cheeks as he slipped out then shot in over and over.

My outbreaths couldn't help but lengthen as his hips hooked and massaged my sweet spot each and every time. It was well and truly my definition of heaven and he was my guardian angel. *Aaaaah...* He retreated leaving my gaping hole of pleasure well and truly void. His passionate kisses impressed deeply into my back, more intense than before. I could tell that he was loving it just as much as I was. My bowed head arched back as I soaked it all up. I craved his kiss and longed to return the favour with just as much vigour but my trapped hands wouldn't allow for it.

"Mhm," he grunted as he thrust himself into me once more and my breast shot forward. His dick felt hungry and I was ready to feed him. His penis pulsated with conviction as he held onto my waist and launched into me harder.

"Aaahh...Take it easy Nelson," I breathed as his force catapulted me forward and my head hit the headboard. He was fucking me fiercer and faster than before. And my walls clenched as I tried to respire through his power. My elbows jolted forward as my latched wrists sought for balance. But he wasn't stopping. In fact, he was slamming into me harder and harder. Pain seethed through me as his dick drove into the pit of my stomach.

"What the fuck Nelson? Calm down!" I hissed as I turned my head towards him to see what on earth was wrong with him. My skin grew cold. My hairs stood on end as our eyes met and his menacing smirk grew wider.

Andrew? It was him that was fucking me so thoughtlessly and the pleasure that he was receiving was written all over his face. My stomach churned in disgust. I couldn't take the thoughtless fucking.
"Wait… wait…" I asked as I tried to capture my breath. And his smirk lengthened even further. He paused for a moment before responding to me with the entire length of his dick plunged deeper inside my weeping vagina. *Aargh! Fuck…* My eyes began to glaze over. My cheeks winced as I tried to take my mind off the pain but he just kept launching into me harder and harder.

"I can't take it…" I told him but his eyes had transformed. Fire breathed from Andrew's eyes as he savagely drove his way through me with gritted teeth. My hands attempted to grab him but I was stuck and my swelling wrists were growing numb.
"Please stop…" I turned to Nelson to save me but his hands had been bound and his mouth had been gagged. His helpless eyes stared into me as Andrew tore his way through

me; my pain threshold was tested to its limits. A tear rolled down my cheek.

"Please!" I begged but he responded with more power. Andrew's thrusts were relentless, no matter what I had said to him, my agony fuelled his fire. Bolts of tears rolled out my eyes as my head collided with the headboard over and over. My brain began to balloon as I saw him powering up.

Gasp!

His final thrust sent me through the headboard and out of my sleep. My head shot up. My mouth gaped open. My hands gripped onto the bedsheets as I re-collaborated. Sweat dripped from my chest as I came to my senses in the pitch-black, alone. My heart palpitations burst through my chest. *What the fuck?* A thousand thoughts whizzed through my mind. Right there and then, I knew that the wedding jitters had gotten the better of me.

~ Chapter 10 ~

"Where on earth are you taking me to?" I curiously asked as Lilah bounded my hands and wrapped a fluffy blindfold around my eyes.

"Stop asking questions and just trust me," she said as she giggled playfully. Secretly, I knew that she loved the control but I was petrified. Despite the numerous amount of times she had almost saved me and guarded my secrets, it was twice as hard to trust her when I was tied up and one of my key senses were removed.

"You better not leave me stranded in the middle of the street or something!" I demanded as the jingle of keys taunted my ears.

"Don't be silly! It's your hen night! You know I'm going to take good care of you. Just relax and enjoy the surprise," she assured me as her voice distanced itself away from me then disappeared. My lips dried up as my mind whipped across all the possibilities that she could have in store for me. I was dressed to the nines so I would have been livid if she had made me look a fool. We'd spent the whole evening getting ready and my sash fitted me perfectly. And now I could see none of it.

"I'm almost ready!" she bellowed from the other room as I sat ever so patiently on the bed stool trying to calm my mind.

Within minutes there was a knock on the door and my heart skipped. "Just a sec," Lilah called back in response and my eyes shifted underneath the blindfold. *Who was it?* I wondered as her footsteps trailed towards the door. The lock shuffled. The door creaked. A loud cheer burst through the door and consumed my ears. My head jolted back. "Congratulations!" a flurry of feminine voices hailed as they rushed towards me and launched me to my feet. My bridal party had arrived to lead me down the halls. My heart pumped in excitement. Though part of me was still on edge, another part of me was eager to know what they had in store for me so I giddily followed their guidance through the complex and out into the open air.

"Here, drink this!" a joyful voice ordered from my party as they shot three rounds of rum down my throat. My cheeks winced as a rush of heat raced through my neck and they all roared out in a merriment that was clear to hear across the hall. "You're going to need those with the night we have in store for you!" my cousin laughed as she encouraged me to have one for the road.

"To Mrs Martin!!" They all screamed as their glasses clinked and my hand was rocketed into the air. It wasn't long before they shoved the fourth drink down my throat and levered me into a vibrant vehicle. Two arms led my steps and plonked me onto a seat. And though the blindfold blocked my senses, I could tell there was a constant flow of vibe through and through. Laughter and music galore. My shoulders were rocked from side to side as the contagious sounds penetrated the speakers.

And though excitement raced through my veins, my mind was full of apprehension. Whilst I knew I had all of my crowd beside me, I felt lonely behind the blindfold and my mind couldn't help but stray to Andrew. The girls had kept me secluded all day and had confiscated my phone so I hadn't even had the chance to speak to him since the night before. His rough sex still haunted a part of me even after my night sweats and I was dying to talk things through with him. It was so out of character. I wondered whether the wait had overexcited him but I just couldn't tell. Either way, I had to be more honest with him because I wasn't prepared to live the rest of my life pretending to enjoy the pain of rough sex. But I knew that any chance of having that discussion was out of the picture, at least for now, so I tried my hardest to let go and put it to the back of my mind.

A loud holler interrupted my thought path. "There it is girls!" Lilah called to the rest of the bridal party and the squeals leapt through the vehicle. Our driver slowed before coming to a stop. I was desperate to know what *it* was exactly.
"When are you going to take this damn thing off?" I asked half annoyed and half keen to be fully immersed in my experience.

"Relax. Once we're inside, all will be revealed." Lilah giggled menacingly and my eyes rolled behind my closed lids. My arms lodged forwards as I was ushered down the steps. I slowed to gather my balance. And the longer we walked, the more the saliva dried from my mouth. My stomach was filled with butterflies and I was hungry to get inside.

***

It wasn't long before the ground below my feet transformed from a hard concrete to a cushioned carpet and I knew we had entered. A strong musk of sandalwood filled my lungs and pretty much relaxed my racing mind. A low sound of rhythms flowed through.

"Welcome ladies to *The Debauchery*." A pleasant voice greeted before Lilah took charge of the conversation. She told the voice that she had booked a booth under the name Raven Martin for the hen party and the voice spoke with glee. Immediately, we were shown to the booth and I was planted on the seat. The sweet aroma of lust intensified as her body heat neared me and I could tell it was Lilah. I could always spot her signature smell from a mile away. The heat from her hands wrapped 'round my head and the blindfold loosened. A slight weight of relief was lifted from my shoulders as my eyes quickly adjusted to the low lights. I briefly scanned my surroundings.

We were sat at a round glass table pretty much enclosed from the crowd but not completely private. In fact, the empty, wine-leather seats in the booth opposite were in our direct view. It was only the panels on the stage that kind of obscured their visibility. It was a rather intimate setting. A flower of booths encircled the stage and made way for a generous path around it. Gold glittered strings wrapped 'round the walls of the booth and gathered behind a hook at the opening like curtains. A group of scented candles dressed the table and complimented the ambience. It seemed like a quiet night at the venue but I was sure that my party would liven it up a bit.

"Ooooh... hello." Lilah flirted as a buffed butler arrived at our table wearing nothing but a collar and an apron wrapped around his waist. His smirk grew as he politely greeted us all. His oiled chest glowed as he manoeuvred his way around the table and his mahogany pectorals perked. He was undoubtedly fit enough for his position.

"Good evening, my name is Troy and I will be your butler for the evening. Please take a moment to look at our menu and I'll be back shortly to take your orders," the buffed butler voiced before turning away from the table.
"Listen, you can take my order any time," Lilah muttered as she eyed his firm behind walking away from the table. His cheeks were tight and looked strong enough to crack a walnut. Even I, had to lower my gaze for a moment to gather my thoughts.

"Lilah, you are too much!" I giggled as I squeezed her thigh underneath the table. I could tell that her decorum was running thin. Her head shot to me.
"What? Are you trying to tell me that you didn't notice that sweet peach? Girl, I could have that for starters, mains and dessert!" Blood drained from the corner of her lip as she gripped onto it lustfully. I could only imagine the thoughts that were running through her mind. My eyes rolled back at her 'carpe diem' attitude. And though it was slightly embarrassing, it was to be expected with Lilah.

The menu was engrossed with an array of Mediterranean dishes with a Caribbean twist. My mouth began to water as I struggled to come to a decision. Troy had been monitoring our table for a while now and he was on his way back. I looked over to see what my cousins had picked as I toyed between two choices. But the pressure from Troy's presence as he addressed all of our guests had coerced me to make up my mind quite quickly. I hated keeping people waiting. In the end, I decided to go for the grilled swordfish and the vegetable moussaka. I thought that it would make a healthy change plus, I was watching what I ate before the big day.

It wasn't long before our food arrived and the table was quickly decorated with Mediterranean delights. Sides of plantain, roti and fried dumplings complimented our dishes and we were all keen to tuck in. The swordfish steak was thick, juicy and almost melted in my mouth. The seasoning was powerful, giving an extra oomph to the smoky taste and the vegetable moussaka was to die for. I could tell that I wasn't alone in my gratitude as the table fell silent. Every single member was absorbed by their food and smiles of glee dressed their faces. The in-between visits from Troy quenched our thirst as our party found any excuse to call his fine behind over. And though my heart kind of sunk as my dinner came to an end, I was keen to delve into my dessert.

Soon after we had enjoyed our meal and Troy had cleared our table, the lights dimmed above us and lit up the stage. My eyes bounced out in excitement and were glued ahead. A soft jingle rhythmically shook from behind the stage and seemed to volumise the more it went on. Then, Mediterranean vibes boomed through the speakers with a Caribbean base.

Boom-boom
Boom-boom
Boom

My head couldn't help but rock, followed by my shoulders. One by one, ladies in red mesh veils took charge of the stage with their winding hips. Their stomachs contoured as their waists rolled sexually and the jewellery that decorated their floor-length skirts chimed. And whilst they never showed their faces, their outfits left hardly anything to the imagination. Their elaborately designed bras matched the colour of the veils and they all moved in sync. We all cheered in delight as they worked their magic. The skirts swayed in time with their sensuality and followed their every move as they worked their way into the crowd. The chimes jingled as they addressed every table in search of a dancing partner.

"Over here!" Lilah hollered as she shot my hand into the air; my breathing halted momentarily.
"What are you doing?" I shot in her direction and all she could do was laugh.

"It's your night girl. Let your hair down and have a dance!" She persuaded me out of my seat as the belly dancer opened her hand in my direction. My bridal party cheered as I accepted her request, egging me on even further. And the jeers loosened me up. At first, my hips rolled to her rhythm then my inhibitions took over my style, as she led me 'round the room. The dancers followed behind as they created a winding path through the aisle that circled around the stage. And the audience clapped their hands in merriment.

Before I knew it, the dancer had led me on stage and all of the other guests had disappeared back into their seats. *How on earth did I end up here, all alone? I'd been duped.* The belly dancer smirked as she led me to the seat in the middle of the stage and the bridal party roared. My neck tightened. I absolutely hated being in the spotlight.
"Mrs Martin! Mrs Martin!" They chanted over and over again as the lady in red snaked her way around me. My face flushed hot as all eyes were on me. Then there was an outburst in uproar and my head swiped 'round. Troy was heading towards me with a chocolate cake in hand. A single

candle glowed in the centre and sparkling flames shot out and upwards as he closed in on me.

"Whoooh!" the audience boosted my spirits as the flames fizzled out. *Congratulations!* The cake read and Troy's arms stretched out so that I could blow out the candle. My lips puckered as I blew and they all stood up to cheer. I felt proud. It was almost as though I had brought home the winning medal in the Olympics and I was the one who had been chosen to proudly wave our flag. I flashed my ring boastfully. Troy pierced a fork through the cake to cut out a slither. It bounced like sponge and looked absolutely to die for. Chocolate fudge sandwiched in the chocolate cake that was wrapped in chocolate icing; now that was my idea of paradise. He lifted the bite to my mouth in an attempt to feed me and I opened wide. They all cheered again. I officially had celebrity status.

All of a sudden, Troy stuck his finger deep into my cake and twirled his finger around. *The cheek of him.* But I couldn't help but taste my lips as he clawed out a piece and licked all around his finger. The cake complimented his smooth, dark skin and the way he tasted it made it look even more appetising. His hips circled as he stuck his finger deep in again and his abdominals defined as they moved in synchronisation. I wasn't sure how much I was supposed to enjoy the vision of him but he was undoubtedly a sight for sore eyes.

But this time when he withdrew his chocolate-smothered finger, he offered it to me. I looked 'round at my bridal party for confirmation that this was okay to do. My eyes met with Lilah and I could see the glee in her face as cheer-led me on. She gave me the pass and I could only imagine what she would have said if she was with me on the stage. *"These are your last nights of freedom. You only live once. Do your thing, girl!"* Lilah always had a way of making the inappropriate seem appropriate. But in this situation, it felt right and that chocolate looked irresistible. So my mouth drew in front of the entire audience and his fudgy finger went in. *Mmmm...* My eyes closed. It tasted delightful. My lips wrapped around his finger, suctioning over the tip and by the time I was finished with him, the chocolate had all gone. Whoops and roars elevated through the room and my eyelids receded.

Wow... I thought to myself as the butler toyed with the lining of his apron. He slowly revealed his v-line as he teased it away from his waist and my grin stretched across my cheeks. *He wasn't going to, was he?* I questioned his actions although a significant part of me wanted him to do it. He fingered the strings on his apron as his print became more visible through the cloth. *Take it off! Take it off!* I chanted to myself as I focused on his movements. He turned to the audience as he flirted with his strings and his dark, golden behind amused my imagination. I wondered whether he was wearing any underwear. There was no denying that he was smoking hot and the more he played with us all, the more I was intrigued to see. His arms stretched and the strings followed behind. His apron drooped as he turned to me. I bit my lip. He held onto the ends as his torso wormed his way into my mind. The apron was loose but he revealed nothing at all. His garments sacheted from side to side, rubbing over his protruding energy as his waist wound 'round. *Was that apron coming off or what?* His moves increased my curiosity as he let the apron drop lower and lower. His groin lines were strong and seemed to be never-ending behind his damn uniform.

The girls went wild as he turned to them and let his apron drop to the floor. And as his behind clenched, so did the curiosity in my underwear. I couldn't wait for him to turn around. From my view, I could see that he wasn't wearing any briefs and I was intrigued to find out how well he packed. He backflipped. I gasped. His cock sock swung. I began to chuckle. His penis was encased in a hotdog; mustard and ketchup inclusive.

Smoothly, Troy approached my chair and cocked one leg up as he rested his foot by my side. His hotdog was eye height and he was levering it nearer and nearer to my body. My cheeks hardened in embarrassment. As exciting as it was, I didn't know how to manage it all in a public space. Slowly, he launched my chair down to the ground and mounted me. There was an uproar of laughter and automatically my body stiffened. *What was he trying to do?* His glistening arms were solid in the press up position as his groin thrust over me. His body looked divine as it neared then left my personal space once, twice and then for the third time. His image caused a fluster inside of me.

And within moments he jumped to his feet and hovered over me. The crowd went wild as his hotdog propelled all 360 degrees then flipped back on top of me. This time, his piece was in my face. I didn't know where to look but the flick of his hips left me stuck with no choice as they started to pop harder and harder. My eyes tapered as his cock sock flashed past my face again and again. His butt cheeks squeezed tight. I wasn't so familiar with this angle but he wore it well.

"Get it, girl!" A voice hollered in the audience and I had no doubt in my head who it belonged to. My stomach involuntarily broke out in a series of contractions as I tried to hold back the laughter. I wasn't usually this clueless but I didn't know what to do with his dick in my face. He grabbed my hand with poise and placed it on his buttocks. And I was inclined to follow his lead as his legs butterflied in and out and his penis hovered over my mouth. I had never experienced anything quite like it and I wasn't sure how much I should have been enjoying it, considering the fact that I was due to be wed. Yet my vagina still tingled.

And as I battled the thoughts of infidelity that filtered through my mind, he rocketed up and off me, smoothly raising my chair to an upright position. He grabbed my hand and kissed it softly before helping me down the stage stairs. I didn't know what to do with myself. My legs felt like jelly. I attempted to compose myself whilst I walked back to my bridal party. As I approached them, their faces all shone in delight and pride, embracing me with open arms. As I sat down, I saw how Troy turned to address the audience in such a gentlemanly fashion. They gave him a final cheer whilst he picked up his apron and disappeared behind the stage. After all of that arousal, I no longer cared about the night before with Andrew. In fact, I was even more excited to wed and have my wicked way with him.

* * *

The evening had been filled with laughter, rum and vibes. And we were all in a randy mood. It had been the most amazing night by far since we had landed and I was ready to explore my next chapter. Liquor raced through my veins and clouded my judgement so I was finding everything absolutely hilarious. A few of us headed to the rooftop to continue our vibe whilst some had turned in early. And whilst our banter thrived on into the night, Lilah had disappeared. After the stimulating evening we'd had though, I wasn't surprised that she'd made other arrangements.

Our cocktail glasses emptied and refilled as we sat gossiping and exchanging our tips for a fruitful sex life. And by the end, we couldn't help but cover the age-old conversation of how to subtly hint our men in the right direction; that was a topic that had particularly caught my attention. And my eyes and ears were open to any suggestion. I always loved when my girls helped to rationalise my thoughts.

But as our eyes grew heavy, our glasses emptied for the final time and we returned to our rooms. My head was full of vibration and my feet clomped as I hobbled back towards our room. For some reason, the journey seemed longer than usual but I blamed it on my disorientation. After a prolonged fumble through my bag, I was eventually able to find my key to swipe into my room. My heavy hands pushed the door open and I rocked straight in. I slumped into the chair with a breath of relief. My feet were finished. As I tuned in, I could hear a low-level squeaking pulse from Lilah's room followed by a rhythm of panting. I smirked to myself as I de-strapped from my bra. From the sounds that crept through her door crack, I could tell that she had found something entertaining enough to keep her occupied after she'd disappeared.

And as I leant down to take my sandals off, a woozy sensation turned in my stomach. One too many drinks had caused my head to feel light. I needed fresh air. And the squeaking mattress in Lilah's room had started to pierce through my ears. Without hesitation, I headed for the sliding doors in an attempt to clear my fuzzy head and my rolling stomach.

My arms rested on the balcony as I looked over and a shot of adrenaline passed through me. My eyes widened then narrowed to focus my vision, not quite sure if my judgement had been skewed. *Was that Andrew?* I doubled my blinking to clear my eyesight. A chill passed through me moderately stronger than the midnight air. My legs numbed as I tried desperately to make sense of the vision in front of my eyes.

I was sure that I could see Andrew getting his dick sucked. *He couldn't be?* But the way how his body arched while he stood butt-naked looked all too familiar. I had already convinced myself but there was no way he would do that, so I had to be wrong. Yet, the numbing sensation still intensified as I focused in on him. I tried to sober up. I was almost sure that I could see a head bobbing back and forth off Andrew's mid-section as his head tilted backwards. His mouth drooped open, as did mine.

And as he moved, I could clearly see that there were two people in the room. Andrew stood behind and the other body was bent over.
And I could spot that golden, curly quiff from a mile off.
Sebastian? Was that Sebastian? A wave of insanity leapt through my mind as I tried to confirm and reconfirm whether my eyes were correctly wired to my brain. Vomit warmed the back of my mouth as I watched Andrew ruthlessly tear into his behind. And Sebastian's scrawny, tanned arms sought refuge on the sofa. *Was this actually happening?*

A strong vibration rushed underneath my skin as I watched the pleasure on Andrew's face as he stroked him over and over. I could see Sebastian's eyes rolling back in his head as he was jolted and jolted forward in front of their wall-to-wall windows. As it continued, I questioned my sanity. There was no way that *my* fiancé was actually fucking *his* best man. But their windows were crystal clear and the more they kept going at it, the more believable it became. Tears filled my eyes as I watched Andrew hammer *him* over and over again.

And regardless of whether I was seeing things or not, I could no longer take it. The view was retching. My stomach was boiling. My eyes winced as I burst back through the sliding doors. And my stomach heaved and heaved as I stumbled over to Lilah's door. *What the fuck? Andrew was fucking gay?* Lilah clutched onto her vulnerability as I burst in on her riding; mid-cowgirl. But I couldn't speak.

My eyes spun back in my head. My throat was gorged. My jaw uncontrollably wandered around and around. I paused. I could feel it coming and there was nothing I could do to hold it back.

Bluurrghhhhh!

I splurged it all out before collapsing face-down on the ground.

~ Chapter 11 ~

The next morning, I woke up to a cripplingly weak sensation haunting my soul. My body was firmly fixed to the mattress like a thick hunk of lead on a magnet. A numbing vibration pulsed through my head and prickled my top lip. My stomach felt loose and an offensive taste sat at the back of my throat. The word hangover could not even explain how I was feeling. And whilst the cogs in my mind were trying to turn, my eyes weren't ready so I laid there, stuck until the last waking moment.

"Good morning sleepy head," Lilah's voice entered my room in the cheeriest of moods and my eyes attempted to open. "I brought you some tea. How are you feeling?" she asked whilst sitting down beside me.
"Rotten… Absolutely rotten," I croaked as I spoke my first words of the day. I sat up before she handed me the cup. My hands blissfully clutched onto the mug like a well-needed cuddle and the warmth embraced me back.
"I can imagine after the mess you left on my room floor last night," her brow rose towards me in a jovial manner and my face flushed with blood.

"Oh my goodness, I'm so sorry," I winced at the thought of it.

"Don't worry. It's cool. Last night I was pissed when I had to jump off that dick to clean it all up but I'm over it now." Lilah reassured me.

"I thought I remembered bursting in on you but I wasn't sure with my fogged up brain," I said as the pieces of my memory attempted to fit back together.

"It's fine, it wasn't all that anyway. I was doing half the work, to be honest, but yesterday, you were fucked up. All you kept saying was "That bastard is fucking Sebastian. How dare he?" at the top of your lungs. I had to put you to bed," she quoted; goosebumps crept all over my skin as my reality dawned on me. *Fuck. I knew it.* As much as I had tried to deny parts of my memory, I knew that the haunting images that kept on flushing through my mind were more than the remnants of a hazy dream.

"Lilah, I was on the balcony for ages just staring at them, trying to convince myself that I was seeing things. A part of me still doesn't believe it now." My eyes glazed over as I glared into the distance and watched it all back in my head.

"That's crazy though. I don't even know what to say. I don't even know what I would do if I saw that shit but all I know is that only God could've saved me from bursting straight into their room. What are you going to do?" she asked in a concerning manner.

"I have absolutely no fucking clue. We're supposed to be getting married tomorrow and he is shagging his best friend." My loose stomach upturned at my words. "I don't know if I could even bring myself to admit that to anybody." A silent tear dripped down my cheek at the embarrassment of it all.

"I know. That's fucked up. I didn't even think that he had it in him to sleep with another woman, let alone another man. He definitely pulled the wool over my eyes." Lilah's head shook in disappointment.

"You're telling me? I'm friggin' marrying the guy; well, I was. I don't even know." My mind rushed past the two possibilities in utter confusion. "I don't even know whether I'm coming or going at this point!" I said as my fingers braised past my forehead.

"I can imagine. I can barely come to terms with it myself-"

"What makes it worse is that I've brought all these people out here to celebrate. To celebrate what? It's a friggin' sham!" Blood boiled underneath my skin.

"Raven, forget about the people. You need to think about you. You need to decide what you want from this." Lilah spoke assertively.

"Well, I definitely need to speak to him. That's for starters. I actually want to see what cock and bull he is going to come up with!" I began to laugh menacingly as I lost a piece of my sanity.

"Yeah, you guys definitely need to talk. I'm actually trying to think of a useful explanation for all this but I can't. It would be a shame to see all your happiness thrown down the drain but I suppose you've got to do what you've got to do," Lilah spoke and her words sunk in. She was right but the problem was I didn't know what to do. I nodded silently as I tried to play out each scenario in my head. She could tell that I was lost in my thoughts. "Well, whatever you decide, I am here for you either way," she said as she held on to me tightly and I held her back; locking her in. Although I wasn't quite sure what on earth I was going to do, I knew that a long hug was exactly what I needed in that moment.

***

In an attempt to sort everything in my mind, I spent the day alone, thinking and thinking again. I didn't want to see anyone until I had straightened things out. I could barely even face seeing Andrew. And despite the "We need to talk," text that I had sent to him earlier on that day, I wasn't prepared for it at all. All I knew was that I needed to see him face-to-face to look him in the eye. And whilst I didn't need any confirmation on whether what I had seen with my own eyes was true, I wanted to know why. *Why would he do that to us? Why would he do that to me?* I took it as a personal attack.

My steps slowed as I reached his hotel room door, almost nervous of what I was about to confront. I walked with a heavy glass of red whilst the rest of the bottle lay in my hand, ready for the next dose. The wine seemed to be the only thing that could calm my racing thoughts and numb the pain in my growing headache. I stood outside for a moment, watching the keyhole as I captured my pacing heart. *Was he there too?* Nausea rose to the back of my throat. I couldn't bear to see them together again especially after I'd specifically requested to speak to him alone. And I didn't know what I would've done if I'd seen him; the guy who thought it was okay to casually fuck my fiancé. My eyes glazed as my thoughts took over. I couldn't help but dance past the same questions over and over again; trying to envisage his response. But each and every time, my mind drew blanks, making it even more imperative that we spoke. I needed answers. I needed closure. I needed to understand how and if we could even move on from this.

Knock.
Knock.
Knock.

My heart paused. I'd done it and there was no turning back. And even though I had been waiting for this moment all day, I had begun to clam up. Fear launched through my chest as I attempted to ready myself mentally. The latch shuffled, the handle turned and the door creaked open.
"Hello," I breathed in an emotionless manner as he peered from the door behind him.
"Hey," he cross-examined me before he opened the door. "Come in," he ushered, opening the door a little wider. "Are you okay?" he asked, sensing the chill in the air.
"Well, no not really," I said, as he shut the door behind me, making zero eye contact.
"Why what's up? Was it your 'heavy night' last night?" he chuckled as he walked towards the lounge area and my eyes caught sight of the wall to wall windows as I placed the bottle down.

So this is where it all happened. Blood boiled at the thought of being right at the scene of the crime and I couldn't even bring myself to sit down. "Partly. But not for the reasons you're probably thinking of…" I eyed him for a moment, waiting to see if he would give anything away but he never. His attitude was as cool and calm as ever, which I found even more bizarre. "How was your night, last night?" I asked out of curiosity. I wanted to see if he would show any signs of guilt.

"It was probably quite chilled in comparison to yours," he jived but I was in no laughing mood. He paused awkwardly; more so at my fixed facial expression than out of guilt. I locked into him, waiting for him to tell me more. "We just hung out at the bar for a while then turned in early," he finished and a single brow rose towards his embellishment.

"Turned in early, did you?" My voice was monotone.

"Yeah, being with the lads took it right out of me. I was absolutely shattered," he said as he helped himself to a glass of red. I couldn't believe how casual he was being. It almost made me feel as though I had imagined things but I knew my eyes hadn't deceived me.

"It's interesting that you say that because I saw you, just after midnight." A lump tumefied at the back of my throat as I recalled it all.

"Me? You couldn't have. I didn't even leave the hotel yesterday."

"Well, I don't know about all that but I definitely saw you yesterday, with Sebastian." My eyes began to well up as the images of them rushed back into my head. And he stared back at me, puzzled. "I was on the balcony yesterday night…

and I saw you… and Sebastian by your window." Andrew's eyes gorged open and the bulge in my windpipe felt heavy as it grew in size.

"What?" he questioned me, rather baffled.

"I don't want you to deny it because I saw everything. I was on the balcony and I saw what Sebastian was doing to you and what you did to Sebastian." My tear ducts began to bloat and Andrew froze, still deciphering my words.

"What are you talking about Raven?" He spoke quietly as he looked me dead in the eye and that slightly sidetracked my thoughts.

"Last night, I saw you and Sebastian by this very window. He was on his knees and you were lapping it all up. Do I actually have to spell it out for you?" I tried to read his eyes but they gave nothing away and I began to question myself. *Had I actually remembered correctly?* But even Lilah had confirmed that I kept on ranting about it the night before so I was sure that my memories must've held some weight.

"Raven, I have no idea what you are on about. Are you sure you never had too much to drink last night?" his tone was slightly condescending and that ground my gears.

"I drank but I know what I saw. And I saw you fucking Sebastian," My mouth spoke before my mind caught up. "So please stop acting as if you don't know what I'm on about," I took a swig from my glass, trying to ease the heat that was building behind my ears. Andrew's eyes hit the distance and his movements slowed. "So haven't you got anything to say for yourself then?" I questioned as I towered over him; one hand filled with wine and the other firmly across my middle. I was keen to hear his response. And though a part of me badly wanted him to deny and convince me that I was wrong, I knew my eyes hadn't deceived me so I just had to know why. I watched over him, awaiting his words. But all he could do was just sit there, tomb-still, either deep in thought or blatantly ignoring my question. *Typical.* He didn't even have the balls to speak and that said it all. A seething heat brewed between my nostrils. "You can't even be bothered to defend yourself. I knew there was no fucking point coming here." I huffed as I turned for the exit.

"Wait," A stiff hand launched around my calf and stopped me in my tracks. "Don't leave," he urged as he held me firmly.

"Why? I've come over to get to the bottom of this and you're not even talking so what's the point?" I launched back at him with a glaze over my vision.

"I'm going to talk. We're going to talk. Just give me a moment." he pressed, his hand still strongly hindering my movement and coercing me to stay.

"Well, you need to start talking soon because this silence is starting to piss me off." I vented as my foot began to relax back into listening. He paused for a moment as he began to gather his words.

"You're right, Raven. It's true... I did... fuck Sebastian last night but you will never see that again." Andrew finally spoke and a chill passed through my system as he confirmed the haze in my memory. I stood silently as I tried to process the confusion in my emotions. I couldn't figure out whether I should've been relieved that he had finally admitted the truth or depressed that the world as I knew it was falling apart before my very eyes.

"Why, Andrew? Why?" I eyed his eerily calm stance. I just couldn't figure him out.

"I don't know, Raven. It just fucking happened," he spoke nonchalantly.

"Just happened? I'm not being funny but fucking your best friend doesn't just happen, especially when you're about to get married." As the words left my mouth my mind fast forwarded to our big day and my eyes began to well.

"Well it did, Raven and I don't know why. But I certainly don't plan on having it mess up my wedding, that's for sure." He shook his head disappointedly as his eyes read the future.

"Well I think it's a bit too late for that, don't you? How could you do that to me?" my voice began to tremble. "I'm meant to be your fiancé." My eyes tracked him for a moment, still trying to comprehend his insensitivity.

"Raven, I haven't done anything to you. We got a bit carried away in the heat of the moment and shit just happened. I messed up and it won't happen again," he spoke as clear as day. And though a part of me wanted to believe him, his blasé attitude wasn't settling at all.

"How do I know that? Only moments ago, you were just trying to make out like I was the one seeing things. How do I know that you won't do that again? How do I even know that you haven't been cheating on me the whole time we've been together?" The questions spurged out of my mouth and Andrew paused as he quietly registered my question. Momentarily, I monitored his body language before a frost passed through me. "Have you been cheating on me the whole time?" His inaction made me anxious and I had to be sure. But the question had left my lips and he still had no response; which was enough to almost confirm all of my fears. "You have, haven't you?" My lips upturned at the idea of it. For the whole time we'd been together, I'd been sleeping with someone who'd been fucking someone else. The disgust began to mount inside. "With who? Sebastian? Others? Who Andrew?" My emotions swirled between anger and hurt as the images of infidelity swarmed to my mind. "I can't believe you've done this to me. I can't believe you made me come all the way to Jamaica to marry you so that you could cheat on me and now you can't even speak. Who have you fucked Andrew?" My voice rose as I questioned him again and he finally spoke.

"Listen, I've fucked around and fucked Sebastian a few times." He brazenly told me and a hurl of nausea began to ferment in my stomach as I attempted to digest his honesty. I just couldn't understand it.

"Why? Are you unhappy? Gay? What?" A thousand thoughts fired through my mind at once and I needed answers.

"No. I don't know." He contradicted himself.

"Well you must be otherwise you wouldn't have kept on at it!" I retorted.

"Look, I've messed around with a few guys but it's not a big deal." His words were emotionless and I tasted the first of my salted tears.

"Of course it's a big deal. You made me wait. You made me come all the way to Jamaica. You made me bring all of my friends AND family here for OUR wedding so that you could fuck your best friend! You've fucking cheated on me, Andrew with God knows who else because I can barely get a straight answer out of you. And you don't even seem remorseful! That's fucked up Andrew!" The tears lined my cheekbones and a heat raced underneath my skin.

"I've apologised to you. What more do you want Raven?" he quietly growled.

"How about a guy that loves me and is faithful to me," a surge of water glazed over my vision as I began to imagine the disappointment on my father's face when he found out. *My father couldn't find out.*

"But I've already told you, Raven. I'm ready to settle down with you." Andrew tried to convince me but my hopes had already started to pour down the drain.

"You're ready to settle? I doubt that. You can't even keep your dick in your pants. How can I be with someone who thinks its okay to fuck me senselessly then fuck someone else the next day? Not even someone else but the guy you've been palming off as your best friend?" Flashes of the night before came flooding back, increasing my influx of tears. And then, I couldn't help but remember how he flung me around like a ragdoll. *Was he thinking of Sebastian when he was fucking me?* The thought of it made me sick and he didn't even seem sorry. All he cared about was himself. "Do you know what? There's no point in even having this conversation. It's clear that you don't care about me." I stormed towards the exit. Immediately, Andrew shot up and launched for my arm.

"Wait. Where do you think you're going?" he questioned as he caught hold of me.

"I'm done, Andrew," I told him, attempting to loosen from his firm grip; he held on to me even tighter.

"But we haven't finished talking," His fingers pressed into me and a numbing sensation began to spread through the length of my arm. And I wanted nothing more than to free myself from his head fuck.

"Look, I came here to sort things out but we've got nowhere. You're obviously gay and couldn't care less about my feelings. I can't be with you. There's nothing more to say," I urged towards the door as the tears fuelled my feet. But his strength yanked me back and flung me against the wall.

Aarhh! I screamed internally as my back thumped in pain. His grip hurled to my open jaw and fear launched through my veins. Rapidly, my eyes read his as I tried to figure out what the hell he was doing.

"You see, I think there is." Andrew's eyes bored through me as his fingers pressed into my cheeks and my mouth began to dry. "I'm not going to let you get away with doing this to us, do you understand? I'm not going to let you mess up our marriage." His hot breath heaved over my face as he backed me into the corner and a pulse pumped through my skin.

"Andrew please," I urged as my wine glass dropped to the floor. I was trying to break free but the more my hands shot to my defence, the more strength he used in his clench.

"Listen, I love you and you love me," he scowled as he coerced his views on us. And I could tell by the intensity of his gaze that he actually believed what he was saying. I tried to capture the air through my distorted mouth and the tears rolled down my cheek.

"No you don't, Andrew," My mouth ached as I spoke up and Andrew launched my head back even harder. *Aaargh! Fuck!* Agony fumed back through my teeth. *What the hell was wrong with him?*

"Are you mocking me? I'm wearing my heart on my sleeve here and you're laughing in my face?" His eyes reddened as they aggressively flitted between mine. And my heart sunk in my chest as the pain permeated. *Why did I even come here?* I began to question it all.

"I'm not laughing but this can't be what you want. You've been with Sebastian this whole time. I can't marry someone like that." My heart sobbed at the thought. "Andrew, just let me go, please," I pleaded and as my words registered in his head, he began to loosen his grip.

"Okay fine, I get the message," he murmured as his chest shrunk into his shoulders and I released a sigh of reprieve.

"Thank you," I smiled weakly as I turned towards the door, relieved that he was finally able to see things my way.

"Aaarhh!" A shriek left my lungs before I could even take one step. His hand catapulted around my pony and hauled me back to his chest. My neck clenched as my head jolted and my eyes bulged out of fright.

"You really thought I'd let you go by? You really thought I'd let you out of my sight for one second so you could air my dirty laundry? Well, you're wrong." He grimaced and yelps of distress left my body as he clamped onto each follicle on my scalp. And a tingling panic began to flood through my veins as I wondered what on earth he was going to do to me. "You're not going anywhere. You're not going anywhere until you agree to marry me." A heat raced to my head as he ripped my skull back towards my shoulders and my mouth let out a cry.

"Andrew, Please! Let me go!" I wailed as I tried to regain control but my cries fell on deaf ears as his rage continued.

"Raven, you're mine. You always will be mine. You think you can end it?" he hissed as he compelled me to the ground. Tears streamed down my face as I struggled to find the air in my lungs but his strength was more than I could manage.

"Help!" I pleaded to anyone that could hear though I knew my attempts were hopeless. *Was he actually trying to kill me?* I couldn't breathe. His hands smothered around my throat as he choked the life out of me and my hands scrambled across the floor.

Smash!

Glass shattered as the bottle crashed over his head and briefly knocked his senses. Red splattered all across my face as the top remained in my clasp and the rage took over.

Whack!
Whack!
Whack!

"Aargh!" I screamed as I smashed into him once more with the broken bottle top and immediately he fell to the floor. Blood gushed viciously from his forehead as he crashed to the ground and his consciousness slipped away from him. My heart pounded out of my chest. Sweat dripped from my palms. Without a second thought, I rushed to my feet and bolted to the door.

~ Chapter 12 ~

My airways restricted. My stomach contracted. My eyes reddened as I launched to my hotel door. *What on earth was he thinking?* I tried to capture my breath but I had a million and one thoughts whizzing through my mind by the second. *He could have killed me. I could have killed him.* My mind panicked as I burst in and darted to my room. Immediately, Lilah shot up from the sofa, absolutely startled.

"Raven? What happened? Are you okay?" She rushed towards me as she searched for my wounds.

"No! I need to get out," I told her as I bound for my suitcase.

"What? What are you talking about? What happened?" Lilah questioned as she watched me pace around my room, haphazardly grabbing my things.

"Andrew's a fucking animal. I went to his room to speak to him about last night and he started fucking strangling me and grabbing my hair. I couldn't even breathe, Lilah. He was fucking with my airways so much I had to bottle him and now I've got this shit all over me." I splurged as I shoved my clothes into my suitcase.

"What? Are you being serious, Ray?"

"Look at my clothes! Of course, I am. He's a loose cannon. I can't stay in the same hotel as him." Water soaked my cheeks as I recalled it all.

"What? You can't leave, Raven. Everyone's here." I could sense the fear of loss in her voice.

"That's the whole point and so is he. He could actually have killed me in there and there's blood all over his apartment. Lord knows what that man is capable of and I have no intentions of finding out. I have to leave now." My mouth spoke before my brain even had the chance to catch up.

"And doing what? Catching the next flight home?" Lilah jumped down my throat as she tried to keep up.

"No, but I'm getting the hell out of here. It's not like I paid for this hotel or anything so I couldn't give a damn," I told her and I could see the calculations behind her eyes.

"Well, if you're leaving I'm going with you," Lilah blurted after a moment or two, her feet edging for her room. "Do you even know where you're going, Raven?" she asked as she hurled for her things.

"Nope but I'll figure something out." And as the words left my mouth, my mind darted past a million possibilities.

***

After a swift checkout, we exited the building with our luggage trailing behind. The tension still thrived in my shoulders as the taxi doors shut behind us and the slam hit home. My wedding was cancelled, I was leaving and I had made a lucky escape. My head flung back on the headrest as my new reality dawned on me. *What a waste;* the persistent thought that I couldn't get past spun 'round and 'round in my head. Andrew had wasted my time, my energy and had almost fucking killed me. *What a prick.* Patches soaked through my hands and stained my top as my mind revisited all the excitement and preparation that I had been through over the last six months which had now resulted in nothing; a false start. *How embarrassing.* All that was left was the repeat explanations of what happened and my readied responses for the "but you seemed so happy." Veins pressurised under my eyelids. I had been fooled and I now had to think of a way to explain that to each and every member of my family and friends. My body heat rocketed at the thought of it. I hadn't travelled all the way to Jamaica to put my private life on blast and bring shame to my family. The judgment seemed way too claustrophobic and I had no idea what to do.

What were they going to think? I froze as I envisioned the look on everybody's faces and imagined what they would be saying about me behind my back. *"I'm not surprised. That's what happens when you don't take the time to get to know each other."* I could see them all consoling me to my face and laughing at my downfall behind my back and it felt horrific. But as much as the guilt of disappointing my family still haunted me, I knew that I had made the right decision. There was no way that I could live a life of deceit whilst my husband casually fucked his gay lover behind my back. My eyes rolled intensely at the idea of it all.

The driver hummed along to the music on the radio as he drove us to our destination with very little conversation;

which made a difference. However, I didn't mind as I needed a moment to gather my thoughts and make sense of my wavering emotions. Whilst a part of me raged inside, it was almost as though I knew that something wasn't right between us deep down. But the idea of my fairy-tale wedding in Jamaica sounded so good that I went along with it anyway. Steadily, I began to wipe the tears from my eyes. And as I sat back, I started to question his every move over the past year. From his trips to the gym to his weekends away and even his love of *Men's Health* magazine. As I watched the cars cross my eyes on the other side of the road, I tried to figure out whether his behaviour was a result of genuine interest or in fact a part of the underlying desires that he had desperately been trying hard to cover up. *How had I been so blind?* I smirked at my ignorance and Lilah glanced over at me.

"Are you alright?" she asked curiously as she eyed my sneering demeanour.
"I'm going to have to be, aren't I?" I replied as my head shook in contrast to my words. And my thoughts drifted back to *The Regal* and the moment I whacked him over the head. I wondered what Sebastian would've thought when he found Andrew in that state. But he deserved it. *Thank fuck I'd got out.*

"Oooo look… Here we are!" Lilah gleamed, paying little attention to my confused state of mind. The car slowed as we arrived at the barriers of our new hotel and an automatic sense of warmth flourished underneath my skin. The bright, green sign glowed and the towering walls protected us as we drove right in. The bell boys posted up at the lobby entrance were dressed head to toe in their beige uniforms and the marbled lobby buzzed with smiles and laughter. It looked just as I had remembered it. The bell boys were keen to help as we stepped out of the vehicle and quickly took charge of our luggage.

"Thank you," I breathed as I turned to the dark, heavy-set man dressed in beige, grateful that he was able to lift the weight off my shoulders and Lilah took care of the driver. My mind was too fuzzy to figure that all out. And as I looked back, I could tell by the smile on his face that she had given him more than enough change. But it didn't surprise me. To be honest, I would've given him my life savings just for getting me away from that beast.

After Lilah had sorted him out, it didn't take long for the welcome staff to usher us to the front desk for check-in.
"Welcome to *The Vacation Lodge*." The suited woman behind the desk smiled warmly and I couldn't help but feel like I was finally home.

~ Chapter 13 ~

My body bounced up briefly as I sludged myself back onto my double bed. Our room was nowhere near as luxurious as our suite at *The Regal* but it certainly did the trick. It composed of two double beds facing the wall-mounted television, a basic but clean bathroom with all of the essentials and a balcony that faced the tennis courts. But somehow it felt like the perfect escape. I could breathe. I could think without having to look over my shoulder. And most importantly, I could look out onto the balcony without having the vision of my fiancé fucking his best friend. I wanted to forget it all. I wanted nothing more than to climb into bed and forget the last year of my life had ever happened.

I hated feeling sorry for myself but I hated humiliation even more. I began speaking to myself to counter-attack my growing, self-destructive thoughts but hearing the words just wasn't convincing enough. I needed support but I didn't know what or who to trust anymore. I had so much on my mind and I couldn't even bring myself to speak to Lilah. The guilt of boring her to death with all my issues weighed heavy on me and I couldn't bear the extra burden on my shoulders. All I longed for was someone that I could vent to in a judgement-free zone.

And as I burrowed into my sheets, I couldn't help but think of Nelson. My mind kept replaying the conversation that we had at *The Tabernacle* over and over again. *"It should have been me."* His voice hummed in my inner ear. And though I knew that it was a ridiculous statement to make, it had still resonated with me. In reality, I knew that there was no way that I would ever end up marrying Nelson but somehow I trusted him. He had always been upfront with me and I knew that he wouldn't judge me or my situation. His own situation was messed up enough. My eyes shut as I clutched my phone in my hand, contemplating. But I was bursting with raw, unstable emotions and I didn't feel as though I had anyone else to speak to. I hit the call button and saliva swarmed into my mouth.

Ring.
Ring-

I couldn't do it. A sharp breath left my lungs as I hit the red button. I couldn't bring myself to say it out loud. In my head, I couldn't figure out what was worse; the fact that I had been cheated on, that my fiancé had just rough-housed me or that my wedding was cancelled. My head slumped into the pillow in search of the courage to speak on my situation and let it all out. My arms bounced into the bed as I flung them back in utter confusion.

Buzz.

My phone vibrated in my hand and my arm shot up.

"Hey. I just saw your missed call. I was in the bathroom. Are you okay?" The message notification popped up on my screen and my eyelids grew. Nelson had messaged me back and I didn't know what to say. My mind ran across the idea of pretending that it was an accident but I actually wanted someone to communicate with, even if I wasn't quite brave enough to admit everything all at once.

"Oh, no worries. I was just calling to see if you were okay." I casually mentioned.

"I am indeed and all the better for speaking to you," he wrote and I smiled weakly knowing how much I could also relate to his words. Then he began typing again. *"I've had a chilled out day but I'm getting ready for tonight at The Tabernacle. How're things with you? Are you all ready to jump the broom?"* Three chuckle faces followed his message as though he was mocking my situation and my chest sunk into my reality.

"No. Not at all." Disdainfully, my blinking slowed.

"Why? What's up? Are you getting cold feet or are you just wishing it was me?" He sent a ballsy face with a playful stuck-out tongue and somehow, I wished he was right. I wished I was having second thoughts rather than the actual situation that I was going through; my fiancé was an absolute maniac.

"If only it was that simple." I huffed.

"I told you that it should have been me but you didn't want to hear it!" he shot back and his cheek sent a weak glow to my face.

"No, I meant that it probably would have been easier if I were having cold feet but its way deeper than that, to be honest."

"What do you mean?" Nelson sharply responded and I paused as I thought carefully about what I was going to say next.

"Last night, I found out some fucked up things and it got even worse today. I can't marry him." My heart broke as my fingers hit the send button.

"Why? What happened?" he asked and my head softly shook in disappointment as I recalled it all.

"If I told you, you would never believe it."

"Well, I am willing to give you a try. In more ways than one," he added in an attempt to lighten the mood and my fingers hovered over the buttons.

"Well," My thumb paused as it synchronised with my mind. *"I saw him with someone else if you know what I mean."* I wrote in the effort to save some face.

"What?" Nelson instantly replied.

"I actually saw him fucking someone else with my own eyes. I couldn't believe it."

His emoji's were shocked.

"I know. And I spoke to him today and he admitted it all and we ended up in a massive fight." Stricken with pride, I couldn't bear to tell him who with.

"No way, Raven. Sorry to hear that." He wrote and he gave my fingers the ammunition that they needed.

"I just can't believe the cheek of him. He actually took the time to convince me to move on from you and made me bring my whole family out here for a pretence while he had been getting his dick into arse since the moment we'd met. And to top it off, he tried to strangle me when I told him I couldn't be with a guy like that."

"What? That's mad,"

"No, he's mad. He'd been fucking around for the whole of our relationship and tried to tell me that it was no big deal. He didn't give a fuck about my feelings. All he cared about was him and his fucking image. His rage was so wild I had to move hotels." I finished as my conscious fingers ran out of steam in the fear of oversharing.

"Oh wow. Well, at least you're safe now. You had a lucky escape." Nelson always had a way of looking on the bright side of life and in turn, it passably eased my tension. *"So have you told anyone about this yet?"* he asked.

"No. Only you and Lilah. It's not easy to admit that my whole relationship has been a sham. I just don't know what to do." I opened my heart to him.

"I understand. Well, you don't have to do anything just yet. Wait until you're good and ready." I read his words and they began to pace my racing thoughts. *"Listen, why don't you come out tonight to clear your mind and I can cheer you up."* He typed and my mind pondered on his suggestion for a moment. But my body just wasn't up for it. My eyes were puffed to capacity and my head weighed a tonne. I was in no state to see anyone, both physically and mentally.

"To be honest, I'm not really in the sociable mood tonight. Plus, I am absolutely shattered." I told him, trying my hardest to keep my word vomit to a minimum.

"Okay, I hear you. I don't want to pressure you but I am here if you need me." His words were clear and for that, I was grateful.

***

But that night, I found it hard to rest. Lucky for Lilah, she was dead to the world but every time *I* closed my eyes, I saw flashes of Andrew. Andrew's hands gripped all over *him;* Andrew's hands gripped all over my fuckin' neck. My eyes watered as my breath became trapped once more, just like it did at the time. *That twisted bastard.* My lids squeezed tight as I attempted to banish him from my mind. And as raw as the aches felt, I knew it still hadn't really sunk in. The guy I had spent the last year with, planning our life, was a sadistic homosexual. I couldn't help but lay there, trying convincing myself that it was all an awful dream and someone was going to wake me up soon if I held on for long enough. But that was almost a dream in itself. The reality was that Andrew had fucked up my holiday and shat all over my future. I hated the fact that his image still held weight in my mind.

I wrapped my arms around me as I attempted to console myself. I just wanted the day to be over so that I could start a fresh. But nothing could seem to shake him from my mind. So I used Nelson's words for comfort as I strove to lick my wounds clean. *"I am here if you need me."* My thumbs ran over my cheeks as his words echoed in my ear. And the more that I recycled his words, the stronger his image became in my mind. His words were like a bear hug and I could almost feel him there with me. Before I knew it, I could feel his thumbs wiping the tears from my eyes and his soft lips soothing my cheeks. Although I knew I didn't actually want him there with me, it took me away from my reality. I wanted to feel special and I wanted to find peace with my thoughts. My hands began to wander as I took solace in his image. And wherever my hands went, Nelson's were not far behind. I rolled onto my back as my fingers first stroked past my neck then down the centre of my torso. My skin felt tender but the feel of Nelson's kisses pacified my pain and enheartened my self-worth. His lips followed my hands as he traced through the centre of my rib cage, right down to my pelvic line and back again; adorning every piece of my torso. My shoulders, my waistline, right up to the crease in my armpits, no place was left untouched. The more my hands explored, the deeper my breathing became as I embraced the feeling of oneness with my body.

Hairs stood erect as my fingers circled the meat of my breast and my eyeballs began searching behind my closed lids. Searching for that connection with a real one; someone that loved and accepted me just the way that I was. I had a firm hold on my breasts as I caressed them with meaning and Nelson's ebony eyes gave me his seal of approval. Both hands clutched onto my nipples as my pelvis began to relax and let go. My toes searched the opposing corners of the bed. To and fro, my nipples rolled between my fingers and a warm glow began fester beneath my bosoms. My inhales extended. Stimulation aroused in the nerves that lived beneath the more I took control of my nipples and a smile crept onto to my face as my jaw broadened. I never even knew that this level of self-love existed until now but I was loving every minute of it. In my mind, Nelson's tongue was obsessed with both breasts and my heart beat started to strengthen. More and more, my hands toyed with the hysteria that was brewing underneath my nipples and my hips started to gyrate. Though I wanted more of my body, I also feared the possibilities. The hums were already stewing and I was curious as to how much better it could get.

Briefly, my eyes shifted to Lilah but she was still steadfast in her slumber and my smirk brightened even more. My head rolled back as my eyes sealed once more and Nelson's spirit goaded me even further. I could see his head of dark, tight curls guiding my senses and I was becoming infatuated with the direction they were heading. And though one hand was still ardent on heightening the senses in my nipple, the other hand delved a little lower. My vagina felt smooth between my hands and it undoubtedly welcomed the new sensations it was experiencing with open arms. And my knees lifted underneath the sheets. Two fingers clamped around my clitoris whilst my nipple was taken on a thrill. Up and down, my clitoris was hauled and my soul began to lighten. *Mmmm...* I quietly breathed as sexual shots began to dart from my nipple to my pussy and then straight to my brain. I could feel Nelson's tongue lacing the life out of my clitoris and vagina humidified. *Mmmm, yeah... Just how I liked it.* My imagination had gotten the better of me but I hadn't a care in the world. All I cared about was how sexy I felt as my body was given the pleasure it needed to forget.

Over and over, my vagina was haled and my self-indulgence was hoisted to new heights. *Mmmm... yes.* My body respired as the love spread inside me and my fingers were fuelled with force. The suction I was imagining with his head between my legs was like no other and it gave me the strength of affection that I needed. The pressure was building in all of my limbs and that was what drove my grasp. Faster and faster, my hips rocked against my hands and I could feel my head imploding. The sensations that were thriving between my breasts and my vagina were ballooning so much and my juices were easing the flow. The more my fingers slipped over my swelling clitoris, the more I chased the next thrust. Until my mind started to blow.

"MMMmmh," I voiced out loud as pleasure gushed through my system and my toes crawled the edge of the bed. I couldn't help it. I felt too good and I could no longer hold it inside. Awkwardly, my head shot Lilah as I came to my senses, to see if I had awoken her, and more importantly, if she'd caught me. But she was still, as dead as a doornail and my eyes blissfully shut as I exalted in that fact. Finally, I was able to relax.

affection that I needed. The pressure was building in all of my limbs and that was what drove my grasp. Faster and faster, my hips rocked against my hands and I could feel my head imploding. The sensations that were thriving between my breasts and my vagina were ballooning so much and my juices were easing the flow. The more my fingers slipped over my swelling clitoris, the more I chased the next thrust. Until my mind started to blow.

"MMMmmh," I voiced out loud as pleasure gushed through my system and my toes crawled the edge of the bed. I couldn't help it. I felt too good and I could no longer hold it inside. Awkwardly, my head shot Lilah as I came to my senses, to see if I had awoken her, and more importantly, if she'd caught me. But she was still, as dead as a doornail and my eyes blissfully shut as I exalted in that fact. Finally, I was able to relax.

~ Chapter 14 ~

After a good night's sleep, I rose to the sounds of reggae transcending through my open window. My head turned on the pillow as I tried to absorb the vibes and come to terms with the night before. The rising sun caressed my skin as I laid half in and out of the sheets and my eyelids slowly peeled back. Thoughts slowly filtered through as I embraced the lie-in. *Today was a new day.* I hadn't forgotten what Andrew had done but I endeavoured to move forward. It was almost as though something had re-wired overnight and I was actually thankful that I had got out before I had said: "I do." Gently, clasping my hands together, I took a moment to say my prayers and ask for strength for the coming day.

As I laid there, there was a brief creak from the hotel door and my head rose up.
"Hey." It was Lilah, holding a tray of breakfast treats and the irresistible smell of fresh toast followed her in. "I weren't sure what mood you were in so I thought I'd bring you something to start your day off right," she said as she sat down beside me and I slid up to receive her hand-picked meal.

"Thanks, this looks amazing," I told her as I ogled the plate for a moment or two. My full English had been blessed with the Jamaican touch. Two slices of buttered toast lined my plate with spiced beans, seasoned scrambled egg, avocado and two sausages. My stomach jumped for joy. It smelt divine and I couldn't wait to get stuck in.

"So, how are you feeling?" Lilah asked as I shoved a piece of toast dipped in bean sauce into my mouth.

"Much better than yesterday, I'm just glad to be out alive," I told her confidently though internally, I was still trying to figure out whether I was still in some sort of grieving stage of denial. "I don't even care about the fact that he's gay. I just can't handle the lies. He was grabbing on to me, trying to convince me that I was wrong. He's an absolute psychopath."

"Yeah. It's sad how some people believe their own lies but at least you caught him when you did," She sighed as she thought. "Imagine… today was meant to be the best day of your life; your wedding day and you're all tucked up in bed. Have you even spoken to anyone?"

"No, and I don't intend to." I was straightforward.

"Your parents are going to be so pissed," she added and my insides saddened as I imagined it.

"I know. Thank goodness I won't be there to see it."

"Well, at least you've got me," Lilah smiled as she headed to the mini-fridge to grab a drink for us both. And despite the time of day, she still proceeded on pouring us both a glass of prosecco and handed me my glass.

"Here's to new beginnings," she said as her glass clinked with mine. And my insides bubbled as I slowly grew accustomed to the taste of the cheaper alcohol and idea of single life once again. "So, what's the plan?" Lilah asked after taking her first sip.

"I have no idea. I just want to find my feet again, to be honest," I told her. It felt surreal to have my ring finger bare once more and I wasn't quite sure what to do with my new found freedom.

"Well, there's no point slouching around here all day. You should get out tonight to let your hair down. What's Nelson doing?" she eagerly asked and my nostrils flared at her tenacity.

"I haven't a clue what Nelson is doing tonight but I am certainly not bed hopping if that's what you are angling at." I cut to the chase. As much as I was grateful to be freed from my bed of lies, I wasn't ready to move in on Nelson.

"Girl, the best way to get over someone is to get under someone else." She laughed and my brow rose at her, playfully disappointed.

"Nah, I'm not into that," Being with someone else was the last thing I had on my mind.

"No, I'm only joking really but meeting up with him is just a good excuse to get you out of the hotel. I could call Akeem too. We could make a night of it; all four of us. No Hanky-panky involved." She tried her hardest to convince me. "Come on, don't be a grandma. It'll be fun and you know it. All you have to do is call and find out what he's up to. You don't have to end the night in his bed," she added and I knew she was right. Seeing Nelson did not have to equate to having sex with him. It had been less than 72 hours since I had slept with my fiancé and less than 24 since he'd manhandled me so I knew that being with him in any other way but a friendship just wouldn't work. And though a part of me wasn't quite sure about meeting up with Nelson so soon, I knew that it would be fun for the four of us to have a night out on the tiles so I bit the bullet and made the call.

It had taken us more than a while to ready ourselves for the night and by the time we had arrived at *The Daiquiri joint*, it had already begun to swarm with people. The pungent smell of cocktails laced the room like a hypnotic drug; the drinks poured then took residence in the hands of the party goers. The tunes that pulsed through the speakers were contagious and that was clear to see from the groups that had arrived before us. Frisky females were already taking centre stage on the dancefloor, winding their waistlines and parading with their friends. The girls cheered as they saluted their shot glasses and downed them all in one gulp. Groups of men began to fence the side-lines, eyeing the flamboyant females that were already making a show of themselves in the middle of the room. I could taste the lust in the air. Though it didn't come as a surprise to me because the girls looked good. Their confidence even had me thinking twice. I tugged Lilah before reaching towards her ear.
"Hey, Li can you follow me to the bathroom?" I asked after eyeing the flouncing females for a moment or two. Their confidence was immeasurable and somehow, it caused me to question mine.
"Sure, no problem," she responded immediately and I headed in the direction of the sign. A few eyes followed us as we shuffled through and that played on my mind. Andrew

had made me feel lousy and I was keen to look the part. And though I had no serious intentions with Nelson, I still aimed for the 'look what you could have on your arm' appearance. But the other girls on the dancefloor seemed just as tempting so I needed to reassess my grading. As we arrived, the bathroom doors swung open and a group of jolly girls walked out with not a care in the world. They quickly apologised after accidentally bumping into Lilah and she tried her best to stay polite. I gently tugged at her as I led us past and her teeth gritted through her smile. But I gave her no reaction as I knew that the girls had not nudged her intentionally.

The bathroom was home to a floor length mirror, which was perfect for assessing my look. I had chosen a skin-tight, off-the-shoulder dress that swept over my curves. The long sleeves travelled from my wrists to my armpit, leaving only my upper chest on-show. My exposed collarbones complimented my sexual appearance but my covered bosoms gave me a sense of sophistication. My hair was pulled high and tight, giving a lift to my eyes and creating more of a cheekbone, though my highlighter probably would have done a fabulous job on its own. And despite leaving our hotel full of confidence, I had begun to question myself.
"Do I look okay?" I asked Lilah for reassurance.
"Girl, you look stunning and a lot classier than I do!" she joked and I laughed along with her. I wasn't sure whether it was the blow that I'd received from my Andrew or the fact that I was back out in the wild but something was causing me to over scrutinise myself.

"Are you sure?" I said as I continued to spruce my afro puff. "With your titties and that back, you'd look good in a bin bag. Stop being silly," she told me as she prodded me out of sorts and I cracked a smile. Lilah pulled her deep, red lipstick out of her purse and prepped for a top-up whilst I attempted to convince myself of her words. My head was messed up. Even though there was no way on earth that I was going to sleep with Nelson, I still wanted to impress. A small part of me wanted him to want me. I wanted to feel like a woman.

"Come, let's go and get some drink down you. That'll loosen you up," she ordered as she popped her lipstick back into her purse and took hold of my hand. She led us straight to the bar and beckoned for the bar staff as they bustled behind the bar. Lilah ordered us two Malibu shots and a Strawberry Daiquiri each to warm us up and they worked a treat. The coconut-infused rounds sent a heat down my back and left my tongue with a sweet aftertaste. And after a few mouthfuls of cocktail, the issues of joining the other girls on the dancefloor had started to dwindle away. Lasers of multi-coloured light darted off the walls as we started to laugh and dance with each other. And after a few more, I couldn't care less how sexy I looked because there was no denying how much I felt it. My body bounced along with the DJ's tunes and we all went wild as he paused and reloaded banger after banger. Our hands locked as we twirled and whirled like a spinning top.

Then suddenly, her eyes brightened and she disconnected as she squealed in excitement. Her eyes were fixed on a sight

behind me. As I looked 'round, I saw Akeem and her arms flung around him. I gave him an energetic wave before leaning into his cheek. And by the glisten in our eyes, he could tell that we were high-spirited.

"Hey, my little black bird," A voice came from behind me accompanied with a smooth press on my waist and I intuitively spun around.

"Hey!" I breathed as my hands instantaneously stretched up to clutch on to Nelson's neck and he embraced me back. I lingered with a stiff inhale. *Damn… he smelt good.* Spiced oak tingled my nasal passage and sent a high to my brain. But after a moment or so, he released which encouraged me to do the same as he eyed me from head to toe.

"Wow, you look stunning," he told me with his sparkling eyes still focused down on me and a warm rush leapt through me.

"Thanks." I smiled weakly as I stared up to accept his compliment with grace. *Stunning;* that was the type of reaction that I wanted to evoke and naturally, it alleviated my insecurities.

"You don't look too bad yourself." I played down how smoking hot he looked. His skin-tight, crew-neck t-shirt sat well over his athletic torso, leaving space for his loaded guns. He wore all black and his ripped jeans were slim-fit, showing all the shape in his muscular thighs; they looked sprinter-ready. His hair was freshly shaven with his fade following into his waved high top. And his low, sharp beard followed on from his sideburns and wrapped around his moist lips like a prickled but polished carpet. And somehow, it stood out from his midnight-bright complexion. For some reason, his deep eyes still had something over me and his towering height still sent chills down my spine. My eyes shut briefly as I reminded my tingling vagina that we were closed for business.

"What are you drinking?" he asked as he shunned off my words.

"I just finished a Coco mania. It was beyond bliss!" I shared as I briefly reminisced on it.

"Would you like a top-up?" he queried, gesturing towards to the bar.

"Sure, why not." I was already in a good place but another drink was sure to add to my buzz. He nodded in confirmation before taking an order from Lilah and heading to the bar with Akeem. Lilah seized hold of my hand, giggling like a school girl as she dragged us to follow behind. And in all honesty, I think I was just as enthusiastic as she was.

It wasn't long before our round was ready and our glasses leapt into the air. Smiles and laughter whipped across our faces as we downed our drinks and danced the night away. Akeem couldn't help but show off all his cutting-edge dance moves and Lilah and I eagerly followed his lead. His hi-fives were sincere as we tried to keep up and give him a run for his money. And Nelson was bowled over in tears as he watched our wretched attempts. In time, Akeem had a small crowd surrounding us as the DJ dropped some soul-shaking rhythms and I could tell that Lilah wanted more one-on-one time. She tugged at Akeem and whispered something in his ear before leaning into me.

~ Chapter 15 ~

"We're just going upstairs to check out what the other DJ is playing. We'll be back," she told me and I saluted her departure, knowing that she wouldn't be back anytime soon. Lilah had a habit of going missing when we were out. I took refuge by the railings at the edge of the room, taking my chance to move away from the spotlight for a while and Nelson accompanied me.

"And then there were two," Nelson whispered into my ear before laughing hysterically at his own joke and my eyes wound back at his corn.
"You're so silly," I added, trying desperately hard to ignore his hovering hand around my waist whilst his other one caught up.
"Care to dance?" He winked as one side of his smile rose mischievously.
"I can work with that," I casually responded as my hands reached for his shoulders.

The DJ thrived and Nelson's hips pressed into mine. It wasn't hard to feel his presence as he ground his piece into me and the feel of him was euphoric. And as our dance progressed, our bodies got closer and closer. The touch of his cheeks left a refreshing feel on my face and added to the alluring bliss that crept through me. Then my chest fell into his like the missing piece to my puzzle because his groove was so magnetic.

And in between my thighs, his strength was emerging, ever so temperately stimulating my box. As I snaked on and off him, my blinking slowed, capturing every feel of his stroke. He always did know how to work a room, but the way he was working these railings was electrifying. His body waved in a hypnotic motion causing mine to fall under his spell. And somehow, I didn't mind at all. *It's only a dance.* I reminded my pulsing hormones as I secretly lusted for his next move and then he spun me around.

His hand held firmly onto my pelvis as his growing meat stroked my cheeks. My teeth grazed over my lip. I couldn't help but roll my behind 'round and 'round, encouraging his growth as I flirted with his emotions. His muscle felt mighty as I purposefully brushed over it and tingles pounced through my pelvis.

Gradually, I could sense the firm in his hips as they locked into my motion. Up and down, my dress flirted over the centrepiece in his jeans. My head tilted back onto him whilst my palms feathered his thighs. Then, his hands began to explore my stomach and gently, he pulled me in closer.

"You are more than teasing me tonight," he spoke close to my earlobe and a subdued giggle leapt out of my mouth. "What did I do to deserve this?" he inquired as he lapped it all up.

"Nothing. It's just a harmless dance," I replied as I continued working my way 'round.

"Well, I don't know what this new found singledom has done to you but your moves are better than I remembered." His compliments were endearing and an emerging smirk took heed of his words.

"Like a fine wine, I ripen with age," I told him, knowing the spirits had gotten the better of me.

"Well, I can't argue with that," Nelson's mouth rubbed the side of my face as he spoke. "I could eat you all up right now," he continued and my lashes fluttered at the thought of it.

"That's too bad. I'm not looking for that right now," I said though the idea of it did sound inviting.

"Why?" his voice was concerned.

"I'm just trying to cool off guys after what my ex-fiancé did to me."

As I spoke, my moves slowed. "Today was meant to be my wedding day." The corners of my mouth turned down in disappointment and disgust.

"No way. I didn't even realise." Nelson paused for a second. "I don't know who in their right mind wouldn't want to have you all to their self. Your man lost a keeper." My lips pursed sourly at his turn of phrase.

"He's not my man. He's my ex." I was firm on that stance. I had no future with that man. Not only had he been sticking his dick into someone else's arse crack but he'd tried to coerce me into marriage after I found out; as if I owed him something. "I don't know what it is but things just never seem to work out for me." I opened up to him.

"Well if I had it my way, I would choose you in a heartbeat," he shared and his words easily soothed my conflict.

"But life is not that simple." I turned to him and stared right into his ebony eyes. And as he gazed back, I wondered whether there was a possibility that things could've been different in a parrallel universe.

"You are beautiful and intelligent but you live a million miles away from me."
"And you are married…" I reminded him and his eyes spun back dismissively.

"And if I'd met you first, my head wouldn't have turned once." He smiled as his eyes stayed fixed on me but mine couldn't help but shift.
"I bet you say that to all the girls."

"No, I don't and I don't need to. But there's something about you. There's something magnetic about our attraction." He held onto my waist as I absorbed his view.

He was right. Whenever we were in company, there was something intrinsic about our magnetism. I was drawn to him. And even after leaving him, it was never easy to get him off my mind.

"I'm just so glad to have you back, even if it is just as friends." My lids painfully shut at the idea but in reality, that's all we could technically be; *friends*.
"Yeah." I smiled though sadness still brewed behind my eyes.

"You look so beautiful when you smile." His index grazed over my cheeks then tilted my head up towards him. His touch felt smooth and encouraged my lungs to fill in his direction. I was mesmerised by his ebonic beauty. He gazed into me, first at my eyes then at my lips.

And though he never said it in so many words, I could tell that he wanted to kiss me. And despite being previously firm on my prude-like stance, a growing part of me wanted to feel his lips as well. My lids shut once more as I battled with my inhibitions.

Whilst so many parts of me screamed *"No,"* the lacksadaisical side of me whispered, *"Why not?"* And naturally, my jaw raised towards him.

Bang!

Howls of screams chased the walls above us and my eyes immediately shot open.

Bang!
Bang!

The crowd ducked and Nelson shoved my head to the ground. The cries persisted and my heart launched out of my chest.
"What on earth is going on?" I barked at Nelson though I wasn't entirely sure if I actually wanted to know the answer. And before he could even reply, a herd of people raced down the stairs and like a Mexican wave, we shot to our feet in the fear of getting trampled.
"Stay with me!" he urged as he grabbed onto my arm. I knew something bad had happened and like him, I wanted nothing more than to get the hell out. The crowds stampeded to the exit in fear and I clutched onto Nelson for dear life. The security tried to manage the panic-stricken party goers as a surf of anarchy swept through the building. A few of the beefier, more senior members of staff headed straight upstairs to secure the situation and corner off the trouble. A pulse penetrated through my temples and my palms felt wet. And as we burst through the front doors, everything seemed to move in slow-motion.

Most of the alcohol-infused troops scaled the streets like an army of ants as they fled from the scenes whilst a few curious cats hovered around. Gossip flew through the crowd like wildfire as they discussed what they saw and what they'd heard. Gunshots re-fired in my brain as I heard them talk and put the pieces together. Rumours swirled about who got hit and my mouth dried as I imagined it happening. *That could have been me.* A raving pulse surged underneath my skin and my brain began to swell. And as the blur of the crowd clouded my vision and the voices meshed into one, Nelson was steadfast on getting through and heading straight to the car park.

Where the fuck was Lilah? My mind triggered at the sound of the gun as it fired once more in my head. She had disappeared upstairs at *The Daiquiri Joint* and I hadn't seen her since. *What if she'd been shot?* I knew how dangerous Lilah's mouth was at times and I didn't know what I would have done if I'd found out that I'd left her in a pool of blood. My mind ran on overtime.

"Wait, hold on a minute," I tugged at Nelson as he dragged me through the street. My breath paced as it tried to catch up with my thoughts and his steps.

"I need to get you home," Nelson urged as he trudged on in full tunnel vision mode but my head was elsewhere.

"Wait! I need to find Lilah!" I launched back in an urge to stop him in his tracks. My mind was racing over a million and one possibilities, none of which I wanted to be true.

"She is with Akeem so she will be fine." He tried to convince me but I needed her more than I wanted to be safe.

"Yes, but she is my friend. I can't leave without her!" I insisted and he paused, still in survival mode and turned to address me.

"Look, I don't know what is going on right now but it sounded like gunshots so I know it's not safe. You need to get home." He grabbed onto me and I could sense his fear but the adrenaline had me feeling impenetrable. All I wanted was to have my friend back.

"No, Nelson. I am not leaving here without her." I dismissed him as I let loose of his grip. And as I shoved him off, he could see that I was serious. He eyed me for a moment as he re-collaborated and took my words into consideration.

"Ok, Raven. If you insist, *I* will see if I can find her but I want YOU to wait in MY car." He was firm in his thoughts. Whilst the adrenaline had me feeling invincible, I could tell that he was determined to keep me out of harm's way. And in the back of my mind, I knew that what he was saying made sense so I reluctantly agreed. He started to look for his car once more and I followed behind. But before we had even reached there, a pleading voice bellowed from behind.

"Raven! Help!" My head darted in the direction of the voice and fear launched through my thoughts. In the distance, I could see Lilah hobbling over to me with a pace and bowl full of tears and I ran up to embrace her. Her cheeks were red and sweat dripped from her hairline.

"Lilah! What's wrong?" I asked as I gave her the once-over. She looked distraught and dishevelled. Her breathing was course and her shoulders were weak. And the guilt of letting her go off without me surged right through me.

"It's Akeem. He's been shot!" she blurted out as she collapsed into my arms. The blood ran cold underneath my skin. And as I reprocessed what she had just said, my arms seized up in shock.

~ Chapter 16 ~

It had been a long night and both Lilah and I was exhausted. Swollen eyelids had weakened Lilah's viewpoint and a heavy head had weakened mine. We had been out until the early hours of the morning so the stress had seeped in. Without an ambulance in sight, Nelson had taken on the responsibility of getting Akeem to the hospital and Lilah was determined to stay by his side. The guilt of leaving him unattended sat strong on Nelson's shoulders and I just needed to ensure that everyone was okay. Throughout our journey, I was stunned into silence. I just couldn't get my head around the fact that Akeem had been shot and Lilah had been there to witness it all. *It could have been her.* The thought spun around and around in my head. And as we drove, intermittent whelps of agony struggled out of Akeem and the pain mirrored in Lilah's heart. She clutched on to him for the entire route, applying pressure to his arm as her salted tears laced the wound. And as he was carted in, her heart was heavy, Nelson's mind was thick and my eyelids weighed a tonne.

In the hope of good news, we sat in the waiting room until the nurse that was working with Akeem reappeared. And whilst we endeavoured to keep ourselves occupied, Lilah found it hard to get over. She began to break down as she clutched on to her sanity, attempting to explain it all. Her tears wept the floor as the guilt swallowed her up. And whilst I tried my hardest to assure her that she had done the best that she could have, she had a hard time believing it. It was almost as if she was telling us half a story but I knew she wasn't in the right frame of mind to form her sentences properly. All she kept saying was, "This could have been avoided… It wasn't even his fault." But to make sense of her babbles was a task in itself so I just did my best to support. Lilah's shivers passed through me like a chronic plague as I held her tight in my hands but I knew I had to be strong. The clock ticked on as we bided our time and eventually a nurse came out to reassure us of his stability. And with the help of the hospital staff, we were able to convince Lilah that it was okay to leave him and in due course, we did.

It was after 5 am before we had finally reached our hotel so I was completely shattered. The sun had already started to peek through the horizon and the cocks had started to crow. And all I wanted to do was sleep. Lilah felt too vulnerable to sleep alone so she hopped in with me. And I was grateful to catch up with lost time. It wasn't until mid-morning that her frequent tossing and turning had begun to interrupt my slumber. Reluctantly, my eyes drew back to her alarm of movement.

"Are you alright?" My voice cracked as I rolled over to her.

"Not really…" Lilah's eyes were fixed on one spot on the ceiling.

"Are you still feeling guilty about last night?" I asked as I wiped the sleep from my eyes.

"Kind of. I just can't get past it. It wasn't even his fault, Ray. And now he's been shot and there's nothing I can do about it." She echoed her worries into the atmosphere and I tried my best to console her.

"Li, you don't have to do anything about it. It's not your fault. He's in safe hands now and I'm sure he'll come around soon. You need to stop beating yourself up. You did the best that you could," I tried to stay strong, for her sake.

"But I didn't. I didn't do my best and that's what even more fucked," she counteracted me as she followed her thoughts and I could tell that something was weighing on her mind.

"You sought help. You made sure that he got to hospital. What more could you have done?" I attempted to be her voice of reason but she found it hard to accept.

"Not let him get shot in the first place!"

"Don't be ridiculous. You wasn't in control of that gun." My eyes tapered as I read her, wondering how invincible she actually thought she was.

"I know but it all could have been avoided. If it weren't for that stunter. It was all my fault, Ray. I could have stopped it…" she paused and her eyes began to well up. I could see the guilt intensifying behind her gaze.

"What do you mean?" I gently inquired, not wanting her close off. "I fucked up and I know it but I just couldn't help it. It was all too much. Ray, if you thought downstairs was good, you would've thought upstairs was a whole other level. Not just the music but the whole vibe. The whole floor was full of stunt men with champers and muscles galore. It was chocolate city, Ray. I pretended not to notice because I was with Akeem but I could almost taste the money in the atmosphere. And I really tried my best to ignore it because I was on my best behaviour so I kept my wide behind firmly on Akeem. And I made sure that we danced our arses off and had a whale of a time. Looking back, I did sort of notice a guy eyeing us but I didn't think anything of it; I thought he was just scoping the room, you know; sizing up the potential. But as soon as Akeem had gone to the bar, he swooped his way in and my head couldn't help but turn. I know it shouldn't have but his clothes were crisp, his guns were tight and I could smell the status all over him. And even though he knew I was there with someone else, he didn't give a damn. That's what got me the most, Ray. His reckless attitude and his menacing stance had my pussy tingling already. I'm not going to lie; a small part of me wanted to slide him my number on the quiet; I just had to figure out how. But then Akeem spotted him. Well, he spotted us and he bolshed right over; all guns blazing. Automatically, I leapt between them. I tried to calm Akeem down but he wasn't having any of it and he squared right up to him; all 6 foot 4 of him, shoving him right out of our space. And I could see the red brewing through the length of him as they rammed back and forth. Can you imagine? Two grown men over little, old me. There was no way I could stop them.

Then bang, he fell to the floor and I froze… It all happened so quickly. I could see the blaze in the guy's eyes and that scared the fuck out of me. It wasn't until he'd stormed off, still half in a rage that I was actually able to move. And when I saw his blood soaking the floor, I just didn't know what to do. All I wanted was to find you." The tears fell from her eyes and I immediately clutched onto her. "I fucked up, Ray. I fucked up big time."

"Aww Li," I murmured, honestly lost for words. I was still trying to process how she always ended up getting herself into these fucked situations. "That's wild;" those were the only words I could manage to muster up.

"I know I shouldn't have entertained it but I knew he was about that life and I just thought fuck it. There's no harm getting a taste of the high life on my holiday. I just didn't think he was about *that* life and now Akeem's in a friggin' hospital bed. I'm stuck here; all alone." The guilt warped her reality and her ability to look on the bright side.

"I'm just glad you're fucking alive, to be honest." Lilah loved the dicey life; that's what made her so unpredictable and made it so hard to be her friend, at times.

"Every time I close my eyes, I just can't get the image out of my mind. That bang, his bloodstained shirt; I just keep reliving it over and over again in my head. I can't even sleep," she explained and my heart wept for her.

"So, you haven't slept at all?" I queried as I rescanned her.

"No. I've tried but the vision of him on the floor and the guilt of me leaving keeps replaying in my mind. I just keep thinking of all the things I should've done but never did," she mumbled as she sought comfort in herself.

"Well, at least you got him to the hospital because now he can get the help that he needs." I tried to change her focus. "You need to stop beating yourself up and get some sleep otherwise the whole situation will just keep spinning around and around in your head." Giving her the once over, I could see that her under-eyes were dark and her eye-whites were tainted with red. Shut-eye had been long overdue. "I'm going to see if I can find you something to calm your mind so that you can rest. Everything always seems better after you have a good sleep." I told her and reluctantly, she agreed. And with that, I got up to see what I could find for her.

After a hearty meal and some calming remedies, it didn't take long for Lilah to fall asleep. She was exhausted and her body needed it. Nelson and I had been messaging since I had left out for the pharmacy and he was keen to find out how we both were.

"I'm fine but Lilah has only just fallen asleep. It's taking a while for her to get over the shock of it all." I told him as I rested my feet on the couch with a cup of tea to hand.

"Wow. Well at least she is resting now, that's the main thing. I just needed to know whether you were both coping okay." He stopped then began typing again. *"If I'm honest, you've been on my mind from the moment I opened my eyes this morning so I had to check up on you."* His message popped up on my screen and my eyes immediately smiled as I took note of his words.

"Aww, that's sweet. I suppose I've been thinking about you too," I innocently shared.

"Oh, were you now?" he replied and the smiles that accompanied were large so I knew that he was swelling with pride. My eyes wound back at the thought of it.

"Yeah but only briefly," I clarified as I poked a hole in his inflating ego.

"Well after that dance we shared last night, it's been hard to think of anything else." As I read his words, my lust couldn't help but reminisce on our moment. His lips did look inviting the night before. But it didn't take long for the trauma to storm back through my psyche and ruin the image that was cultivating inside of me.

"Yes, last night was eventful in more ways than one," I reminded him before my eyes shifted to Lilah.

"Well, it definitely was a roller coaster but at least we've lived to tell the tale." I could tell that he was trying to keep the mood light but I found it hard to ignore the fact that my friend was in tatters because of some puffed-up pricks that were trying to prove a point. *"Anyway, what are you doing today?"* He tried to change the subject.

"Nursing duties," I replied flatly whilst Lilah still resided in my thoughts.

"Nursing Lilah? Isn't she asleep?" Nelson seemed confused.

"Yes, but after leaving her alone last night, I just feel like it's my duty to make sure that she's okay," I told him after glancing over in her direction once more.

"Well, there's not much you can do while she's sleeping...Sounds a bit boring to me." Though I could tell that he was mocking me to some extent, I knew that he had point. But something inside of me just wouldn't leave her be.

"So, what are you suggesting?" I asked though I had an inkling of what he was about to say.

"That I should keep you company." he typed and a single brow rose as I read. *Typical.* I could have guessed that he was trying to somehow inveigle his way into my plans. And though part of me wanted to keep him at arm's length whilst both Lilah and I healed, a tiny slither of me enjoyed it. I thought for a moment before replying.

"Nah, I can't…" I eventually wrote, knowing that Lilah was at the top of my day's agenda. But something in the back of my mind was tempted by his suggestion.

"Why?" Nelson's response was quick and as I read, I had to re-ask myself the same question.

"I'm just trying to stay dedicated to Lilah until she's back on her feet." I declared as I put myself aside for a moment to re-align my fluctuating morals. But after reading my message, his response was not as quick as the last and a part of me felt sorry for turning him down. I hated having to say no. I sat with my phone in my hand, patiently awaiting his response

"I understand. You're just being there for your friend. I respect that. I would love to see you though," he eventually wrote back and a warmness grew inside of me at his willing but considerate response. And that resonated with the part of me that wouldn't have minded seeing him as well. But I couldn't bear the guilt of triggering any more shock into Lilah.

"I'll tell you what, I'll see how Lilah feels after she wakes up and then we'll take it from there," I told him and we both had no choice but to be content with that.

~ Chapter 17 ~

It wasn't until the next day when Lilah arose that she seemed to be in slightly better spirits. Though she was still riddened by Akeem's attack, the sleep had helped her to rationalise their situation and she was fervent on lifting the heavyweight from her shoulders. Lilah still had a strong concern for Akeem's welfare and their relationship status. I could tell that she was keen to see how he was coping in his new found situation; a situation that she'd had a heavy part to play in. Though she never said it in so many words, I knew she was fixed on getting back on Akeem's good side in the hope of some holiday dick. So she made her best efforts to show her support. And whilst I also offered her mine, she was adamant that she wanted to see him alone so I allowed them the space to breathe.

As the boredom of watching Lilah sleep had tired me out so quickly the night before, I had risen at the crack of dawn and was feeling full of energy. I had woken up to an abundance of calls and texts. Though there had been more than I expected, a part of me wasn't surprised as I knew I had turned in extra early. When I routinely scrolled through my notifications, I noticed that there were quite a few missed calls from some of my friends and family who were probably concerned as to why I hadn't turned up for my wedding. My thumb tired as I copied and pasted the same message as a response to them all, purposefully avoiding the *"Call me."* messages from my wedding guests. I was in no mood to explain myself to them nor did I want to keep reliving the whole situation time and time again. I just wanted to move past my set-back the best way I knew how and that certainly didn't involve apologising or finding excuses for my absence.

And as I continued down my list, my eyes paused on a message that had been sent from Nelson.

"Hey. Is Lilah up yet?" The message read, then I noticed his 3 missed calls. Even after leaving him on standby the day before, he still seemed keen on knowing how we both were. A small smirk grew on my face. Seeing his message had moderately shifted my mood away from the drone that came with my deflective auto-responses to the failure of my marriage. All I wanted was to be away from the constant reminders that my ex-fiancé was a narcissistic bastard and my wedding had been a sham. Nelson seemed to be the only one who wasn't concerned about what went wrong. Instantly, I came off autopilot and gave him a call in the hope that he was still interested in meeting up. And given the fact that Lilah had other plans for the day, I knew that meeting up with Nelson would've given me a healthy distraction from my reality.

It didn't take long to convince Nelson to meet up after I'd hit the green button and I couldn't help but beam with pride at my powerful persuasion techniques. We'd only been on the phone for a few minutes before Nelson took the wheel and decided when and where we were meeting. But he was adamant that he wasn't going to tell me what we were doing. And a glowing smirk filled my cheeks. There was something thrilling about not knowing the full capacity of our plans and I silently enjoyed the mystery of it all. And despite my constant questioning, all I could manage to get out of him was what I should wear. By the end of the call, I could hardly tell who'd been persuading who but I didn't mind. I was only glad that I had found a way to positively fill my day.

***

It was just after mid-noon and the almighty sun rays possessed the blue sky. The light was blinding and the heat was draining so I took comfort in my daiquiri as it briefly cooled my insides. I sat on the couch in the foyer with my gold rimmed shades as I awaited his text. And despite the fact that both my vest and shorts were light and loose, a moist sheen still persisted on coating my skin. The Caribbean weather was a force to be reckoned with and the sweat that sat on my upper lip was proof of that alone. The longer I sat there, the more desperate I grew to get the show on the road.

"Where are you?" I wrote to Nelson as my patience began to wane. My glass was quickly draining and I had no intentions

of refilling it before he arrived. But only moments after I had hit send, my phone started to flash and it was his name on my screen. My eye-whites glittered. In an attempt to compose my heightening emotions, I let it ring on for a moment before answering the call.

"Hey beautiful, I'm outside." His voice rung in my ear and strengthened the drum in my chest. Not only was I eager to get out of the heat but I couldn't wait to find out where we were going. I took a final sip of my daiquiri and placed it down on the table in front of me before responding to him.

"Okay. Give me a sec." I played down my impulses as I grabbed all of my gear and slowed my legs from drilling to the exit.

Passing the gates, I noticed a white vehicle parked up by the entrance but it wasn't the car I was expecting. I paused for a moment as I scanned the area briefly but there was only one car in sight. It was a sleek and sporty four-seater with freshly-shined, black wheels. It possessed that just-washed look and there wasn't an inch of rust in sight. *That couldn't be Nelson.* I questioned the vehicle as I attempted to peer 'round the grand wall of the hotel in search for Nelson or his car. But there wasn't a slowing car in sight so I began to head to the hotel car park ahead of me.

As I moved closer, the roof lowered on the white car and tucked itself into a compartment in the trunk; that caught my attention. I had never witnessed a convertible convert so I took a moment to watch. But then, red lights flashed at the back of the vehicle and the horn sounded along with a signal of a wave. I peered over to the driver's seat.

"What are you waiting for? Jump in!" Nelson ordered from the convertible and my cheeks rose, fairly impressed by his new ride.

"Sorry. I didn't realise it was you," I told him as I jumped inside. The interior was black and his seats were leather. My eyes gently shifted around as I quietly admired his new vehicle.

"I suppose you were expecting that rusty, old banger," he chuckled.

"Yeah. I didn't realise you'd changed your car," I revealed as I eyed his digital screen and his Bluetooth-ready gadgets. It wasn't even the car he'd used to take us to the hospital.

"Well, this is one of Mara's but I thought I'd borrow it today for the occasion," he explained and I swallowed the lump of disappointment in my throat. The mention of her name made my blood run cold after the way she'd treated me the last time I was on the island but I didn't want that to show.

"I see…well, it does look good," I said as I strapped myself in and plastered a smile on my face.

"And you look good in it." He winked as he eyed my loose attire and my head shook submissively at his charm. It was probably the most casual he had seen me. And though he was still full of approval, I found it hard to believe. "Just accept the compliment," he ruled as he revved his engine and we zipped down the highway.

The wind rushed past my face as his music roared into the road. His base was unforgiving and it pulsed right through me. As I looked out, the vision of the landscape rushed past my eyes and graced the scenery. I tried my best to keep up with it all whilst my plaits blew back behind me. And though I knew it was hers, my chest still rose at the thought of being a passenger in such a sleek ride and my gold-rimmed shades complimented the look. My chair reclined and I sat back in delight. I had never felt the breeze of a convertible before but I welcomed it with open arms.

It was just under an hour before we had left the highway and entered a quieter side of the island. The roads were narrower and the trail was bumpy. As we drove on, the light from the sun became hidden and we'd been surrounded by a sea of greenery. Nelson's car slowed as we arrived at *Windsor Café* and within minutes, the roof had climbed up and over our heads. I peeled the shades from my eyes as I adjusted to the new light. And as I assessed my surroundings, I became more curious as to why he had taken me here.

"So are you ready?" he asked as he unclicked his seat belt.
"I suppose so," I spoke with a questioning tone in my voice as a series of theories possessed my thoughts. Nelson opened the car door for me and ushered me out into the forest of greenery. And with a chirp, the car locked as it sat by the abandoned café. Briefly, I looked back as Nelson took hold of my hand. The spanking car stuck out like a sore thumb but Nelson seemed unbothered by this as he sauntered through. He'd obviously been to the area before and was more focused on getting to our destination.

As I followed his lead, the twigs bristled and collapsed underneath our feet. The ground below was rough and crunched as we stepped. And the natural light dulled right before our eyes. An army of timber trunks shot up towards the sky and lined the path as we ventured through. The more we walked, the more my heart filled with anticipation.

"Where exactly are you taking me to?" I asked, seeing no clear destination and Nelson turned back towards me with a satisfying sneer on his face.
"Oh, you'll see," he replied and my eyes couldn't help but extend. Whilst a part of me was thrilled, a growing part of me was rather petrified by our abandoned environment. It was only me, Nelson and a few stray pigs in the midst of a sea of trees as far as the eye could see. Subconsciously, I squeezed onto his hand a bit tighter. "Don't worry, you'll love it," he reassured me as we delved in deeper.

As the winding path came to an end, we approached a series of wooden spokes that led down to the bottom of the rocky terrain. "It's just down here." He beamed as he turned to climb down the makeshift ladder. As I watched, my head felt light at the thought of climbing down such a steep cliff with no strings attached. Snaking stalks climbed 'round the ladder and scaled the depths of the rocks. The ground below was more than a stone throw away: in fact, the ground wasn't even in eye's view from where we were. After taking a few steps, Nelson paused waiting for me to join him and momentarily, my feet froze. "Come on, don't be a scaredy cat." He joshed with me. "I'll be right here behind you, admiring the great view." He chuckled as he gestured towards the view that sat between my back and my thighs; my eyes rolled back sassily. Nelson held out a hand towards me.

"You better be right there!" I exclaimed as I took in a deep breath and took my first step down.

"Just don't look all the way down and you'll be fine," he called up to me and my hands steadied on the wooden spokes. The further we descended, the dimmer it got and the stronger the sound of nature grew. Looking up, I could see a crevice of light inching between the cracks in the trees. From where we were, the café grounds were so far above our heads, that the birds looked like flies as they darted past the treetops.

As we arrived at the bottom, there was a rising sound of water crashing in between the rocks and a zesty smell of freshness consumed my lungs. When I turned around, my eyes became witness to the crystal clear water that zipped through the centre of the mountainous rocks and into a shallow river that trailed along the path. I was stunned. Immediately, my eyes shot to Nelson with an eager look in my eyes and he knew exactly where I was heading.

After reaching the edge of the stream, I dipped my barefoot into the water and shot of life burst through my system. The water was stone-cold but it gave me the boost that I needed. Twiddling my toes in the flowing course, millions of minuscule fish rushed past my feet. A hue of rose tinted their murky scales as they flurried through and a tickling sensation crept through my nerve endings. It was beautiful to watch and I absolutely adored being at one with nature. My eyes gleamed as I turned towards Nelson. And the crystal streams reflected in his eyes as they glistened at my gratification.

Before long, my body acclimatised to the feel of the stream and Nelson led me along it. Pebbles pounded the soles of my feet and the flowing water ricocheted against my calves. Wrapping my hand through his arm, I held onto him for balance and his bicep locked me in. Ahead of us, I could see a dark, vast gap in the rocks and Nelson lit up as we approached it. My examining eyes shifted to him. Then, my system paused as I realised that we were heading towards it. *Why would he take me here?* I questioned Nelson's motives as I tried to keep hold of my bearings. I had convinced myself that there had to be something compelling inside if we'd ventured this far. With the deepest of breaths, I trusted his lead and launched into the space of darkness.

~ Chapter 18 ~

From the moment that we stepped into the bleak hole, an eerie sense of quiet consumed us. Only echoes of drops bounced from the ground and hopped 'round the walls. But the sound of the outside world had stopped. A strong musk of earth possessed the air as we took a moment to adjust to our new dimension and I tried desperately to clutch on to the moist rocks. I couldn't see. I attempted to steady myself with the feel of the walls but a silky substance was making it hard for me to catch a firm grip. I held a squint in my eyes as they grew accustomed to our new surroundings then I reached into my pouch for a light.

With the click of a button, the torch shone and I held the light towards the view. The hole was vast. A maze of rocks travelled down the hole and above our heads for as far as the light would stretch. I stood in silence as I mapped it all. Cumbersome pebbles of differing sizes graced the concave walls and expanded through the space. Above our heads, a parade of shining stones pierced through the rocks and decorated the roof. The light bounced off it and created a sparkle in the trinket of water that crept through the cracks below us. "Wow." My voice echoed as I consumed the view and Nelson smiled. It was absolutely mesmerising.

"I knew you'd love it down here," he told me as his chest rose at the thought of his excursion. "And this isn't even the best part. Come with me. I want to show you something else," he told me as he took hold of my hand and I inquisitively ventured through with him.

I took the time to stabilise my steps as we followed the path of light that I had set out for us. And the further we trekked, the smaller the glare of natural light appeared behind us. It wasn't long before the ground below changed from a landscape of jagged rocks to a thick ooze and my feet sunk in. My face squirmed at the feel of it. Nelson stopped.

"What on earth is that?" I queried as the sludge thrived in between my toes.

"It's healing clay," he said as he bent down to scoop a handful of the brick coloured gunk. "The natives come down here when they are in need of restorative remedies or just to relax. Have a feel of it." He offered a handful to me and my eyes assessed it before I stuck my finger in. Smooth gunk slimed around my fingers as I clawed a piece for myself. And the smell of earth intensified as I brought it to my nose.

"Wow. This smells phenomenal," I told him as I absorbed the aroma into my fibres. It reminded me of my ritual Sunday night facial masks.

"I know right. I thought this would be perfect for you, considering all you've been going through. Come and sit on this rock," he suggested as he supported me into a seated position. I sat, still obsessed by the musky smell that came from the clump in my hands. Every time I inhaled, a weird sense of euphoria came over me and I couldn't help but feel easy. And after getting comfortable, he took hold of my feet and rested them on his thighs. Naturally, I leaned back to rest on the stone wall.

"I know you've been feeling stressed these last couple days so I thought this might ease your mind," Nelson continued as he proceeded on sliming a handful of clay over my feet. My head hit the rocks as I savoured the dripping scent that consumed my hands. And with his palms, he began painting the entirety of my sole; from the heels to the toes and back again. My lungs filled with air. Nelson had barely done a thing but with the encompassing scent that filled my hands, I had already started to unwind. Gently, he began squeezing my foot in between his hands as he rubbed back and forth against my inner and outer base bounds. With each movement, a tender tingle began to spread through my veins and my blinking started to slow. Briefly, my mind questioned what kind of drug was in the clay, but with the way that his fingers were making me feel, I found it hard to care.

Sandwiching my feet, he began his thumb work and my eyes couldn't help but roll. One by one, he stroked my toes down, down, down and the vibration in my feet rushed to my head. And as he rubbed, he spoke softly about the foot anatomy, describing how each pressure point alleviated different parts of me. *Mmmm...hmmm...* I tried my hardest to focus on his words but the sensation made it hard to do anything but relax. *Andrew would've never thought to bring me to a place like this.* My thoughts crossed over him as I compared him to Nelson. *In fact, he'd never even touched me like this before.* My mouth softly turned down at the thought of it. Andrew's hands were so heavy and clumsy and somehow, I'd always been the one to put in the groundwork. Although in hindsight, his lack of enthusiasm kind of made sense, considering the fact that I probably was the wrong sex. My eyes wound under my closed lids. I hadn't realised how much I loathed being the one to keep our ship afloat but Nelson had always been giving in nature. As his thumbs possessed each part of my sole, I had no choice but to submit and allow the stress to drain out from inside.

"Wow. You're good..." I whispered as my head rolled against the rocks. I knew Nelson was good with his hands but this felt electrifying. And as he circled his way around the arch of my foot, I couldn't help but reminisce on the way he used to run rings around my clitoris. *No, Raven. Your soul is healing.* My subconscious firmly spoke in one ear before it drifted out of the other. I bit my lip between my teeth as I wondered what part of the body he was triggering with his reflexology. Wherever it was, I didn't mind because it felt too good to deny. *I suppose a kiss wouldn't hurt. It's just a bit of fun.* My lust tried to convince my wounds as Nelson's fingers persisted. Blood rushed to my vital organs as he stroked my Achilles between his thumb and index. And the more he caressed my tendons, the more that I grew weak.

Smoothly, he worked his way up to my calves and down again. My chest rose towards him. *Touch it...* I begged on the inside as he reached up but I never uttered a word. Andrew's brand of burn wasn't even a week old and that scolded my principles. *Raven, you've been with Nelson before. It doesn't count.* I spoke to myself as a growing part of me longed for him to work his way up further. But he didn't. His handy work didn't even surpass the knees. And though a part of me clutched on to the air in my chest in frustration, I appreciated the respect that he was giving me. Nelson knew that I still had some things to disentangle in my head. But by the time he had finished, I'd already started to loosen up; in more ways than one.

***

After a quick wash off underneath the mountain falls, we headed back to the car for a bite to eat. Though the excursion had helped me to relax, it had also worked up an appetite in me. Nelson ordered the Steamed fish and hard food special for two at the *Windsor café* before driving off to a quiet spot to eat. He lowered the roof from above our heads to release the insulated heat and allowed the natural air to flow through the vehicle. The trees lightly danced in the late afternoon breeze as they towered over our heads. And in the distance, the city populated the ground below. I could just about make out the movement of the cars from how high up we were. A few birds had fluttered by us intermittently but not a single soul could be seen for miles. Quietly, I admired the peace and the thought of just us and our food in the middle of the mountainous greenery. Boiled dumpling, boiled yam, boiled banana, fried plantain and steamed fish. The sweet mixed with savoury titilated my taste buds and curbed my hunger but my thirst still lingered.

"Thank you for today," I declared as I scraped the last of the morsels into my mouth.

"No problem. Anything to cheer up your sad, old soul." Nelson chuckled before continuing. "I'm playing but seriously, I really adore you as a person and I just hate seeing you upset," he shared as his volume lowered and the guilt tripped inside of me.

"I know, I've been a drag but I am just trying to get over it all. I'm sorry if I've been a pain." My gaze lowered as my thoughts shifted inwards.

"You haven't been a drag at all. And you're feelings are expected considering all that you've been through. I know you've not been yourself but that's okay," he reassured me and my regards slit towards him. He always knew the right things to say to put me at ease and that echoed in my heart.

"Thanks. I really appreciate it," I told him before a huge huff left my chest. "I just want that happy Raven back again." My shoulders shrunk into his leather seating.

"And that will come over time. You just have to allow yourself the chance to do what feels right rather than what you think is right." He consoled me and I knew that what he was saying made sense. I was so caught up in what people would've thought of my situation and how others would've perceived me that I was burying my inner self. I was burying my own happiness just to keep up with appearances. But I didn't want to wait for happy Raven to arrive, I wanted her here with me now.

My aching eyes gazed up at Nelson as he dug his fork into his food. And I knew exactly what I wanted, even if it was just for a moment of happiness. I wanted to feel again. Leaning over, I stopped his fork in its tracks and his eyes glanced to me. His look alone made me giddy and I yearned to feel his soft lips against mine.

"I've got something… a little more satisfying for you," I plucked up the courage to speak and a glint sparkled in his ebony eyes.

"Really, now? And what might that be?" he asked as his fork dropped into his box. My chest began to thump. His gaze focused on me and my eyelids sealed as I silently went in for the kill.

Instantaneously, a breath of life launched into me as my lips pressed against his. And as he received me, a shot of energy hurled through my veins. The aroma on his breath smelled like cinnamon chocolate. *His taste was sweeter than I'd remembered.* I revelled in the very moment. And as his nose began to graze against mine, I could tell that he was beginning to enjoy himself as well. He paused for a moment and my eyes crept back open. A bright smile shone on his face as our eyes connected and his expression reflected on mine. A sheen of sparkle tinted his dark eyes and his gaze was intense. I wanted nothing more than to smother his adorable face and his edible lips once again so I delved back in. Smooth bristles of hair crept through my fingers as my hands automatically graced the back of his head. And with every kiss, I slowly savoured the flavour of his thick lips.

Before long, his food had dropped to the floor and his fingers had begun to caress my waist. *Aahh...* My mouth dilated as I embodied the feel of the tingles that crept up and down my side. It was only the smallest touch but it made me feel so alive. I clutched onto his skull tighter, absorbing his every sensation. As my head tilted back, my body drew closer to him. Tender kisses pursued the outline of my throat whilst his hand searched underneath my flimsy clothing. My lashes fluttered endlessly. I wanted him. I needed him. And though the roof was bare and we were in the open air, I didn't care. I knew that he knew how to satisfy me and that was what mattered to me most in that moment. I missed the normal, cheerful Raven and I had no doubt that Nelson knew where to find her.

Touch it... I internally urged once more as his hand scaled up my side and my chest craved his connection. He inhaled my aroma and my heart began to pound. His lips plunged deeply into my chest and little by little, his tongue slipped out in between kisses, tasting the essence of my bosoms. Throat protruding, my head rolled to the skies above. *Oh yes... taste more...* I yearned for him to go further. Then his thumb slipped into my bra and my head began to float. Between his thumb and index, he rubbed my nipple back and forth, back and forth and my body levitated towards him.
"Mmmmhhh..." Each breath felt fresher than the last, irrespective of the fact that we were in the midst of the

mountains. And every time I exhaled and his nipple twisting persisted, I longed for my next hit. His tongue began to graze over my areola; amorously sweeping the tip over and over again whilst his other hand tantalised my inflating emotions. Wonderous sparks shot straight to my vagina; swelling the tip and moistening my walls. My hands began to drift.

Rock-solid muscles rippled between my finger trail and I couldn't help but lick my lips. He seemed to be firm in all the right places. My hand took refuge on his cock and my mouth began to water. His bulge protruded through his jersey shorts and was ready for action. Whilst his tongue travelled back and forth between each breast, I stoked him down then up; gently squeezing the tip. And every time I did, my lusting vagina rocketed towards him. The more I rocked, the more of his body I wanted to feel.

With the reach of my wobbling knee, I climbed on top and straddled his groin. His piece stood loud and proud between my gap. Gently, I lowered his shorts so that I could feel him, up close and personal. His top lip rose on one side of his face and his chin elevated towards me. And as his hand braced onto my meaty cheeks, my teeth couldn't help but grip my lip. His hold quietly dominated my soul and I relished in the submission. My arms wrapped 'round him. My jaw fell towards his and our lips locked. 'Round and 'round our tongues swirled whilst he held a firm grasp on my behind, softly massaging my cheeks in time and drawing me towards him.

Progressively, my swelling clitoris began to graze his firm dick more and more. *Mmmm...* my thoughts began to wander as my tip was stroked with sexual delight. And my passion for him fortified. As our tongues played tennis, he just kept squeezing, squeezing and squeezing my cheeks onto his lap. And my tip just kept stroking, stroking and stroking his cock as my walls expanded in pleasure. And like the clouds in the skies above, my chin aimlessly strayed away as our romping intensified. As I looked around, everything became tinted with bliss. Even the spears on the grass began to shine. And the more my cherry danced on top of his firm rod, the more I yearned for his piece to fill my wet, wide hole.

I levered up to lower his boxers whilst I stayed fully clothed. Though I hadn't seen anyone else for the last few hours, I had no guarantee that a wandering stranger wouldn't pass us by. And nothing would have prepared me for that embarrassment, nor did it need to. My shorts were loose, my vagina was panty-less and now he was bare as well. My eyes gawped in delight as his underwear dawdled around his ankles. And I couldn't help but lick my lips hungrily as I readjusted myself on top of him. His chocolate sausage looked delicious enough to eat but my gaping valley craved it more. So I slit my shorts to the side and sat down on his lap.

"Aaaahh..." A gush of release exhaled out of me as he slipped in. And my walls gleamed in delight at the feel of his first stroke. A buzz raced to my cheeks, forcing my eyeballs back. He took control, gripping on to my waist and his hips struck again. The buzz spread like wildfire from my head to my toes. And my cavity sopped in response to his penetrative pleasure. His tongue wept my neck heavily as he sucked the life out of my soul and my desire welcomed his feasting. And as he lathered and licked down and over my chest, his dick searched the circumference of my essence. My mouth hollowed and my lids grew weak.

Welcome home, baby... My mind couldn't help but run across the phrase as his thick, broom swept clean. He knew all the right corners and was stroking all the right spots. His hands held me firm. Then his dick struck, struck and struck again deep inside of my being. Sounds of sultry slipped out of my gorging mouth as he thrust and thrust his way past my sweet spot. And my eyes began to water. His head buried into my chest as he sucked my breast like a thirsty leech. And I had all the juices he needed. Up and down, he pulsed me onto him and my lungs filled with euphoria.

"Ooohhh," I couldn't help but moan as he continued to pound his penis into my pleasure zone over and over again. And my spirit writhed in rapture as he kept on going and going. A protruding vein enlarged on his forehead as his work rate thrived and a glowing sheen tinted his dark skin. *Mmmm...* The harder he worked, the hotter he looked. Breathlessly, my tongue wept my lips as I admired his chocolate masculinity. And my breasts pranced up and down as he continued to rock my world. Even more so, the feeling of ecstasy swelled and swelled. His thrusts were relentless.

My vagina was overloading with pleasure. And his hits were getting stronger and stronger. *Ohh... yeah...* Suddenly, a flurry of tingles fuelled my consciousness.

"I'm coming baby... don't stop..." I breathed as I overfilled with opium. Wearily, Nelson's mouth gawped as he tried to process my words.
"I don't know if I can hold on," he confessed as he drove me on to him harder. And my eyes filled up. My heart pounded.
"Don't stop, Nelson. Don't stop," I repeated as I levitated on and off his dick. Each thrust got sweeter and deeper and my limbs grew weak. *Oh... Oh... Oh...* He lunged once again and a gush of exaltation blasted inside of me. "Aaaaahh…" My lungs impelled. He had finally triggered the thriving implosion that was lying dormant and my head shot back. My body burst with pride and my juices ejected straight onto Nelson's pulsing penis. As I gazed at him, I was bewitched by his ebony eyes. And as we continued our compelling connection, his eyes grew feeble and his own body started to convulse.

"Aaahh, Raven," he whispered my name and the sound of his voice graced my eardrums. Instantly, breath raced into my chest, sharper than before. His force powerfully peaked inside of me. *Wow…* My heart began to smile as our souls tied. I could feel his spirit entwining with mine in a way that I never had before. That fusion felt empowering. His clutch strengthened. Our eyes locked. *He looked so damn handsome.* And in that moment, I knew that I could possibly begin to feel again.

~ Chapter 19 ~

Buzz.
Buzz.

My heavy eyelids peeled back at the feel of the vibration and my hands clambered for my phone.

"Raven?"
"Are you alive?" The messages appeared one after the other. They were from Lilah. I stared at the phone blankly for a moment as my brain fog attempted to clear. Then my eyes shifted to the time at the top of my phone screen. *Midnight? How on earth did that happen?* I had only closed my eyes for what seemed like five minutes after we had reached climax and somehow it was midnight.

I peered over to Nelson, who was still conked out on his reclined seat with his hand protectively resting over my thigh. A whisper of leaves rustled in the trees and the quiet rubbing of crickets echoed through the pitch-black sky. My eyebrows rose as I looked up. *The rooftop was still open? Wow! We must have been shattered.* Briefly, my hands rubbed over my clammy face as I adjusted to the silver, sprinkled night. Then, I went to re-open my messages.

"Hey," I managed to type as I came to my senses and within seconds my phone started to flash. My ears stretched. And the violent ring automatically cleared my bleary eyes. Trying to not wake Nelson, I swiftly slid my hand over the green button.

"Raven? Are you taking the piss? I haven't heard from you all day!" Lilah's voice blared through my handheld speaker and instantly I removed the phone from direct connection with my ear.

"I know. I'm sorry. It's just that Nelson took me out for the day and I suppose the time ran away from me." I spoke in a hushed tone as I edged myself up onto the car boot.

"But you can't not keep in contact with me for the whole day. What were you thinking? We're not in England you know!" she bellowed.

"I know. I suppose I just thought that you wouldn't be bothered 'cos you were with Akeem all day." I quickly thought of excuses.

"Yes, I get that. And to be honest, I was fine when it came to dinner time. I assumed you were probably going to eat out so I had the buffet for one. But when the clock struck midnight and you still weren't back, my whole head started to spin. I hadn't even received a text!" Her lecture went on.

"I know, I should have messaged you. Sorry, mum," I quietly mocked and Lilah let out a slight giggle.

"I don't mean to sound all naggy but after what went on, I'm just a bit on edge. I wouldn't usually worry 'cos I know you're *Sensible Sally* but when I didn't hear from you, I couldn't help but think the worst. Anyway, where are you? And why are you whispering?" she double questioned me after airing her thoughts.

"We're still in the mountains. Nelson's still asleep," I casually spoke.

"In the mountains? What on earth are you doing in the mountains?" I readied myself for her inquisition.

"Oh, Nelson took me to the muddy caves by the falls in Trewlany and gave me the most amazing massage. And afterwards, we ended up resting by the mountains," I explained and a grin smeared across my face as I remembered it all.

"Just resting?" she queried, sensing the joy in my voice.

"Well, we did get involved in a bit of extra-curricular activities but eventually, we cooled off. We were so wrecked that we couldn't help but fall asleep." I quietly filled her in on the gossip.

"He wore you out that much, did he?" Lilah sassily snapped back and I couldn't help but snigger.

"Well, you could say that." I tried to keep it demure.

"Well, at least one of us is getting something. The most action I've had today was from watching the shuffle of Akeem's hospital sheets as he rolled over." Her voice sounded bitter.

"I can imagine. How's he doing?" I asked, fairly concerned about his welfare and hers.

"He's okay but he's still high on painkillers so the conversation between us wasn't much to write home about." Lilah's voice trailed off.

"Well, at least he's speaking." I tried to look on the bright side.

"Yes, true and hopefully he'll be able to come out once they lower his dosage. So I can at least get some use of him before we fly back." She tried to hide the disappointment in her tone.

"I'm sure he'll be out in no time," I reassured her and Nelson began to stir.

"I hope so. It's only been a day and I'm already climbing the walls. Anyway, when's Miss Cinderella coming back? I miss you, girl," Lilah eagerly asked.

"Soon. I'll check with Nelson but I'll definitely be back before sunrise then we can do something fun together tomorrow." I tried to make up for lost time.

"Thank God! Well, I won't wait up for you but I can't wait to catch up. I'm in need of some *real* stimulation," she emphasized.

"Yes. Definitely. I'll message you once I know what I'm doing." As my volume rose, so did Nelson's head. "See you later," I whispered before shutting off the phone and Nelson peered 'round.

"Do you want to talk any louder? I don't think they could hear you in Miami." His voice snarkily croaked.

"Sorry, it was just Lilah wondering where I was. I tried to be as quiet as I could," I guiltily mumbled.

"Well if you call that quiet, you'd probably deafen me if you were actually trying to make a noise," he sniggered as he thought. "Though, I don't think I'd mind taking the chance." Nelson's smirk grew as his corn sewed deep into the soil. My eyes rolled playfully. "What did she think? You were kidnapped or something?" he curiously asked.

"Basically, but after hearing my voice she soon calmed down. I told her that I would make up for my absence tomorrow as it's too late to do anything now. When are you actually planning on taking me back, by the way?" I needed confirmation, for Lilah's sake and my own. Nelson paused as he thought. Then his smoulder grew.

"After I've had my dessert." He turned to me and planted a kiss on my outer thigh while his hand began to run idle. Automatically, my walls warmed as they clenched. I attempted to asses his words. *Dessert?* But his feather-light touch transmitted tingles that flowed from his every movement straight to my central nerve endings, making it hard for me to think straight. Then his moist lips impressed on me again and I knew that he wasn't interested in just any old dessert parlour. My toes curled into the seat as I sat on top of his trunk. He wanted my creamy cake and my lips had already begun to salivate at the thought of it.

Gently, he levered my leg to eye-level as he sewed sweet kisses down the outer length of it. And my inner innocence leapt out in laughter as my eyes shifted through the night sky. "I didn't realise you were still hungry." I toyed with him as he adorned my body with affection.

"I wasn't," his tongue slipped out, "until I saw how sweet and sexy you looked on top of that trunk." He held onto my heel as he dipped my toe deep into his warm and wet mouth. My breath hummed through my closed lips. And the sleeping birds in the towering treetops hummed along with me. Sensuous signals began to wet my sexual appetite as his tongue stroked over my soaking foot. And my mouth began unsealing.

My, oh my. I oozed at the feel of the intense attention he was giving to my body. His suction had strengthened as he laced the white of my sole and my chin began to lift. The shadow of branches danced in the sky above and the glowing moon gave them the spotlight. And in the midst of open darkness, I tried to capture my swelling emotions but his tongue felt too good. The feel of his soothing tongue on the base of my feet only made me crave him more and the erection growing in my clitoral nerves was evidence of that alone. Kiss by kiss, he worked his way around my ankle, my calf and then my thigh. His tongue began skillfully tasting the meat of my cheeks whilst his hands held a firm grip on my inner thigh. And with his every massaging movement, my muscles relaxed and welcomed the thought of his oral pleasure. It wasn't long before my foot was lifted over his head and his tongue travelled underneath.

Mmmmhhh... My lids slowly sealed as he inhaled my inner thigh and naturally my legs loosened even more. His warm breath hovered near my entrance and his nose brushed the cushioning meat that protected it. But I knew that my meat was ready to unearth what lived in between. Tenderly, his thumbs began groping my behind as his teeth pulled the fleshy skin near my groin. And intermittently, his tongue assessed the taste of me. My eye-whites drew back as I longed for my taste to be good enough; good enough for him to get even closer to my centre. His carnal bites were driving me wild and my teeth sunk deep into my lips. I was definitely ready to be eaten alive. And the more he teased me, the more I needed his pleasure right there and then, on the boot of the convertible.

And eventually, his hands began to creep up and gently tugged at my shorts. My cheeks began to glow. *It was about damn time.* I craved the feel of his wet lips on mine down below; his face treasuring the taste of my crotch. And with the lift of my hips, I was more than happy to give him a helping hand. Firmly, his fingers stroked my outer legs as he clawed my shorts towards the leather seats. The solid metal sent a chill up my spine as my bare behind came into contact with his trunk. And my back stood erect. His eyes lit up as he chortled at my slight discomfort; only inches away from my vagina. Then his tongue whipped his lips.

"Mmm, that looks delicious," Nelson spoke to me whilst his eyes fixed on the dessert that was spread between my legs. "But I haven't got a fork." His mouth pouted down, impishly disappointed.

"Don't worry, you can use your hands if you'd like," I joined in with his act, "or even your mouth, that is, if you don't want your hands to get dirty, of course." I had worked the art of subtlety down to a tee.

"Can I use both?" He looked up to ask for my permission and my heart wept.

"If you'd like," I weakly replied as I caught contact with his midnight eyes and almost instantly, he began to delve in.

"Aaaaah…" I breathed as the strength of his tongue launched over my clitoral glands. Weightlessly, my head fell back, revealing the austerity of my Adam's apple. A growing glow illuminated inside of me as he began to lick my plate clean. *Mmmm…* I relished as he began to savour every inch of my glory; all 360 degrees; leaving no place untouched. And wherever his tongue went, he dragged my hood with him. My kitty began to hum as it wilfully followed his lead. He held my legs apart, making space for his face. And my hands dropped back on the trunk in an attempt to support my weakening spirit.

Up, up, up; his tongue stroked along the middle and my back arched in time with his rhythm. Each stroke triggered my ignition and sent sparks to my essence. Silently scratching, my fingers sought for grip on his car as I tried to process the pleasure. My eyes scanned our solemn surroundings for confirmation that what I was feeling was actually happening, but the whistling bushes gave me nothing back. And not a single soul could be seen. But his tongue was gliding across my vagina like it was the best piece of dessert he had ever tasted and I exalted in that honour. Every lick was deliberate, every taste was cherished and it felt smoking hot. I couldn't help but look down in adoration as his head bobbed 'round. Breath leapt into my chest as his tongue bounced from east to west over my sensual tipping point. And my jaw dropped lower. *Oh, Nelson...* He looked so sexy in between my legs and I felt like nothing less than a queen. And he was my humble servant; willing to adhere to my every whim and desire.

"Aahhh," I exhaled as he continued his amorous worship. Then my elbows dropped back on the trunk and my legs spanned even more so. *Oh yes, eat that pussy, baby.* I gloated internally as his tongue made love to me. Kiss after kiss. Suck after suck. A flush of radiation blared inside of me each time his tongue soothed my point of bliss. And a hue of utopia glowed around him as I absorbed his sexual solace.

"Mmmm…" I purred as his finger slipped in like a thick, silk wand through a soaked sponge. I was already dripping wet from the motion of his tongue and he had now decided to enter me. In then out, his finger began to slide whilst he passionately lapped my cherry. *Now that felt good...* I smiled to myself as I lustfully tasted my lips. *That's right baby; pet that kitty.* I was fixated on his fleshly indulgence. My hips urged towards his motion. In then in; he grazed over my g-spot. 'Round and 'round; his lips kissed it better. My eyes rolled in delight at his twisted contradictions. His tongue played nice while his fingers played dirty and I was loving every minute of it.

Harder and harder his fingers began to thrust whilst my clitoris was warped into a whirlwind of pleasure. "Mmmm…" I buzzed as the hum of ecstasy began to germinate. Circles of suckles wrapped 'round my vagina whilst he continued to dive in and out. Then a glaze of rapture blurred my vision and my neck began to clench in his direction. "Oh, Nelson… Oh, baby…" I voiced as the sensation spread inside of me. And my words spurred his actions. On and on, his tongue whipped 'round and the swell in my sexuality thrived. And though an evening chill lingered in the midnight air, my heat levels were still rising.

"Oh Nelson," I couldn't help but repeat as my voice volumised in synchronicity with the height of my gratification. My heart pumped, my femininity pulsated and my head began to float. "Mmmm," I oozed as oral pleasure seeped out of me and my abs began contracting. I was on cloud nine. I had lost all control as Nelson's heavenly host took possession of my body. And with every contraction, a shot of stimulation thrived through my system. I tried desperately hard to cope with the heights of euphoria that I was experiencing. And like a true gentleman, he held me down; never once giving up until my body gave in.

~ Chapter 20 ~

"So, where are we going?" Lilah asked as she lined her lips with the third layer of gloss.

"To let our hair down!" I replied, adding the finishing touches to my up-do in the mirror. Lilah's brow flicked over to me, hiding the depths of her smile as she tried to decipher my vagueness. She had been waiting all day to spend the night with me after her stagnant spell the day before and it was now our time. My family had been hounding my line since I hadn't turned up to my wedding but I still couldn't bear to face them. All I wanted was to move on and forget about it all. Having a night out was the perfect way to find my feet once more. I hadn't told her anything about the night's plan as I wanted to keep it as a surprise but Lilah's inquisitive nature always craved it all. My eye's caught contact with her in the mirror as I continued perfecting my look. She was still staring; waiting for answers. "There's an event going on at *Paprika Beach* right in the heart of town. There's going to be a few performances there and the vibe is meant to be amazing. Trust me, you'll love it," I divulged some more to uphease her curious cat.

"I hope so because I'm in need of a boost right now," she emphasized as she dipped back into her make-up bag.

"Well, I'm sure there will be plenty of opportunities to boost your spirits tonight," I paused to give her a naughty wink. I was fully aware that Lilah didn't know how to sit still for too long. She always needed something to capture her attention.

"Yeah, it's about time I found a hot guy with all his limbs in working order!" she chuckled, taking a break from her last minute spruce. "I just want someone that treats me good, like how Nelson treats you. And they better have the bank balance to match. I'm not trying to leave here broker than when I came!" She looked me dead in the eye and my chin drew back in shock. Though she spoke in jest, I could tell that Lilah was actually serious.

"What about Akeem?" I asked.

"Akeem's still there but he can't do anything for me while he's in hospital. I'm abroad and I'm trying to live my best life. I can't do that while I'm stuck in A and E." Her eyes rolled as she paused. "I want to be treated like royalty. You're not the only one who wants to get their foot rubbed and their pussy sucked for no reason at all!" Her lips pouted playfully in my direction as she mocked my late night rendezvous. I couldn't help but smirk.

"Girl, you can't have everything you know, even Nelson's married." I laughed as I tried to bring her back down from the pedestal that she had put herself on. And for a moment, I reassessed her ridiculously high expectations; wondering if my own were too low.

"Raven, life's too short to limit yourself. I say, get what you want while you still can." Her tone strengthened as she stood up to pack away. And I thought for a moment as I strapped my high heeled shoes on. I knew that Lilah was right.

***

We arrived in town just after seven and the strip was already thriving. The queue for the beach stretched down the length of the road and the music from the other side of the barriers blared onto the streets. *Already?* I was silently shocked by the movement in the streets, though a part of me had put it down to the genuinely lively nature of the island. The girls were dressed to the nines in the queue, proudly peacocking their interpretation of beach chic as they waited to get in. I eyed them all as we walked to the back, secretly validating my own style against theirs and wondering how long it would take until we were finally inside. But the queue moved quickly and it wasn't long before we had reached the front and a silent cashier stood before us pointing to the sign for the event.

After reading the cost on the poster, we gathered our money for the cashier, she handed us our bands and we bolted right in. A gust of wind from the music blasted my ears and filled the venue to the brim. Only a few chairs were lined out in front of the stage and they'd already been occupied by the early-comers. As I looked around, I could see that the beach was filling fast. An array of outdoor bars and food stalls marked the parameter of the barriers and the smell of it was glorious. The frying festival had already begun to titillate my taste buds but the enormous queue for the food alone was enough to curb my appetite. Instead, we headed to the bar for a beverage that would lighten our spirits and loosen our inhibitions. After a short deliberation, we ordered two glasses of Rum and Red Bull each. And the stools by the bar aided in lightening our load. Our eyes smiled as our glasses clinked and a shot of energy launched down our throats. We watched as the crowd sat tight and a short, stubby man dressed in black intermittently appeared on stage, checking the mic and the speakers. It was rumoured that some serious acts were to be performing that night so we were in for a treat. And even if they didn't turn up, I had no doubt in my mind that the night would be one to remember. The tunes that the D.J. had already started to spin were on point and the crowd was full of healthy specimens. Topping that, the sips in our drinks were lethal. They were so strong that within a few minutes, they had already begun to make us giddy.

It didn't take long for the first artist to appear on stage. He was short, brown and held a thick, spinning medallion around his neck. His plaits sprang up and bobbed as he walked to centre stage in his skinny jeans. "Yooow!" his voice echoed down the mic and the crowd went wild. The roar made my hair stand on end. Within seconds, he had commenced; performing the latest of music that had hit the island and automatically, I jumped to my feet. The strength in his vocals penetrated right through me and set my waistline on fire. Instinctively, my waist wound 'round to the rhythm and Lilah wasn't far behind me. Our eye's smiled as we absorbed the vibes that pranced through the air and our energies bounced off each other.

Act after act, drink after drink, the good vibes flowed and I knew that we had both started do what was intended; that was to let our hair down. Sand leapt up as we brushed our feet through the ground and the stage lit up. The crowd was filled with buzz as I looked around and the sweating bodies were consumed with joy. The girls cocked their behinds while the guys crept up in an attempt to steal a dance. But the girls didn't seem to mind and I had no doubt in my head why. The guys that surrounded us were looking thick and strong. And there were quite a few smooth-skinned, bearded beauties glittered around the place. But as I looked over by one of the barriers, my eyes caught sight of him and my grin sprang up.

His all-white caught my attention. And his fitted t-shirt sat well around his torso as he leaned against the bar. The bulge in his white, slim-fit shorts had been accentuated by his cross-legged stance. Casually, a bottle of *Magnum* hung steady in between his fingers. He looked fresh and fine. Plus his newly-shaped beard chiselled his jaw-line and brightened the melanin in his chocolate complexion. And though his dark shades concealed the direction of his attention, it enhanced the mystery behind him. And whether he had actually intended on increasing his mystique or not, it was definitely working because I was dying to get closer to him. Like an excited puppy, I dragged Lilah in his direction.

"Hello, you," I greeted him with a smooth hand on his bicep and as he turned around, his teeth instantly shone.

"Hey, Raven. Long time," Nelson giggled as he leant down to embrace me and my arms naturally sprung around him. And though I had just spent the night with him, a flurry of butterflies still fluttered inside my stomach as though it was the first time. I held onto him tighter, steadying my waving inhibitions and my bursting emotions. And I couldn't resist giving him a sly kiss on the cheek; he just looked so sexy. My eyes glowed as I turned back to Lilah and her eyes glowed approvingly as she slickly pulled me towards her.

"You didn't tell me Nelson was coming?" she quietly questioned me with a quiet smile plastered on her face.

"Because I didn't know myself. I told him where I was going tonight but I didn't think that he would turn up!" I laughed as I danced, trying not to make her enquiry obvious.

"Ray, this was supposed to be a girls' night on the prowl for some fresh meat." Lilah's teeth glowed as she danced along with me.

"Well, there's no harm in hanging out with him for a while then we can circulate, I promise," I told her as I wrapped my arms 'round her and reluctantly, she clutched onto me also.

Cordially, Nelson greeted Lilah then introduced her to his friends. In the spirit of it all, she embraced them and engaged in their friendly chit-chat. And it wasn't long before she had convinced them to buy us another round. Lilah had a way with men, casually getting them to do things for her, even the ones she didn't like. And they were always happy to give her a helping hand. So the buzz in our cheeks spread as our glasses were filled then re-filled, adding to the fluffy mood that we were already in.

The music vibrated through my entire system and the vibe thrived so I couldn't help but wind my behind on Nelson. And his crotch was obliged to welcome me. His chest felt warm behind me and the thought of prancing around in front of such a fine human being sent a heat to my rising bosoms. Reaching behind, my arm held on to the back of his neck as my body snaked down and back up his. His body stood firm. Lilah couldn't help but join in on the action as she backed herself up on me and rotated her round peach in time. A giddy giggle leapt out of my mouth as she confidently showed the crowd what she was all about and it didn't take long for her to catch some attention with her Asian persuasion.

I held a piece of her beach chic as I jeered her on and she swiftly spun around. Her eyes connected with mine as I rubbed myself on Nelson and her green eyes shone. She grabbed onto me in merriment and I held her back as we danced our feet off. Our high increased as I encouraged her moves and she encouraged mine. We were feeling sexy as fuck. Nelson's friends celebrated that fact as they encircled our moves and goaded our lack of behaviour. Sweat seeped through my pores as we partied on and there was no doubt that we were having the time of our lives. But with the mix of the alcohol and the strength in our moves, my energy began to wain and my head felt a bit *too* light. The vision of

Lilah had started to subtly waver in front me. And for a moment, the sound of the music muffled in my eardrums. So I reached over towards Lilah's ear as I tried to steady my stance.

"I think I need to get some food to soak up some of this alcohol, you know. Do you want anything?" I managed asked her. Briefly, she sized me up; assessing the status of my rookie drinking behaviour. My legs reached for balance as I awaited her response.

"Nah… I'm good," she signalled back with a smirk on her face as she continued her prance around. She could tell that I was pretty waved but she didn't seem too concerned. And even with my head in the clouds, I could still tell that she was loving every bit of attention that she was receiving so I had no plans on raining on her parade.

"Okay. I'll be back in a minute," I slowly mouthed before heading towards the food station.

My footsteps were heavy as I filtered through the bouncing crowds and the vibration in my cheeks was at its highest. The party-goers smiled, briefly pausing their buffoonery as they parted for me. But I was far too gone to show any signs of gratefulness as I lumbered through. In fact, the only thing I was able to be grateful for was the selection of hot food lurking at the back of the beach. My eye whites brightened as my eyes met with the lights and my nose met with the adorable smell. Almost immediately, I was drawn to the Jamaican patty stool.

After assessing the menu for a moment or two, it didn't take long for me to come to my decision. I made a swift order of the beef patty in cocoa bread with a side of jerk wings. With delight, I plonked myself on a chair that sat beside the vending truck whilst I waited. My feet exhaled in joy at the thought of some respite and my fingers itched to be filled with warm Jamaican delicacies. And as I sat, I took a moment to enjoy my new surroundings. The sounds of the speakers were reasonably duller so the voices around me were clear to hear. It was a lot less congested where I was and the people seemed a lot calmer. In fact, most of the people that hung at the back were either interested in the meal they were about to receive or the meal that they were already diving into. And I couldn't blame them.

My own stomach even leapt for joy when I noticed a woman in a red apron heading in my direction with a steaming-hot package.
"Order Number 74?" she called with a questioning tone in her voice and my hand automatically soared towards her.
"Thank you!" I gleamed as I welcomed my order with open arms and she nodded back hospitably before returning back to the vending truck.

Almost immediately, my teeth sunk into the freshly toasted cocoa bread and my taste buds tingled. The soft loaf melted whilst the spicy pastry crunched and my mouth drifted in harmony. Leisurely, I inhaled the delight as I took note of every flavour that flirted with my tongue. And intermittently, I dipped the wings in the sticky sauce and took a bite as respite from my blissful sandwich. The bread was sweeter than I'd expected and the ground beef was seasoned to perfection, or at least it seemed so in my drunken state. And bite after bite, the alcohol was mopped up, my stomach was satisfied and my energy was rejuvenating. I smiled as I sat; savouring every moment. Slowly but surely, the focus in my sight was starting to settle.

But then as I lingered, I noticed a trembling mess coming towards me and a gust of wooziness floated through my system. I double blinked as I tried to focus in. But the image shook as it moved. *How was this alcohol still getting the better of me?* I pondered as I watched them. And though I wasn't in the best state of judgement, they still appeared broken. I could see a head rising and falling over a hyperventilating body. And their hands were firmly wrapped around their chest as they hobbled over. As they looked down to their feet, I noticed that their hair was dark and scraped into a top knot but their skin was light. And that neon co-ord looked all too familiar.

Lilah? I had begun to recognise her features though she didn't look like the same girl that I'd left. And as she got closer, I noticed a stream of dried black tears down her cheeks and immediately, I shot up.
"Lilah? What's up?" I said as I headed to her and as she noticed me, she tried desperately hard to compose herself.
"Hey, Raven. Are you okay?" she tried to play it cool but I could see right through her weakened state.

"I'm good but you're not. What's wrong?" I inquired as I placed a hand on her shoulder and scanned her body for damage. But either consciously or subconsciously, she shunned me away as she spoke and my hand lowered to the ground.

"Nothing," she smiled weakly at me but I could tell that she was lying.

"But your eyes are red? What's wrong?" I asked her again and without realising, she tried to hide in plain sight.

"Oh, I'm just tired and ready to leave now," she mumbled with her head in her chest and her eyes cast down to the sand. My brows furrowed as I sought to understand her newfound stance and the reason she'd left everyone.

"But why? We were having so much fun. What happened?" I curiously pried. *Why did she look so defeated?*

"It's nothing. I just… want to go now," Lilah repeated, with her arms still firmly across her stomach as her body turned from mine. I followed her 'round and watched her, this time giving her space. And as I eyed her cowering stance, I knew that something dire had to have happened to deflate her usual-sized ego. This wasn't the Lilah I knew and it certainly wasn't the Lilah I'd left. My ears grew hotter the longer I stared at her vulnerability and a heat began surging through my nose. I needed to know what or who had shifted her mood.

"No Lilah, you've been crying. It's definitely not nothing!" I pressed her and she paused for a moment.

"Look, I don't want to spoil your night so I'd rather not speak about it," she told me as she tried to deflect but I needed to know why she'd been so wounded.

"Lilah, if your night has been ruined then mine has too so you might as well spit it out. C'mon, I need to know what's going on." I sought to capture her gaze. And slowly, her eyes slanted towards me then dropped again. Her neck clenched before she gathered the courage to tell me and my head urged towards her with open ears. *What on earth happened?* Lilah inhaled a deep breath and then her jaw motioned to speak.

"It's... Nelson," she paused and my eyes froze open as I waited for her to finish. *What about Nelson?* I stayed silent, pretending to patiently wait whilst a million thoughts whizzed through my mind. *Was he hurt? Was he dead?* But she wouldn't talk. She seemed choked up and selfishly, it was starting to drive me insane. I desperately needed her to finish. The longer she stood there, the more my mind came up with all the possible things that she was about to say; all of which I didn't want to be true. And I started to feel a palpitation growing in my chest. Slowly I inhaled, trying to calm my racing nerves. Then I finally decided to speak.

"Lilah, what happened?" I asked calmly though blood surged right through me. I needed to know now more than ever. "You know you can tell me anything." I gently reminded her and as my words registered, a force of silent tears began to fall from her ducts. *Oh my goodness. It was bad, wasn't it?* Lilah's eyes reddened once more and her jaw wobbled as she tried to regulate her emotions. Yet I stood there and said nothing though my thoughts were going at a mile a minute. *"Give her time, Raven. She will open up."* I tried to convince my inner urges then her voice began to hobble.

"He… just… tried to… violate me…" Lilah murmured as the tears rolled down her cheeks and my heart froze. *Nelson?*

"What?" I queried in utter confusion. *Nelson?* My eyes locked into her as I re-attempted to process her words. Though she hadn't said it in so many words, I knew exactly what she was trying to say. But it just didn't make sense to me. And a growing part of me was almost waiting for her to tell me that she was joking or to somehow convince me that I had misheard her. But she didn't. And as I stared at her, her eyes looked weak. Her soul looked bare. Her cheeks were blushed with red. *He couldn't have?*

"I was just dancing and… Nelson… fuckin' groped my pussy, Raven," she repeated with more certainty as the tears flooded from her eyes. And this time, there was no denying what I'd heard. "Can you imagine?" she queried as she sobbed and in an instant, the awful image of his ogling eyes and his wandering hands flooded into my mind. They were all over Lilah's curvaceous body. *Nelson?* A part of me was still in disbelief though I'd heard her loud and clear. But as the tears streamed out of her eyes, I knew that her emotion was raw and that pierced deep into my heart. *That fuckin' Nelson.* My eyes slid tight as her words finally hit home and my weeping heart dropped into my stomach.

~ Chapter 21 ~

That night, I couldn't sleep a wink. My eye-whites gazed into the darkness of our hotel suite whilst Lilah slept peacefully in the bed beside me. *How pathetic.* It should have been her that was tossing and turning after her ordeal. Instead, it was me who couldn't help but flit between glaring into the black and staring past the back of my eyelids. I had even switched my phone off for the night in an attempt to find some inner amity. But no matter how hard I tried to relax, my body remained on high alert, sensitive to every single sound. I tried emptying my cluttered mind but the hum of the extractor painfully droned through my ears. I made a strong effort to block it out and for a moment or two, it actually worked. But every now and then, there was a slam of a door or a laughter from outside that instantly opened my lids. The world just wouldn't let me rest, neither would my thoughts. Nothing seemed to work.

Why me? It was that question alone that kept me awake and persisted on haunting my consciousness though I used my best efforts to move past it. A large lump grew in my throat as I tried to figure out what I had actually done to deserve all this. *Why on earth would Nelson think that it was okay to grab a feel of my best friend's vagina? Was I that easy?* My eyes searched my thoughts. But the more I looked for answers, the more questions kept on flooding into my mind. *And how did I end up with a gay psychopath? Why did I have to be punished?* My leg slipped in and out of the sheets as a wave of heat and then frost passed through me. I was racking my brain for answers. But no matter how hard I'd dug, I couldn't find anything in my archives that would allow Karma to deal me such a rotten hand.

I had been nothing but kind to those guys but somehow I was the one that had ended up with the raw deal. Solemnly, my shoulders sunk deep into my chest. Instantly, a wave of regret clouded over me. I couldn't help but regret allowing them both in and letting them both walk all over me like a rubber doormat. But they'd probably seen me coming; *"Yup, she definitely looks like the type of girl that will buy my story and believe my every word."* My eyes wound back at the thought of it. I had been so foolish. All I ever wanted was to feel good about myself but no matter what I'd done, I'd somehow ended up feeling worse. A wet heat crept over my nostrils. *Why was I never good enough?* My theories continued to eat away at my confidence. And with each tick of the clock, another morbid thought entered my mind, then another. Then another until my body had enough. In fact, it wasn't until the sun had started to rise that my mind had begun to settle and eventually I was able to drift off.

***

Knock
Knock
Knock

"Housekeeping," A muffled voice attempted to interrupt my slumber but I was too exhausted to answer. There was still a groggy weight from the night before that hung over my head and I craved more peace. Casually, I rolled over to reposition myself more comfortably on the bed whilst my eyes stayed shut.

Creak…

The door began to open.

Gasp.

Slowly, my eyelids peeled back at the sound of her voice.
"Oh, I'm sorry ma'am," a humbly dressed maid apologised as she backed out of the room.
"No…its fine," I began to croak, "You can come in," I spoke nonchalantly though my body longed for a few more hours in the sheets. A deep stretch extended my muscles as I attempted to wake myself up.
"It's okay, ma'am. I'll come back later." Her voice muffled once more behind the door then trailed off down the corridor. She hadn't even given me an opportunity to respond. Briefly, my eyes rolled back in my head as I accepted her statement. And as a matter of fact, I was rather grateful for her disappearance; firstly, because I was still tired

but also because my bladder was filling fast. And the longer I laid there, the more noticeable it was becoming that my body was in need of a morning release.

As I sought for the bathroom, I caught sight of Lilah's peeled sheets and her empty bed. *Where had she gone?* The thought crossed my mind as I walked past but I thought nothing of it. I was more interested in relieving myself and getting comfortable again. And as I sat on the toilet seat, the fluids tumbled out of me like a fresh spring. My body exhaled in respite. Though a dark cloud still hovered over my head, I felt one step closer to lightening my load.

Lost in my thoughts, I just sat there for a while, reflecting with my pyjamas around my ankles. I had a lot on my mind and I was still trying to make sense of it all. But I knew that somehow, I had to find a way to get over it. And I reminded myself of that fact as I found the motivation to move. I'd caught a glimpse of myself in the mirror as I washed my hands in the sink. Straight away, I noticed the deep bags that sat underneath my lids. My cheeks dropped in disappointment. *What a state.* I shook my head in disgust as I turned away from my broken view. The deflated part of me found it harder to bear the sight of my reflection and I had only myself to blame for that; me and my sloppy decisions. My weight dragged as I tried my hardest to come to terms with it. But in actuality, I wanted nothing more than to curl up under a rock and stay there until the whole situation had been forgotten.

As I walked back into the main room, I noticed a note on Lilah's pillow that stopped me in my tracks. I hadn't realised it before. I must have been so inward on the way to the bathroom that it missed my eyesight. But it was obvious that it was for me so I reached towards it to get a better view.

"Ray, I'm at the beach if you need me. Lilah x," it read. I stared at the paper for a moment as I tried to figure whether I did, in fact, need her. And though I knew that I wasn't particularly in the right frame of mind, I wondered whether she needed me as well. But Lilah was always a lot more resilient than I was, or so she liked to make out. So she was probably sunning it out with a large cocktail and zoning in on her next target. But I couldn't forget that easily. And I was in no mood for people or pretence so I knew that the suite had to be the best place for me.

I whipped the sheets back over me as I climbed in and snuggled into my comfort ball. And though I knew that I wanted to be alone, a part of me still wanted to touch base with the world. I didn't even know what the time was. My phone had still been off from the night before when I craved that extra piece of serenity. But now the sun was up and so was my mind and I needed a distraction. My fingers fumbled through the sheets as I sought for my phone and switched it back on. A slight fizz shook out of the phone as I held it in my hands and it reconnected me with the outside. *Oh wow, it was after 1 already.* My brows rose as I took note of the time, patiently waiting for the rest of my phone to fire up.

Buzz Buzz Buzz
z zz zzz

My phone began to vibrate as a stream of missed calls and messages registered on my screen; all from the same person.

"You're taking your sweet time."
"Hurry up and come back."
"Hey. Where are you?"
"I tried calling but it's not going through."
"Raven. Are you okay?"
"I tried calling you again but it went to voicemail."
"Call me when you get this message."

My heart sunk as I read Nelson's messages. The time stamps had marked the concern in his thought trail but I knew that his actions had proven otherwise. A draft passed over me as I analysed then reanalysed every inch of his messages. *Hurry up and come back?* He played such a slick game but I could see right through it. Anyone would have thought that he actually cared about me from the number of calls I'd received and the messages he had sent. But he wouldn't have touched *her* if he did.

All of a sudden, a misty haze began to cloud my judgement as I re-read into his words and a growing part of me wanted to believe that he actually cared. It was that burning part that wanted to text him back; even if it was just to tell him that I'd got back to my hotel safely. But the disappointment that I was feeling wouldn't allow me to respond. *Why Nelson? Why did you have to fuck up?* My thoughts transcended into the atmosphere as I exited his messages and sought another distraction. The contents of my phone were nothing but a healthy reminder of why I couldn't trust men. *It wouldn't have even been so bad if it was anyone else. But Lilah? Why her?* My head struggled to come to terms with it all but I knew I would have to, and that was the hard part. My phone locked as my head collapsed back into the pillow. And my eyes began to count the cracks in the ceiling.

Ring
Ring

The vibration from the phone in my hands pulsed through my skin and my eyes shifted to my display. And as soon as I had caught sight of the name that was highlighted on my screen, my heart instantly froze. *Nelson.* I stared at the call for a moment as my mind swung to and fro. I was torn. Whilst a small part of me wanted to hear him out, a growing urge in me desperately wanted to give him a piece of my mind.

Why had he been so blatantly disrespectful? I still wanted to know but it was my pride that was stopping me from answering. I watched as my thumb hovered over the answer button, then it stopped. The ringing had stopped. I paused as I tried to process the weird sensation of dissatisfaction that was passing through me. I was the one who wanted to be in control of the decision to speak to him but my indecisiveness had caused me to miss that opportunity. *Fuck.* My chest sunk as I stared blankly at the missed call; thinking of all of the things that I could've done but hadn't had the chance to. The control had been swiped from underneath me and I honestly couldn't decide how I felt about that. But then, a notification popped up on my screen followed by another.

"Raven, I know you've seen my messages."
"Are you okay? Why haven't you called back?"
My pores dilated as I read Nelson's new messages. The ball had swung back into my court. Though I wasn't sure how or if I actually wanted to reply, I already had a million and one responses lined up for him.
"Because you seem to think that it's okay to grab my best friend's pussy." I had begun typing, then I paused as the image of his hands on her resurfaced in my mind. And in an instant, an inflammation of nausea began to mount in the back of my throat. *Was he even worth the energy?* My eyes started to roll as I questioned it all.

"?" Nelson sent, fully aware that I had been typing then stopped. I was angry and still disappointed yet I knew in my heart of hearts that loose flying word vomit just wasn't my style. My thumbs readied as I deleted my message and sought for the right words that I wanted to send.

"Because I'm tired of being disrespected, Nelson," I blankly stated. My eyes rolled back once more at the thought of it.
"What? Where's that come from?" he wrote confused, which sadly, didn't surprise me.
"Last night at Paprika Beach. Have you forgotten already?" I probed his selective memory further.

"Oh yeah. Don't think that I forgot about you yesterday. I was looking for you everywhere but you were nowhere to be seen." He wrote back, conveniently missing out a key part of information. *I was nowhere to be seen so you decided to make a move on Lilah.* I automatically replied in my head. I had the knowledge but I had no plans on divulging it before he did. Somehow, I had convinced myself that him admitting to what had happened off his own accord would soften the blow to my stomach. So by hook or by crook, I was going to make sure that he voluntarily confessed it all. And in pursuit of my mission, I prodded him for more.

"That's because I left but I'm not talking about that. I'm talking about what happened with Lilah." I wrote, knowing her name was sure to ring alarms bells in his head.

"With Lilah?" Nelson confirmed although the words I'd written were as clear as day.

"Yes, Nelson. I know what happened although I actually can't believe it. How could you?" An uncomfortable tingle rushed to my sinuses. Then Nelson began typing.

"What happened? Wait… What did she tell you?" He wrote as he continued his clueless act and my skin grew cold. He was trying to buy time. My eyes scanned over his query once more astonished by his shiftiness, but I was adamant that I wasn't going to buy into his mind games.

"Well, what do you think? You know what you did?" I played the accountability card.

"No, Raven. I don't know. Care to explain?" My jaw dropped in disbelief as I read. He was still pleading innocence and it was starting to piss me off. *How shady could one person be?* I searched deeper into my toolbox of confessions. He was

going to admit it, even if it was the last thing that I made him do.

"No, Nelson. You were there so you can explain." The heat spread underneath my skin as I persisted. *How dumb did he think I was?* But this time, he took his time to reply and I could tell that he was in deep thought.

"Look, Raven. I don't know what Lilah has told you but we definitely need to talk."

"We sure do." I wrote back in an instant. I was adamant that he was going to confess what he did; for my own sanity at the very least.

"I'm just in town at the moment but I can swing by you in an hour," his message read and an instant chill passed underneath my skin. I wasn't expecting a meeting. But, I was definitely expecting answers. I thought carefully before I responded.

"Fine… Call me when you are here." I sent the message and my lids instantly shut down as I re-thought my decision. The thought of seeing Nelson slightly unsteadied me. But I knew that there was no chance of him hiding the truth when we were finally face-to-face.

~ Chapter 22 ~

My heart pounded as I walked through the lobby and towards to exit of *The Vacation Lodge* in an awkward state of limbo. And whilst the lobby still lived up to its usual busy status as I passed through, somehow it didn't feel the same. I couldn't help but pay attention to the weird outer body experience that had crept all over me whilst I paced. Not only was I able to observe the groups of people that casually loitered on the lounge chairs, but simultaneously, I was also able to observe the droplets of sweat that formed on my upper lip as I caught eye contact with them. And though none of the loiterers knew what I was experiencing or what I was about to experience, I still felt vulnerable. Anxiously, my sight lowered as I tried to come to terms with my surreality. But I still had to complete my mission. I had finally received his call and it was now time. I was going to find out what exactly was going through Nelson's mind when he ambushed Lilah.

My feet hit the concrete ground of the car park and instantly, I paused. My tongue re-lubricated my drying lips. I knew Nelson was near but I just hadn't located him yet. Silently, my eyes scanned the vicinity in search of him and his vehicle.

Beep Beep!

A horn sounded and my eyes shot over in the direction of the sound. There he was. The palpitations recommenced. He was at the back of the car park in the same car he used to fuck then suck me. *Still driving around in his sugar mother's car, eh?* The concrete clutched onto my feet as my mouth winced at the tainted memory of it all. Nelson obviously didn't take his union seriously and neither did I. Casually, he signalled and I hesitantly walked over.

The car door opened as I closed in on his radar and he instantly stepped out to greet me. His face read warm whilst mine read cold and that changed the direction of his embracing arms. Instead, he greeted me with a formal nod; something which my crossed arms were a lot more receptive to. Then he forwarded to open the passenger door. Cordially, I nodded back as I took the reserved seat in the convertible.

"Afternoon," I remarked as he finally climbed in on the driver's side. Vacantly, I examined his body language from head to toe as he sought comfort on the seat. He looked nervous and the petty part of me took pleasure in that fact.
"Hey, Raven. You good?" he asked though I knew that he already knew the answer. My eyes slid over to him briefly before removing my eye contact.
"No. Not really but you already knew that." I mumbled towards the windscreen in front of me.

"Yeah, I know… You were… trying to tell me something about Lilah but you never got around to it," he hesitantly spoke and my brows instantly lined as I took heed of his words.

"No, Nelson… You were going to tell me what you did to Lilah. That's why you asked to meet up," I conveniently reminded him.

"What I did?" he queried, taken aback by my words and my eyes fecklessly rolled in response to his poor act; it was growing tiresome.

"Yes, Nelson. Lilah told me all about what you did so I don't know why you keep on acting like you don't know what I'm talking about. I'm just shocked that you would disrespect me like that, to be honest," I told him as I gently tugged at the sleeve that was revealing my breaking heart.

"The thing is Raven. I'm not acting like I don't know what you are talking about. I'm just confused as to why you are angry with me," Nelson spoke and I could feel his eyes burning through me as I continued staring forward. But I refused to make any eye contact with him.

"Well, it's pretty obvious, isn't it? You know what happened when I was gone last night," I frostily spoke as I tried to mask my hurt.

"Yes, I do. And I get that maybe I should have been with you instead or maybe I should have told you what happened. But have I really done anything that bad to warrant this cold reception?" he queried and my brows crossed in confusion. I couldn't believe how naïve he was acting.

"Well, according to Lilah, you have," I confidently affirmed. And he paused, still staring at me whilst he came to terms with my statement. Then he smirked. And a short breath huffed out of his nostrils. And though his attitude towards it all vaguely knocked me, I was still ready to stand firmly alongside my assertion.

"So all this," Nelson gestured to my body language, "has come from Lilah?" he asked in a rhetorical fashion. "Wow. That girl is seriously dangerous. Now I really want to know what this is all about," he sounded intrigued and that caught me off guard. *Dangerous? Why would he say that? Surely, he was trying to sidetrack me.* I sat in silence for a moment as I tried to figure him out from my peripheral. But I couldn't. I had no idea whether he was actually oblivious or whether he was just playing oblivious. But either way, the ping pong mind games were getting tedious so I decided to come out with it. My chest rose as I gained the courage to speak.

"Well… Lilah told me that… after I left you guys, you tried to violate her," I aired as I watched for Nelson's reaction and his mouth gaped open.

"What? Me?" he confirmed with a choke of astonishment and my eyes narrowed in on his movements for a second.

"Yes, you. I found Lilah in tears, Nelson. She could barely speak. But then eventually, she told me all about how you grabbed her crotch and rubbed your dick all over her arse." I began to address the elephant in the room and his chin searched his shoulder. A glaze began to blur my vision as I recalled the rest of what Lilah had told me. "And then, when she asked you to stop, you had the cheek to laugh and tell her to that she was playing hard to get." I finished, carefully grabbing hold of my emotions. My lids closed slowly as I attempted to control the liquid build-up on my eyeballs; the car stayed silent. I knew his brain cogs were turning so I waited. I was waiting quietly for his reaction but he wouldn't utter a word. *Why wasn't he speaking?* All I wanted was an answer; some sort of response. *Did he or did he not?* So I turned to him. His brow began to rise in my direction and his smirk branched out. But he never said a thing. I watched him closely as I tried to figure out why the cat had got his tongue but his smugness had thrown me off. He hadn't even denied it. *Was he proud of himself?* I couldn't tell, all I knew was that the silence was deafening and I needed some sort of closure. "Well, did you?" I urged for a response and eagerly awaited his confirmation.

"Raven, are you actually being serious right now?" He answered my question with a question and that sent a burning heat behind my ears.

"Yes. Did you try it on with Lilah last night or not?" I looked him dead in the eye. All I needed was an answer.

"No way, Raven. I washed my hands with those types of girls a long time ago. I can't even believe that you are even asking me this," He spoke directly to me and that messed with my mind.

"So, why would she say that to me then?" I centred in on his body language. He wasn't showing any signs of deception and that scared me the most.

"I don't know. She's probably jealous of you or something." As Nelson spoke, my brain sought to make sense of his words.

Why would Lilah be jealous of me? "I told you, girls like her are dangerous," he reiterated.

"Listen, I've known Lilah for years. She has no reason to make something like that up. But you, on the other hand, do." I stood in solidarity with her in her absence. There was no way I was going to allow him to work our friendship apart so that he could work his way back in.

"Well, she obviously does because she did. And I have no reason to lie to you, Raven. You and I are not together." Nelson's words pierced deep into my chest and gave me the reality check I needed. My breathing halted for a moment as I tried to gather the pieces that were shattering inside of me.

"Yes, you are right. We are not together but Lilah is my friend-"

"Your friend?" Nelson spoke with a sardonic tone. "And do your friends usually send messages to the guys that you like?" Nelson cut me off before I had even had the chance to finish. I paused as I tried to untangle his trivia.

"Erm, no," I sought to speak with confidence, though I knew it was wavering. He began to snigger as he noted my response and that toyed with me even more. *What was he getting at?*

"So why is it that your friend, Lilah has been messaging me, then?" Nelson's head shook in dismay and the hairs on the back of my neck instantly rose.

"What?" All thought paths in my head began to freeze up.

"Lilah has been messaging me, Raven." Nelson regrettably declared. And for a split second, a seed of doubt sprouted in my mind.

Why would Lilah be messaging Nelson? I sought all avenues as I attempted to uproot my growing paranoia. *She was probably trying to find out about Akeem. He was probably reading into it.*

"That doesn't mean anything, Nelson and that certainly doesn't excuse your behaviour," I spoke boldly, actively trying to overpower the negativity that was germinating inside of me.

"Look, Raven, I've already told you. I haven't done anything wrong. I haven't even touched the girl but the messages she has been sending me have been far from innocent." He seemed distracted as he felt around his pockets. "Even up until this morning, she was texting me," he told me before handing me his phone. And a chill passed through me as I received it. Silently, my eyes slid together before hitting his screen. *Please be mistaken. Please be mistaken.* My psyche longed for Nelson to be wrong as my eyes met with the messages that had been flying back and forth between them.

"Hey! I saw your moves on stage last night. You sure know how to work a room don't ya?"

"Well, they don't call me Mr Vendetta for no reason!"
"I can see that! Any chance of loosening Akeem's hips a little? He could probably learn a thing or two from you."

"Ha ha! Sure. I'll tell him you sent me."

Their banter had begun and I tried my hardest not to think anything of it. But I found it hard to ignore the fact that Lilah had found him online and not mentioned a word of it. Yet, I strove to see the innocence in it all as I read on.

"Hey, Mr Vendetta!
I had a naughty dream last night and guess who was in it?"

"Who? Akeem?"

"I'll give you a clue... I'm texting them right now."

"...?"

"It was you, Nelson. It was you."

"Oh right! Haha. That performance at The Tabernacle must've really gotten to you then, didn't it?"

"It sure did..."

"That darn imagination! How's Akeem getting on anyway?"

"So-so. It's just a waiting game now really…"

And though I could see that Nelson had actively tried to change the subject, I couldn't help but notice that Lilah's message was accompanied by a water splash. I questioned her motives. *What on earth was so wet?* I pondered as my own mouth began to dry.

And though a part of me could understand what it felt like to dream about someone else's man, I couldn't fathom why she had actually admitted out loud. *Why would she do that? She hadn't even told me.* Lilah's messages were beginning to piss me off and I was finding it harder and harder to sympathise with how she felt about Nelson mistreating her. *Did he even mistreat her?* I began to question it as I scrolled down.

"Hey, Raven told me about your sexy escapade on the mountains last night and it really got me thinking. I feel like something's missing in my life."

"Oh really? What do you think it could be?"

"Probably you between my legs."

"Oh, Lilah! You're not serious!"

"Oh, I think I am..."

Nelson had tried to laugh it off but somehow, I was adverse to the funny side of it all. Lilah was now blatantly trying to flirt with my guy. *How fucking dare she?* My blood began to boil. There was no excuse for that one at all. My eye movements began to quicken as I sought to find the lengths of her nerve.

"It's still not too late for you to come and get this pussy, Nelson."

"What are you talking about Lilah?"

"I saw the way you were looking at me tonight. I know you want me as much as I want you."

"No Lilah. You're drunk. You don't know what you're talking about. Go get some sleep."

My heart ferociously pounded as I continued to read the messages that had been sent earlier that morning.

"I still can't believe that you rejected me last night. I'm hurt."

"Sorry, I wasn't trying to offend you but I've been with Raven. That's way too close to home for me at the moment."

"So if it was another moment would you have ever gone there with me?"

"I don't know. Probably not, to be honest."

"Why?"

"No offence but Raven's more my type."

"Oh please. You're a guy. Pussy's your type. How are you going to deny this round booty?"

"Believe me. I've had pussy on a platter before. I don't just sleep with any girl, contrary to popular belief. Plus you're with Akeem. I wouldn't do that to him. Especially while he's in hospital."

"Listen, I'm not with Akeem. I'm single and I'm tryna get my pussy to tingle. I've already heard that you're that guy so I don't know why you are trying to move tight with your dick."

Lilah's lyrics were on fire and the audacity of her was burning a hole through my brain. Her words were so remorseless that I could barely believe it was her writing it all. But there was no denying her screen name online so it had to be her. I was seething. I knew Lilah was wild but I never for one second thought that she would ever do something like that to me. *Did she even consider me in all this?* Blood raced to my eye whites as I continued down.

Then my eyes froze on the image that she had sent. *What the actual fuck?* It was a picture of her bald eagle spread wide right in front of my eyes. *She'd actually sent him a picture of her pussy.* I was stunned. I couldn't believe that she would send this to anyone, let alone Nelson. My jaw dropped to the floor. I read the accompanying caption.
"I know you can't deny all this."

"Nah... I'm good."

That was Nelson's final reply and I had no doubt in my head why. *Was she actually serious?* I thought as I handed the phone back to Nelson. But she had to be; she was bold enough to send a picture of her rotten vagina. The thought of that alone was enough to bring vomit to the back of my throat.

"I had to block her in the end because she was moving too mad. I told you those types of girls are dangerous."

I sat there for a moment as I stared past the glass window. *She had actually been messaging Nelson the whole time.*

"I can't believe what I've just read, Nelson. Why on earth would Lilah do that to me?" I aired my thoughts aloud.

"The thing is, it doesn't surprise me, to be honest. You know it was actually her that tried to rub up on me and I had to put her in her place last night. That's probably why you found her in a fit of tears." Nelson's face soured as he spoke. "And she had the cheek to make out that it was you that abused her? Wow." My mouth began to catch flies as my eyes locked in on the distance. I knew Lilah could be manipulative but I never for one second thought that she would ever try to manipulate me like that.

"Some girls have no morals what so ever. When they're lonely and they see you with a piece of happiness, they want it and they think it's their right to have it. Even if it means stepping on other people's toes in the process. They will use you to get exactly what they want when they want. But for me? I'm not into that. Girls like that only think about themselves and that's exactly the reason why I stay far away from them," he told me and my heart sunk into my chest. And though the painful truth was wrenching to hear, in the back of my mind, I knew he was right.

~ Chapter 23 ~

The car door slammed, the engine roared and just like that, we were off. I was completely done. The thought of spending another night with Lilah by my side actually sent chills down my spine. At first, I thought that what Andrew had done to me was bad but Lilah had swiped the trophy right from underneath him. My friend for over ten years had blatantly tried to make a move on my guy, even after she'd found out what my ex-fiancé had done to me. And the lengths that she went to had taken me completely by surprise. If she was capable of that, I had no idea what else she was capable of but I had no intentions of finding out. The word dangerous was an understatement.

Since being on this island, it felt like I had received blow after blow from the people that I had considered closest to me. And though a part of me felt slightly guilty for ignoring my family and friends, I needed the time out. And I'd finally built up the courage to tell my parents so; their opinions were the only ones that really mattered to me now but enough was enough. Andrew and Lilah had previously been in my small circle of trust but their actions had proven that our relationships were just a fallacy. To be honest, it seemed as though Nelson was the only person that had shown me any remote signs of loyalty outside of my family. And his company came judgement-free. Nelson was the only one left that I had even an inch of faith in so it didn't take much convincing for me to stay with him in *Runaway Bay*. After my mass phone blockage, I began to pack every last thing that I owned and stuffed it into his trunk. I was over it. I had no intentions of ever going back to that hotel, seeing or even hearing from Lilah or Andrew ever again.

We arrived in town just after 6 pm when the evening haze had just begun to transform the skyline from a dainty blue to fiery orange. We parked just below the apartment which sent a sense of nostalgia through my being. Automatically, a weight of tension was released from within. *Freedom. Finally.* A warmth graced me as I gazed up to the coral orange building in relief.

"Shall we?" he confirmed after switching off the engine and gesturing towards the car door. And I eagerly agreed. After unloading all of the luggage, we took an elevator to the second floor and walked down the long, parqueted corridor. And though the key code on the door remained the same, the insides of the apartment looked completely different.

The marble floors had transformed from a cream to a grey which really brightened up the place; especially whilst complimented with the still brilliant white walls. But all the cupboards had been replaced with white framed glass which made the contents inside clear to see; though hardly anything lived inside the cupboards anyway. To top it off, all of the kitchen surfaces were still layered with a white, shiny granite. The sides were still so clean that I could, in fact, see my reflection in them. The colour scheme had really opened up the apartment. And the lounge seemed even more spacious without the kitchen island in the middle. There was now only a grey, L-shaped sofa that differentiated the kitchen from the living area; which added a nice touch to the room. Whilst one leg faced the wall-mounted television, the other faced the balcony which was now home to a full-sized Jacuzzi. My eyes magnified in astonishment as I took a moment to scope the view.

"Wow. Your friend really did up the place, didn't he?" I noted as I admired the décor.
"Yeah, I'm not sure whether it was part of some sort of early mid-life crisis but he seemed desperate for a change." Nelson chuckled as he took refuge on the sofa. And I took that opportunity to join him.
"Well, either way, the upgrade has worked wonders. It feels like a 5* hotel suite in here now," I added as I checked out the new bathroom from a distance.
"I know right; the perfect escape for you to unwind," Nelson joshed as he casually placed a hand around my shoulder. "So what's the plan for tonight?" he inquired and my eyes couldn't help but cynically slide over in his direction.
"Plans? I have no plans at all. I am completely shattered, to be honest," I told him as I took note of my mental exhaustion. "But I am a little hungry," I added.

"Yeah, I understand. It definitely has been a long day. Why don't you put your feet up whilst I go to the shop and grab us a bite to eat? How does that sound?" One side of his cheek rose as he spoke. I could see that he took pity on me.
"That doesn't sound bad at all," I agreed as I got used to the idea of unwinding.

***

Whilst Nelson popped out, my eyes grew heavy so I took the opportunity to sneak forty winks on the sofa. It was the first chance I'd had to recoup after hearing the appalling news and it felt sweet. But after resting for what felt like only five minutes, I heard the beeps of the lock and the shuffle of the door. I gradually began to resurface. As my eyes peeled open, they zoned in on Nelson, carrying two over-sized shopping bags.
"Hey," I groused as my voice caught up with my thoughts. "What's all this?" I queried his abundance of shopping.
"Oh, I decided I wanted to whip you up a nice, fresh meal instead so I stopped by the supermarket to pick up some snacks," he glowed as he spoke; quietly proud of himself.
"Ooooh, that's nice. What did you get?" I asked now positively intrigued.
"Well, I thought I'd cook up some Escovitch fish with rice and peas so I bought us some bits and pieces to snack on while we wait," Nelson said as he began unloading one of the shopping bags, item by item. "Crackers, cheese puffs, pretzels, popcorn, grapes, guineps, mango and wine," he listed boastfully and my mouth watered at the sight of it all.

"Mmmm… sounds amazing," I smouldered as my eyes zoned in on the snacks.

"I'll put them by you so you can eat to your heart's content." Nelson forwarded to the lounge table, his hands full of snacks.

"Thanks but I think I'll just take a few pretzels for now. I don't want to spoil my appetite," I mentioned as my hand reached for the snack pack.

"Trust me, when you smell my food, you'll most definitely have an appetite," he boastfully told me and that caught my attention.

"Mmm, well I'll look forward to it. You better get back in that kitchen," I playfully ordered and he joined in on the act.

"Yes, Ma'am," he saluted as he marched back through.

I watched as he began laying out his ingredients, group by group. It was so specific that I could tell it was about to go down. I sat back as he washed, chopped and seasoned everything so precisely before he began cooking. My brows rose up as I eyed his cooking style. I knew that he could be flamboyant when it came to drinks but I didn't realise that he had such flare in the kitchen as well. I was keen to see if the taste matched up with his style and within half an hour of him starting, my senses had already begun to tingle. The warm smell of coconut milk enriched my nostrils whilst the seasoned rice and kidney beans boiled inside it. Quietly, the fragrant fish sizzled in the pan and my mouth started to salivate.

And with the sprinkle of some peppers and a dollop of coleslaw, my dinner was served. Nelson headed over.

"Mmm… that looks amazing," I voiced as I admired the plate before my eyes. A whole fried fish blessed my plate toppled with sweet peppers and onions doused in vinegar. It sat pretty next to a perfectly portioned side of auburn-hued rice and kidney beans. His home-made coleslaw was professionally placed alongside a rainbow of sweet salad and I just couldn't wait to delve in. The smell alone was enough to trigger my taste buds. After grabbing his own plate, Nelson took a seat beside me and waited for me to take the first bite.

"Well?" Nelson eagerly asked whilst his fork lingered in mid-air and my head nodded in approval. I had no time for words. The perfectly salted crunch from the fried fish had captured my tongue whilst the spicy-smooth rice danced with the beans in my mouth. And though I had never doubted his cooking skills, I was honoured to have the chance to experience the extra string on his bow. My fingers kissed my lips.

"I'll take that as a job well done then," Nelson poked as he began digging into his own dish.

"Most definitely," I confirmed before resuming my love affair with the meal that sat on top of my lap. Forkful after forkful, my mouth was blessed and before I knew it, my plate had been cleaned and my stomach was stuffed.

"That was heavenly, Nelson," I finally declared after taking a moment to reminisce on my blissful meal.

"Thanks," he acknowledged as he took my plate from me and headed over to the sink.

"Any room for dessert?" he asked and almost immediately, my eyes lit up.

"Oh darling, there's always room for dessert," I confirmed, accentuating the courtesy in my voice.

"I thought you would say that," Nelson chuckled. "It's such a lovely evening out, why don't we have it on the balcony?" he suggested.

"Sure, why not?" I agreed as the night did look captivating.

"Okay. Why don't you get changed whilst I make dessert and I'll fire up the Jacuzzi," he subtly ordered and a spark of excitement triggered inside of me. I'd never had dessert in a Jacuzzi before but I certainly wasn't going to turn down the opportunity.

***

The glass squeaked as the door slid open and I stepped out. It was pitch black on the balcony. The only lights that could be seen were from the lounge area inside and the ones that glowed beneath the water. The spotlights caused the water to glow a magnificent blue as the air pulsed through and I couldn't wait to sink in. The wrapped towel dropped to the floor before I began my descent and the warm water instantly embraced my presence. I released an exhale and automatically, the tension started to slip away. The thunderous bubbles pounded against my back and my thighs. *I need one of these in my own place.* My thoughts drifted off. It was the perfect way to end such a stressful day and what a day it had been. I took a moment of peace to enjoy my surroundings while Nelson readied himself inside.

But it wasn't long before the glass door slid open once again and a less modest version of Nelson walked out. *Had he oiled up?* I began to question the status of his pre-shined pectorals and abdominals as he walked over with my dessert in his all-black, skin-tight swimming shorts. *What took you so long?* My stance had been skewed. Not only was I excited to see what he had whipped up but the view of what was hidden behind those shorts added to the vim that was infusing in my own bikini bottoms. Admirably, I eyed his chocolate physique as he neared. His muscle definition was incomparable.

"Oooh, thank you." My hands reached out to him as I received my bowl and he placed my glass of wine beside me. It took a moment for my hands to adjust to the hot and cold fusion that had been placed in my palms but my stomach was more than ready to receive it. Warm apple pie sat on top of salted caramel ice cream and it quickly slipped into my mouth. I sunk back in bliss as I soaked up the party that was going on inside of my mouth and outside of my body. I had the perfect harmony of sensations both internally and externally. And the sight of Nelson stepping into my space made the ambience even better. Together, we ate, we spoke and sipped on some wine. And to be honest, it was just nice to know that I could unwind and indulge in good company.

"Thank you for the dinner and dessert. It was such a pleasant surprise," I shared as I reminisced on the delicious tasting two-course meal with snacks.

"No problem. I know what kind of day it has been for you and I just wanted to make it all up to you," Nelson declared with a sorrow look in his eyes.

"I appreciate that but it wasn't really your fault," I told him as I took a sip of my wine.

"I know it wasn't directly but I can't help but feel guilty for not speaking up. I should've told you from the moment that she started messaging me but I suppose I just didn't think anything of it at first," Nelson began lifting the weight off his chest.

"You should've blocked her slimy behind from day one," I corrected him as my eyes rolled back at her corny moves.

"I know and I'm sorry," his sight dropped to the water.

"It's fine though. It could've been worse. You could've fucked her for goodness sake!" I tried to see the humour in the situation and Nelson's lips instantly winced.

"Not in this lifetime. Even if it weren't for you, I would have never gone there with Akeem's woman. That's just not my style," he reiterated, expressing his warped sense of morals.

"But you don't mind stepping out on Mara though," I reminded him and the truth of the matter moderately unsettled my chi.

"That's different. I told you already, Mara and I have an arrangement so that doesn't really count. Besides, we barely sleep together these days anyway. But the point I'm trying to make is that I would never sleep with someone knowing that I could potentially hurt someone I care about in the process," he cleared things up and in a twisted sort of way, what he said made sense to me. It was at least what I wanted to hear.

"Well regardless, I appreciate the fact that you batted her away, even if you weren't honest at first. You didn't need to do that but you did," I expressed as I was consumed by his nobility.

"And I would do it again in a heartbeat. I respect Akeem and I care about you," Nelson's eyes rose towards me and my heart began to melt. *Nelson cared about me.* My lashes fluttered as I absorbed his every word.

"That's really refreshing to hear," I revealed as I gazed up at him and his dark eyes began to glow.

"And I mean it, Raven." Nelson placed a gentle hand around my neck. "So don't for one second let anybody else tell you any different." His thumb traced my jawline and his conviction penetrated my psyche.

A powerful silence writhed through me as I nodded. I was truly lost for words. All that could be heard were the bubbles that brewed beneath us and the pounding pulse in my ears. He smiled as he received my seal of approval, then he removed the glass from out of my palms. And our magnetic field strengthened. He drew closer to me and my body devotedly adhered to the laws of science. I just couldn't resist the pull. My jaw raised towards him and zealously, his lips locked with mine.

Aaaahhh... A transfusion of energy bounded back and forth between us as our liquids started to exchange. *I love you...* My inner being spoke though I knew the words would never dare to leave my mouth. His energy was infectious and the way that he made me feel was electric. Our rhythm synchronised as our lips softly boomeranged time and time again. And I cherished the feel; they were so thick and juicy. Warm hands wrapped around my neck firmly as his mouth took charge of mine. His kiss alone was enough to make me feel like the most important woman in the world. *Did I love him?* I wasn't entirely sure but I undoubtedly loved the way that he made me feel in the moment.

Bubbles bounced between us as our tongues massaged one another and my insides craved for the depths of his scent. *Mmmm...* His aroma was addictive. And the longer our noses stroked each other, the more of his body I needed. Water dripped down his back as my hands searched upwards and pulled him in. Carnally, his suction intensified as I clawed my way down him. Blood raced through my veins and my fingers spoke a thousand words. I still needed him nearer despite our ever closing proximity. And by the strength of his motions, I could tell that he needed me too.

As Nelson's hunger pervaded, his teeth began to clasp the skin on my neck like a bear trap, leaving me hankering for a deeper lungful of air. *Mmm... that shit felt good...* Bite after bite, his sultry suction strengthened on my neck and forced my head backwards. My mouth hollowed in fruition as my Adam's apple laid bare. Gratified, my cheeks swelled at the sensation of him cravingly consuming me as if his life depended on it. And I took solace in the idea of being his lifeline as I knew that he was now mine; at least for the duration of my stay on the island.

Cords unloosened as his fingers toyed with my strapline, slowly revealing the meat of my bosoms. And as the water waved, my areola peered from around my slack bikini. Nelson's hands stroked my chest and the straps flopped into the hot tub. My teeth gripped my bottom lip as my nipples stood at peak position. Momentarily, they floated on top of the rippling water. Then Nelson slipped in between my legs and draped his loving hands around them. My heart pounded in pleasure. Massaging them deeply, his mouth clamped on to one breast as he began to swallow it whole, over and over again. Lustfully, my hands scraped through the tight curls on his head. Then Nelson's tongue swivelled 'round to make love to the other and my eyes climbed back. Sparkles raced to the tips of my nipples and my legs began to unfold. His hands were taking the floor and I was grateful to give him that opportunity once more as I willfully wrapped my legs around him.

I stared down at his glistening, chocolate skin as his head flirted between my breasts. His moves were silky smooth. I admired his tenacity as he grabbed my breasts together and energetically tasted both nipples in sync. Up and down, up and down his head repeatedly bobbed and my eyes glazed over in awe. His tongue had the strength of a thousand men and my pearl couldn't help but pulse. And though we were already surrounded by water, I could tell that it was about to get wetter.

His hands crept underwater and in front of my bikini bottoms. My breath momentarily clenched. I could feel his fingers stroking my clitoris as he continued to suck my breast. *Aaah...* My mouth steamed as I embodied the feel of his provocative hands on my swelling sex drive. Nelson's tongue toyed with my nipples and it drove my libido wild. I started to thrust towards his hands as they rubbed against the grain, back and forth, back and forth. And an electrical current began to surge through my seeping sexuality. His breast suction was unyielding as he rubbed and hauled my clitoris around. And in response, my hole thirstily amplified. The more he tugged at my pleasure spot, the more I hungered for a piece of his meat.

I grabbed his face for a smooch and my legs yanked him closer. I could feel the girth of his cock as it rubbed against my vagina. *Mmmm...* My pelvis wound as it searched the length of his penis. He was thick and hard and my clitoris was loving every minute of it. An upsurge mounted in the peak of my pants as the friction between our privacy's intensified. I wanted to feel him. I needed to feel him. I tugged at the waist of his swim shorts. Then he paused to pull them down. *Now, that was what I was talking about.* He kissed me gently. Then I began to smirk. I couldn't help but notice his floating shorts in my peripheral as they bobbed around the Jacuzzi and my bikini bottoms longed to join them.

One string, then two; my swimsuit untangled and swam off in the water. I suspired a release. Finally, our bodies had been liberated on the second floor of the coral-orange building, in the pitch black of the night. But it didn't feel naughty; it just felt free. I grabbed hold of him for a celebratory kiss and his wet lips soaked mine. My soul awakened as our bare bodies connected and our energies interlocked. His skin felt velvet smooth and his touch felt so right. I only longed for him to fill the void that was growing inside of me.

I need you. My eyes swelled as I stared into his and automatically, I held him close. My tongue slathered all over his sleek chest of mahogany. His firm cheeks squeezed in the palm of my hands. All the way up, my mouth planted soulful kisses over his chest, neck then lips. Our hips drew closer together. Back and forth, our genitalia bounced on top of each other in the water as our kissing reached climbing heights of intensity. And my hardened nipples grazed against the ripples of his chest. *Mmmm.* The drum in my heart solidified. His dick was teasing my entrance as it slid up and down over my grinding grain. More and more, my lusting lady was craving the penetration that it was missing. *Fuck me already.* I internally pleaded yet I never uttered a word. I held onto him tightly as I swallowed his lips and he held me back with just as much vigour. And even without the verbal cue, he knew that I wanted him.

"Aaaahh…" I breathed as he finally slipped inside of me. I tasted the sweet savour on my lips. His thrust rocketed up me like a shooting star and his sensational remnants scattered deep into my darkness. A rush raced to my head at the first hit of his addictive drug and like all fiends, I knew that once could never be enough. Then he thrust again. My jaw searched for more air. His reach was deeper and sweeter than before and by the look in his eyes, I could tell that he was searching for something buried inside of me. Pound, pound, pound; he hit me with the hat trick and my head dropped back. Waves wafted as he perused my neck with the base of his tongue. And his dick took solace in my purring cat. Nelson's mouth was devouring me like I like a dog after a long run and that made me even hornier. My hips wound on top of his lap and he plunged into me even harder. *Oh...Oh...Oh...* My mouth dilated as he dug. My heart thumped out of my chest. His force penetrated through my entire being and sent a buzz through my skin. Nelson's mouth extended then rested on my bouncing breasts as he continued to drive me wild. And the gentle grazing of his tongue on my nipple added to the sexual voyage that he was taking my body on.

Swiftly, he exchanged positions with me and then spun me around. Nelson's penis was still snug as I sat in reverse on his lap. My essence pulsed around it like a throbbing heart. His soft lips proceeded on tracing the expanse of my back whilst his hands began to explore my breasts. My chest rose into the night sky as I sought to recapture all of the fervency leaving my mouth. My arms reached back for balance. The sensation of his philandering fingers all over my bosoms left my head in the clouds whilst my vulnerable body sat all too comfortably on top of him. Pins pricked through my lips as my breathing deepened. I could hardly tell where I was. All I knew was that the way his hands took command over my body was enough to not want to be anywhere else.

I looked back at him and a rose glaze tinted my view. *What would I do without you?* His eyes lusted as he held me closer. One hand slipped through my breasts and gripped the base of my throat whilst the other took charge of my nipple. And his tongue returned to mazing through my back arches. Sexual energy raced round my triangle like the night lights on speed. The pound in my chest pumped. And whilst my jaw dropped in submission, my sexual core yearned for control. I couldn't resist curling my behind on and off him as I savoured the waves of emotions that were flowing through my system. His dick felt sweet as it rubbed on every internal crevice and my walls revelled in delectation.

Gradually, his fingers slipped down; over my belly button and on to my clitoris. My breath cut short. He was circling against the motion of my hips and my essence expanded in excellence; as did my thighs. His handwork was so precise and so sensitive to my every need that it felt exalting. My lungs captured that honour as my eyes began to fill. And as our movements syncronised, I rode his cock 'round and 'round like a royal jockey. And the volume of his moans got louder and louder.

Whoosh.
Whoosh.
Whoosh.

He grabbed on to both breasts like gear sticks as he shoved his penis in and out of my hole. It wept in delight. Each time he pounded, a burst of desire vied through my fibres, leaving me yearning for more and more. My lashes flashed my eye whites. His punch was powerful and sent my joy through the roof. And the more he pounced me on to his cock, the more the love flowed through the tub. My limbs grew weaker and weaker.

I reached forward for respite; my hands gripping on to the edge. Promptly, he clutched onto my wobbling hips.
"You good?" he leaned in to ask as he took heed of my feeble stance and my heart began to pour.
"Never better," I breathed as I looked back at him, noting his genuine concern. *He was just so endearing.*
"You sure?" He confirmed as he slowly rotated his dick clockwise inside me. My eyes rolled anti-.
"Mmm hmm…" That was all I could manage to muster as his penis stoked my g-spot and he took advantage of that.
"Good," Nelson rumbled before shooting his cock straight through me.
"Uhhh," I mouthed as I took pleasure from his thrust and his smirk spanned. His hands clenched onto my hips and he struck me again, again and again. And a warm ripple splashed around us. *Mmmm…* His dick soothed my insides and made my sweet zone swell and swell. My bottom cocked up to receive his cock and I gripped onto the sides even tighter.
"Oh, Nelson," I called out as he hammered his way into me. Each shot filled my vagina with bliss and that seeped through my lips.

Splash. Splash. Splash.

A tsunami whirled between our bodies as his hips slapped against my backside and his golden balls crashed against my clitoris. He was giving me double the pleasure and he didn't even know it. *Or maybe he did.* But the more his balls collided with my love bud, the more blood flooded to my v-spot. And the pleasure in my zone continued to mount and mount. Full tilt, I pushed back on his cock.

"Aaaah, Raven," he groaned and I bit my lip at the sweet sound of him calling my name. And that alone was enough for me to push back some more.

Uh. Uhh. Uhhh.

His penis swole. And with his expansion, his hammering became even more euphoric. Back and smack, our bodies bounded off each other; my pleasure bubble grew and grew.

"Ohhh baby," I groaned as the girth of his penis multiplied. Nelson's thrusts had tripled in power and my eyes began to water. In... In...

"Aaaah, Raven," Nelson breathed as his juices squirted inside me and his power began to diminish. My eyes reached back as I absorbed his last hit. "You are... everything," he told me as he collapsed onto me and my eyes couldn't help but smile. His chest rose and fell on top of me as he recuperated and it was my pleasure to capture his fall. *I'm everything... wow.* Those words alone were enough to look past the negativity and look towards our clean slate.

~ Chapter 24 ~

This was perfect. My cheeks rose as I laid still stroking the curves of his chest and Nelson's hands repeatedly graced my hairline as we tucked into our 4th movie of the day. After an exhausting night, we hardly had the energy to do anything else; nor did I want to. It felt safe being in the clasp of Nelson's arms and it helped me to forget the betrayal of *him* and more importantly… *her*. My eyes recoiled as I cursed the image of her bald pussy out of my mind once more and returned back to my serenity; my safe place. Since noon, all I had been doing was mindlessly eating the snacks that were left over from the night before. In fact, the most active thing I'd done all day was lifting my backside to squat on the toilet seat. But I loved it. I had never really had the chance to chill with Nelson all day before. But we were cosy in *our* little apartment away from everything and it felt so right.

We took turns choosing our movies with Nelson starting first. Inadvertently, we had a slight competition going on as we strove to choose the best movie of all time. Whilst I went for the usual *Poetic Justice* and *Baby Boy*, I was fairly surprised by Nelson's choices. His first was *Waiting to Exhale* and his second was *How Stella got her groove back*. And as I delved into each one, they both got me thinking. I wondered whether he'd actually held a genuine interest in those films or whether he was just trying to send me subliminal messages. Whilst I wasn't usually a fan of awfully imitated accents, it was still good and food for thought, none the less.

We'd ordered pizzas and ice cream to accompany our binge along with all the trimmings. I opted for the Hawaiian with pepperoni whilst Nelson opted for the Vegetarian, claiming that he didn't like the idea of meat on his pizza. I found it quite ironic considering the fact that Nelson had always been partial to a bit of extra meat on the side. But that was something that I was trying to ignore for the moment. The olives and dough balls were the perfect addition to our meal and they went down a treat with the reconciliation of Jody and Yvette.

"I've got to give it to you. That film actually wasn't too bad you know," Nelson silently applauded me as the film closed.
"I know. It's a classic. I still can't believe you've never seen it before. I watch it all the time at home." I rose up, boastfully proud of my choice.
"I can imagine you sitting at home, cheering her on and hoping for your Jody to come along," he mocked as his thumb playfully slipped into his mouth.
"Well, it would be nice to finally find someone that was ready to step up and play their position," My eyebrow rose as I subliminally dug at him. "I'm not getting any younger, you know," I made light of the situation.

"I know and I'm sure your time will come. But that's just a movie. Life is not always full of happy endings like that,"

"You're telling me?" My eyes rolled as the thought put a dampener on my good mood. We'd had such a nice day so far and I liked the idea of movie land so I strove to keep the happy boat afloat. "So anyway, what's next? I want to see how you top that one!" My mouth rose as I batted the challenge back in his direction. I already had a few more classics up my sleeve but I was keen to see what else he could come up with.

"I'm not going to lie, I'm not even sure I can. Plus, I'm sure my eyes are turning square from all this television watching. I need a real challenge. How are you with games?" he asked and my eyes sharpened in on his motives.

"Well, it depends on the type. What game are you thinking of?" I inquisitively asked.

"Maybe some truth or dare," one cheek rose with his suggestion and a sharp breath swept through my teeth.

"Okay… this could get interesting," I aired as I thought of all the things I could possibly discover under the umbrella of the game. "I'm down for the challenge. What are the rules?"

"It's simple, you just keep choosing a truth or a dare until one person folds. The first person to give up loses the game and has to do a forfeit,"

"Okay, I can work with that. But the loser has to do whatever forfeit the winner chooses," I offered him a firm hand as we agreed on the terms and he happily accepted.

***

The coin flipped into the air and landed on the lounge table. The silver head shone and I knew what that meant. My heart began to thump as Nelson smirked at my vulnerability.

"So, truth or dare?" he asked as his arms smugly crossed over his chest. My lips dried as I thought. *Should I take the easy route or should I just get one out of the way?* My mind flitted past both ideas before my voice spoke.

"Truth…" I gulped as I awaited his question.

"What's your wildest fantasy?" his tongue brushed his cheek and I thought for a moment as I explored his question.

"I'm not sure if this counts as the wildest but I definitely would like to be blindfolded and tied up while someone had their wicked way with me," I shared more freely than I thought I would've and a breath of relief left my nostrils. *It could have been worse.* I smiled as he accepted my answer, knowing that it was now his turn.

"Fuck it…Dare," he spoke before I had even had the chance to ask the question and my tongue slipped out between my lips. After a moment of contemplation, I dared him to strip and head to the balcony. His challenge was to do ten naked jumping jacks while shouting the numbers out loud. Not wanting to quit before the game had even begun, he rose to the challenge and stripped down immediately. My brows rose at his bravery as he bolted to the balcony. I couldn't help but chuckle as his long john flapped up and down between numbers but he completed it all too easily. I knew that I needed to up the ante.

Biting the bullet, I made my choice and rose to my feet. It was my turn again. My breath held as I rejected my inhibitions to stay safe and dove back in at the deep end. And though part of me dreaded it, another part of me got thrills from the mystery of it all. My breath clenched as he declared my dare but yet, a part of me was still pretty excited to complete his challenge.

My hands clamped against the wall and my legs spread as I stood butt naked in the room. Then the lights shut off. *Was this how he prepared for a frisk?* My nostrils flared at the idea as I waited patiently to be checked. Suddenly, I felt his cold crotch against my behind and my head shot up. *Oh, Nelson.* My brows lifted surreptitiously. Although he was unusually close behind for my search, the frisky side of me didn't mind at all.

Calmly, his hands brushed through my flat fingers and down my arms. My hairs stood on end as they followed his sensation from my fingers to my shoulders and then underneath. His hands paused as he leant in for a closer inspection and the tip of his nose brushed over my back. My lungs halted as I waited. But after a moment or two, he signified that they were all clear. Then smoothly, his hands began to search up the centre of my chest and around my breasts.

My eyes spun back as I internalised the feel of it all. His hips flexed towards me as he gave my nipples a thorough forage;

it sent triggers to my vagina. And as his search continued to titillate my every nerve ending, my back arched towards the wall in front. My upper lip began to perspire. But then, he released my nipples from his captivity as he confirmed that there was nothing to be found. So he began working his way up from my ankles to my thighs, carefully checking in between. I captured my breath in its tracks.

"Hold on, I think I found something…" he whispered as his fingers examined around my clitoris again and again. And my jaw began to lower. He then clamped my v-spot in between his index and middle finger as he probed me up and down for a moment or two and my mouth steamed against the wall. Soppily, my vagina began to prepare for further investigation.

"Nope, you're all clear," he confirmed as he gently slapped my behind and my heart immediately dropped. I was nowhere near ready for that search to be over. The lights turned back on and a rosy feeling still festered inside of me.

"Do you believe in fate or free will?" I asked as I sat forward, intrigued.

"Probably," Nelson took a minute to formulate his answer. "I'd say fate. I believe that everything happens for a reason. Sometimes, we don't know why at first but as time goes on, the reason is gradually revealed to us," he explained and automatically, I questioned his stance.

"So you don't believe you have a choice in the matter?" I challenged his thought process and slowly his index began to stroke his chin.

"I don't really think you do," he continued and I was surprisingly saddened by his view. It was as though he was admitting to not having any control over his life. My ears tuned in to understand his perspective. "Even if you choose one thing, somehow it has a way of leading you back on the path that you were meant to follow," Nelson divulged and as he went on, I thought back to my plans of marriage.

Were things meant to be like this? I questioned my situation, then his. And though I weren't entirely sure, a part of me understood his line of thinking.

"Okay," Nelson joyfully rubbed his hands together "Now this time, I'm going to make the choice for you," he smirked. "Now let's see if you'll sink or swim…" a cunning smile grew on his face and I tried desperately hard to keep my game face on.
"Let's see what you've got," I fired back, still eager to win and his eyes lit up.

"Your dare is to get naked, sit on my lap and rub the hell out of your pussy," he declared and a plastic smile smeared across my face. He was really trying to push me to my limits but I wasn't ready to give up. So I stripped down once more and straddled my legs around his lap. Nelson's hands cupped his head as he leaned back against the bedstead. "When you're ready," he nodded towards my bare clitoris as it sat over his groins. Hesitantly, my hands slid down.

"Mmm…" Nelson groaned as he saw my hands clasp my vagina and my head buried in my shoulders. "Don't be shy. You look good," he reassured me as I coyly rubbed my fingers around my clitoris. Nelson's tongue slipped out to shine his lips. "You look fucking hot," he breathed and his words sent a slight chill down my spine. Slowly, my eyes closed as I got into the groove and took charge of my vagina. Up and down, my hand searched around my tip and my entrance began to tingle.

"Mmm…" I breathed as the sensation spread through my limbs and my hips began to curve. *Aaahh…* His cock was firming as I rubbed myself all over it and it was stimulating my entrance.
"Yes… that's it," he egged me on and my eyelids slowly slid open.

A fluorescent glow illuminated off his dark, golden skin and he looked so damn sexy with his arms cocked back. My tongue chased my lips as my fingers continued to repeatedly expand my hole and my crease began to weep. It was me who was in control of my own pleasure and I was loving every minute of it.

Ring! Ring!

The 5-minute alarm rang and I was pissed. Masturbating on top of him was nicer than I thought and a buzz still vibrated around my cheeks. But now, it was his turn and I was still determined to win. I climbed off his lap as I prepared to put him in a predicament. But still, the opium fermented in my system.

"Alright Nelson," I bit my lip as I built the courage to speak. "Would you rather divorce Mara or kill me?" I asked and my eyes tapered to scrutinise his body language.
"Wow," Nelson's eyebrows rose. "I can't actually believe you are asking me this," he chortled before he took a moment to ponder.
"Yes I am and you have to be honest," I reminded him as my inner system almost halted as I awaited his verdict. Out of all of the questions that I had asked him, I wanted to know the answer to this one the most. *How much did he really value me?* I had to know.
"Okay. If I had to pick, I'd divorce Mara." Nelson smiled.
"Really?" I questioned whether he only chose that option because I was there with him.
"Of course. I'm a lover, not a fighter," he told me and his glowing smile subconsciously reflected inside me. And even if it wasn't true, my heart wanted to believe him.

"Right. Now let's see if you really have balls." Nelson's eyes shone with a menacing look on his face. "I dare you to knock next door and ask for a cup of sugar in just your bra and panties!" Nelson chuckled as he finished and my tolerance levels instantly shut down.

"What? I can't do that!" I retorted as I laughed along with him in astonishment. And his eyebrow rose.

"So are you folding?" he asked with a seeded look on his face.

"No, but the dare is outside, that's unfair!" I exclaimed and his laugh got even louder.

"No one said anything about where the dare has to be... That sounds like a fold to me." His chest rose and my head shook in shock.

"No I'm not quitting but I'm not doing that!"

"Then you are quitting," Nelson mockingly shook his head. "That's your dare." He eyed me to see how ballsy I really was but I knew there was no way on earth that I was going to embarrass myself like that.

"Wow, I can't believe you're actually doing this," my eyes centred in on him and his smug smile grew. I could tell that he wasn't going to give up on this one. "Fine, whatever. Do your worst." I huffed as I patiently awaited his forfeit.

~ Chapter 25 ~

The next day, we left the apartment bright an early for breakfast and headed to *Mother's,* the local café. Nelson was keen to treat us both as he had woken up with an enormous appetite. *Mother's* was one of his favourite restaurants and he had been fantasising about it since the moment he had lifted his lids. When we arrived, I could tell that he wasn't the only one who had food on their mind by the sizable queue that snaked through the fast food restaurant. But after overeating the night before, I was too full to go large so I decided that I was going to keep my order modest.

When we finally reached the till I only ordered the ackee and salt fish in coco bread. However Nelson, on the other hand, persisted on ordering all of his hearts desires; hard food, mackerel rundown, a beef patty and a cornmeal porridge to wash it all down with. And I couldn't help but side-eye him when finally he regurgitated his order. I just didn't understand how he stayed so trim with such a huge appetite. But who was I to complain? Whatever he'd been doing had obviously been treating him well thus far so there was no way that I was going to stop him now.

After receiving our meals, we took respite on the diner seats as we began to devour it all. The more I ate, the more I perked up. It made a nice change to get up early and grab the day by the horns. And a good meal always did start my day off right. But despite the deliciousness that was working its way through my system, one thing was still bothering me. It had been more than half a day since I had lost the game and Nelson still had me pondering. *What on earth was he going to come up with for my forfeit?* I wasn't even sure if he knew but he was definitely holding his cards close to his chest.

"So is your meal living up to all of your fantasies, then?" I toyed with him as he delved into his third course.

"Of course," he smiled as he gulped down a hefty mouthful of food. "Probably more so than yours!" he joshed and my eyes rolled at his insensitivity.

"Well after what I had stuffed last night, my body definitely needed the break," I explained, destroying his attempts to mock me even further. "But my sandwich sure did taste good," I told him.

"Good. Then my work is done," he grinned as he tucked into another bite of his patty.

"Well, they do say the way to a woman's heart is through the door of a good restaurant," I carefully folded the napkin in a manner only suitable for a Michelin starred gastronomy.

"And look where we are!" he chuckled, rather proud of his budget achievements. "You see... It's not about where you go, it's about the company you keep," Nelson stood firmly behind his choices and I had to agree with his stance.

"Speaking of company, a few of my friends have invited me out for dinner tonight." Nelson casually slipped the extra information into the conversation which took me aback.

"Tonight?" I confirmed as I attempted to prevent my heart from sinking. I had grown used to the idea of just 'us' and actually looked forward to spending another night alone with him. But now, it seemed as though that was out of the picture.

"Yes. It's not very often that I'm in town so I thought it would be nice to catch up with some of them before I left," he explained but the selfish side of me found it hard to understand his point of view. *It's not very often that I'm here with you either.* My inner ego sulked but there was no way that I wanted him to brand me as the bunny boiler that made him change his plans.

"Oh right, I see," I tried to maintain a chirpy tone. "That's nice," I told him as I attempted to remove the sour taste from my mouth.

"And I wanted you to come with me," Nelson added and my eyebrows jolted back in surprise.

"Me?" I had to double check that I'd heard him right; surely they must've known Mara.

"Yes, of course. They've heard a lot about you and are dying to meet you," he told me and my ears couldn't help but prick up.

"What have they heard exactly?" I confirmed, trying to figure out my place at the table.

"That I'm in town with a dear friend for a few days. But when they heard you were a she, they got all excited and told me to bring you along,"

"Oh right. Okay," I said as I assessed his answer, though it still moderately unsettled inside.

"Don't worry, they are good people and so are you. So as long as you're yourself, you'll be fine," he reassured me.

"And are you sure you'll be okay with me being there?" I had to ask.

"Of course. Besides, I can hardly keep you locked up in the apartment twiddling your thumbs all night now, can I? What kind of host would I be if I did?" he joked and my cheeks began to rise.

***

The gold jewels shone as they rolled over my collarbone and sat perfectly around my neck. I had already chosen my outfit so all I needed to do was add the finishing touches to my look. My hair was scooped up high into a ballerina bun, pulling my cheekbones up and showcasing my thin, gold, dangling earrings. And I wore a deep, emerald dress. It was long-sleeved but plunged low, allowing for a bit of extra decoration around my neck. The lace material hugged over my torso and flared out at the waist, leaving just enough space over the knees for sexy sophistication. And whilst my thick, oiled legs laid bare, my diamante-strapped, heeled sandals wrapped around my feet. The look was perfect for the occasion and my eyes glowed as I admired my reflection.

"You look beautiful," Nelson spoke as he entered the room and the vision of him stood behind me in the mirror.

"Thank you," my cheeks shone as I accepted his compliment. "You too," I casually told him though I knew he looked effortlessly hot. His pale, pink shirt fell loosely over his shoulders and roughly tucked in at the waist. I could tell he was going for the breezy look as his shirt was only half buttoned up and revealed a slither of his chocolate chest. His chinos were fitted and black, sitting perfectly over his athletic thighs. And to top it off, he smelt phenomenal.

"Well, I'm sure that I'll look even better with you on my arm tonight," he told me as his reflection eyed me up for size and I couldn't help but blush inside. "I have a little something for you to wear also," he added as he revealed two shining, metallic balls in his palms.

"What is it?" I queried as I tried to decipher the purpose of his gift and his lip began to rise.

"It's your forfeit," he breathed and my brows began to taper. "You didn't think that I'd forgotten, did you?" Nelson's smirk had redeveloped and my expression began to reflect his.

"No, I didn't. In fact, I've been wondering about it all day. I just don't get how *they* can be a forfeit," I explained as my eyes shuffled down to what he held in his hand and Nelson began to snigger.

"You have no idea what these are, do you?" he confirmed and my mouth turned down in befuddlement. "Raven, instead of underwear, your forfeit is to wear these tonight, between your legs." One cheek rose as he spoke and my eyes closed in on his words. "I want you to put both these balls up your pussy and keep them there until the end of the night," he told me as he handed me the balls. "And don't let them drop," Nelson added and as they landed in my hands, I realised that they were a lot heavier than they looked. But casually, I agreed. And though Nelson had forbidden me to wear underwear to the dinner as part of my forfeit, having a pair of balls stuck up my vagina hole seemed a lot easier to do than some of the other forfeits that I'd imagined.

We parked up in the centre of town where the night lights jazzled and the streets were full of energy. Nelson hadn't told me much about where we were going but by sounds of the streets, it was sure to be a good time. Like a gentleman, he jumped out first to open the car door for me when we'd arrived. And he held onto my hand as he guided me out. From where we'd parked, the restaurant was in eye's view but was still a fair walk so I held onto Nelson's arm as we strolled towards the entrance.

Cobbles crunched underneath my sandals and a rosy feeling began to fester inside of me. At first, I couldn't put my finger on why as I assumed it was from the excitement of meeting more of Nelson's friends. But the longer I walked, the more I realised the reason for my internal glow. Those balls were rubbing on my inner walls and it was making the walk a lot more pleasurable than usual. *The cheeky bugger.* My eyebrow rose as I side-eyed Nelson. Though I'd been none the wiser, he knew exactly what he was doing when he gave me those weights. But somehow, I found it hard to be mad at him. I only hoped that I could keep them up me for the remainder of the night.

It wasn't long before we'd reached the doors of *The Hippodrome* restaurant and we swiftly slipped inside. The room was dimmed and hued with violet lights by the bar.

And a grand, long table dressed the centre of the intimate restaurant. A small crowd had already begun to take their seats and his friends were already sat at the long table, awaiting our arrival.

"Hey!" A petite female jumped up as we neared the table and flung her arms around Nelson's neck. Without thinking, I stepped back from their embrace. "You must be Raven," she smiled as she let go of Nelson and warmly leant into me. "I'm Ash. It's so nice to finally meet you," she exclaimed as she ogled me for a moment. I had no idea whether she was admiring me or my outfit but I could definitely tell that she liked what she saw. Enthusiastically, she bought me over to meet her partner and the others.

Nelson and I sat at the end of the long table, in between both sets of couples. Nelson sat next to Jay and his partner on our right whilst Ash sat with her girlfriend on our left but the spotlight seemed to be solely on us. Back and forth, they fired questions in our direction in their pursuit to find out how we'd met and what we'd been doing since being in *Runaway Bay*. All the attention was so overwhelming and a part of me found it hard to figure out what exactly was appropriate to say. Luckily, Nelson handled the questions like a pro and kept my eminence intact whilst I sat pretty, speaking only when I needed to.

And after our meals had arrived, the focus began to switch and everyone tucked into their plates. For a moment, the only sounds that could be heard were the scrapings of the plates and the smiles of filling stomachs. The smooth sounds of jazz floated on in the background and my soul began to lift with each bite. The more I sat with them, the more I began to find my place at the table as everyone welcomed me with open arms.

"You are just so darn sweet," Ash gazed over at me for a minute, taking a break from her steak and my head began to shrink into my shoulders.

"Thanks," I replied as I took a sip from my glass.

"If only Nelson could've found a girl like you a long time ago," Ash continued as she directed her attention to Nelson and I couldn't help but silently snigger. *If Only*.

"Yes I suppose so but everything is timing," Nelson replied.

"And situational," I couldn't help but add as my thoughts shifted to Andrew's storm of a lie then to Mara. I knew that no matter how much I'd pretended or tried to forget, Andrew's callousness had scarred me and Nelson's status meant that he could never truly be mine.

"What do you mean?" Jay asked and I thought carefully about how I wanted to phrase my response.

"I know Nelson is a good guy but he's lived his life and I've lived mine. I've had my fair share of frogs back in the U.K and Nelson is married. So I suppose it just wasn't meant to be," I shrugged as I tried to rationalise my situation in my head and Ash burst out in a laughter.

"Married? To Mara?" Ash could barely contain herself and that put me on the back peddle. "Please, that marriage isn't nothing but a contract," she spoke bitterly and my head gawped back in shock. "Which for the life of me, I can't figure out why he's still in. Must be the money!" She joked and the whole group roared out in laughter. My brown face blushed crimson.

"Listen, money is the least of my problems. Life is not as simple as that," Nelson shot back in defence and I felt a sudden urge to protect him.

"So you keep saying," Ash quickly interjected. "You have a beautiful woman on your arm right now, who seems so loving and genuine," she gestured towards me and my heart began to warm. "So what's stopping you?" she asked. And though I was highly intrigued, I consciously slowed my eager head from turning as I awaited his response.

"Raven is a beautiful soul and she knows that I respect her," as he spoke, Nelson slid his hand over my thigh under the table. "I would never intentionally bring her into anything that wasn't right. We both have some things that we need to figure out. And if it is right after that, then we will see how things pan out," Nelson explained as his endearing hand reached for mine. Suddenly, my heart was comforted by his words.

"Yeah, I agree. Things don't just happen in the click of a finger. What will be will be," I found myself seeing things from his perspective as I tried to protect how we were viewed. Despite my growing feelings for him, I had already convinced myself that Nelson could only ever be a holiday fling. So I decided to make the most of my situation whilst I was with him and figure out the rest when I needed to. But Ash wasn't buying any of it and was quick to dismiss our statements as spew.

"No, Raven. What you make happen, will be," she eagerly corrected me and the strength in her words echoed in my ears. And Nelson sat silently as he registered her stance. "Anyway, Nelson is a smart guy so I'm sure he knows what he is doing," her eyes briefly met with his and so did mine.

"Don't worry. I'm sure everything will work out just as it is meant to," Nelson finally spoke as his hand stroked over mine and I had no choice but to believe him.

~ Chapter 26 ~

After our plates had been cleared, the backlights dimmed and the spotlight shone in the middle of the grand, long table. The smooth jazz powered through the dark restaurant and I knew a show was about to commence. Casually, a slim, slender woman floated onto the table wearing nothing but a sparkling leotard. Her hair was scraped back and tucked into a tight bun and her makeup was pale. Her feet were light on the ground and she commanded the stage like a graceful gazelle; sliding and gliding as she travelled the length of it.

And my eyes locked in on her. I could tell by the stretch in her stride that she was more flexible than the average female and I was intrigued to see what tricks she had up her sleeve. And eventually, she addressed the hoop that dangled from the tall ceilings above and reached her hands up high. Effortlessly, she wrapped her hands around the spinning hoop and began to levitate off the ground. *Wow*. I admired her strength as she found her balance in mid-air then contoured her body around the hoop. And the crystals glistened on her leotard as the spotlight bounced off them.

I grabbed Nelson's thigh in excitement as I watched her flex her leg right over her head then spin her body through and through the rotating hoop. Her flexed control was like no other and that truly enthralled me. Slowly, her body stretched upside-down and her legs drew open and a wandering hand crept up my thigh. Briefly, my eyes slit to Nelson but his eyes were locked in on the floating gymnast. The hoop spun as she reached up and curved her head back comfortably on to her toes. Her breast stood firm as they rotated above our heads and the soothing hand began to move higher and higher up my thigh. My eyes shut momentarily as I tried to maintain my focus but the soft strokes that were running up and down me were making my hairs stand on end. I reached under the table to grab the hand and Nelson's cheeky eyes turned to me.

"Are you enjoying yourself?" he whispered underneath the sound of the music and I nodded back at him meekly. "Good, then sit back, relax and enjoy the rest of the show," he finished and he gently squeezed my thigh, intentionally massaging it with enough sensual strength to allow his hand to wriggle free. My vagina pulsed as the inner meat on my thighs stretched into his grasp. The more his hands dominated my legs, the more my body relaxed into the sensation and allowed his hands to continue.

I watched as the skilled gymnast reached her leg upwards around the rotating hoop and allowed her body to drop down as she clutched on with only her thighs. And my own thighs began to unlock. Little by little, Nelson's hands were nearing my crotch-less line and his touch was causing a sexual swell in my vagina. His strokes were adding to the entertainment that stood before my eyes. Sporadically, his finger strokes would transition from light to firm and that sent a thrill down my spine. More and more, I was becoming torn as to where my attention should be drawn to. And whilst a growing energy inside of me urged for him to continue, I would've been damned if one of his friends had noticed. So my eyes stayed stuck on the aerial artist as Nelson's hands lingered by my vagina.

Smoothly, she climbed up with poise and wrapped her legs around the top of the hoop while her upper body hung. Her upside-down smile addressed all 360 degrees of the audience as her flexed chest stood strong. And a rush raced around me as his fingers progressed. His middle finger was tenderly stroking over my centre and a waft of wind whipped into my lungs. My blinking slowed as I wrapped my head around the growing sensation that was festering between my legs and they, in turn, loosened even more.

From the view in front of me, I could see that the gymnast had smoothly transitioned into a vertical position with her legs wrapped 'round the dangling rope. And Nelson's hand began to move in synchronicity with her as she searched up and down the length of the hoop. And my tongue wept in delight. Up and down, up and down, Nelson took my vagina on a thrill. And the more he toyed with my clitoris, the more the magnetic balls moved inside of me; stimulating the spreading vibration underneath my skin.

'Round and 'round, her body began to flip as her crotch hung tight on the hoop. And my eye whites began searching the back of my lids. *Mmmm...* My inner Goddess wanted to breathe so badly but it was only the company that surrounded us that kept her tame in her cage. A gentle, more controlled breath exhaled between my lips instead as Nelson matched the speed of the spinning lady. 'Round and round, he dragged my hood underneath the table and my heart began to pound. Sexual secretions began to seep through my hole as the balls rubbed against my inner sweet spot. His hands had started to flirt over my entrance more and more and I longed to feel the taste of his dick.

I leaned back on my tucked-in seat as my pelvic bone unlocked. And the performer's head hung over the hoop as she reached back for the tip of her toes. Her crotch laid bare, as did mine as I slowly circled against Nelson's rhythm. Surges of joy circulated around my body as his hands heavily petted my kitty and my clitoris began to throb; forming a pulse of its own. And the way that my inner walls were contracting over the metallic balls made the feel of his movements a lot more intense. The longer he continued to tease my crease, the harder I was finding it to stay discreet.

Firmly, I grabbed hold of his hand as I let out a silent huff of frustration. His eyes slit to me whilst his head stayed in the same direction; towards the floating woman. And I gave him a gentle tug.

"Excuse me," I whispered to the group as I gestured for the toilet and Nelson followed closely behind.

"You... are a naughty boy," I breathed as we finally shut the door in the cubicle.
"Me? How?" Nelson's jaw innocently dropped as his hand clutched onto his chest.
"You knew what you were doing when you gave me that forfeit," As I spoke, he couldn't hide the growing smirk on his face. "And now, all I can think about is the taste of your dick in my mouth," My eyes rolled as I shook my head at him in disappointment.
"Hmm," a short huff flared out of his nostrils. "I was wondering how long it would take you to crack." He smiled towards me as his thumb stroked over my chin.

"You don't even understand how fucking horny I am right now," My teeth gritted as I spoke and my hands rubbed over the bulging zip in his chinos. "Mmm..." I licked my lips at the feel of his package. "You're so fucking thick and firm. I need to taste every last piece of you. Right here, right now," I asserted as my hands fiddled with his zip.

"Well, who am I to say no?" He playfully spoke rhetorically as I dropped to my knees and inhaled the scent of his dick. My mind exploded with joy as my nose swallowed the spicy musk on his meat stick. The tip of my nose ran against the length of him. His skin was soft but his dick was hard and his girth was turning me on even more.

Gently, my tongue began to lace the back of his shaft from his balls to his tip and my taste buds started to tingle. His salty, sweet aroma tasted better than I'd imagined and I let out an instant moan in satisfaction. Automatically, my hands wrapped around his base and my sweating mouth drew open to devour his girth.

"Aaah," Nelson breathed as my tongue caressed the back of his tip and my insides began to glow. His penis fitted perfectly inside me my mouth and his skin felt smooth. I smothered him in kisses as I showed full adoration for his pretty, thick piece. Then, I relaunched him back into my mouth and he let out yet another moan. My sexual crease contracted at the sound of my name seeping out of his mouth. *Raven*. He made it sound so fucking hot and his enjoyment spurred me on.

Up and down, I massaged his skin as my mouth sucked his tip. Sounds of slurping multiplied as my thick lips met with my hand ring and then bounced in the opposite direction. His dick was mouth-watering and the dribble dripped down my fingers. And the wetter his dick got, the louder he began to moan. Back and forth, my head bobbed with passion and my hands caressed his length.

Over and over, I forced his tip to the back of my tonsils and my desire for him intensified. The more I rocked back and forth over his dick, the more those damn balls stimulated my insides. And it wasn't long before my sheath began to salivate. A warm moisture started to crawl in between my thighs and my heart pounded in pleasure. At that point, I knew that there was only one thing that could cure my undying thirst. I sprung back on to my feet.

"Oh fuck, those fucking balls. I need your dick right now," I urged as I wrapped my lips around his and my hands pulled his head even closer.
"Oh, do you now?" he flirted as he flexed his bare dick over the flare in my dress. My vagina sopped at the feel of it.
"Yes," I breathed as I curved my craving cat on and off him; dying for him to push it in.
"Then turn the fuck around," he ordered and automatically my hands searched the wall as I eagerly awaited his penetration.
"Ohhh," My eyes watered as he slipped inside and his hips pounded off my round rear. His hit was strong and firm and my vagina began to weep in delight. Again and again, he drove into my behind and forced the sex balls up. My eye whites drew back. Every hit came with a sensational rush and my legs were beginning to weaken. Nelson's hands clutched onto my hips and mine clutched onto the wall for dear life. *I love you. I love you.* I captured the phrase as my breathing began to deepen. And for a moment, I almost spoke it out loud but my inhibitions knew better.

Undeniably, his carnal pounds were spinning my world and those twin balls were making me even weaker. Each and every time he shoved his way inside of me, they massaged my ego and naturally, my sweet spot couldn't help but swell. A warm vibration started mounting in my head and my moans got even louder.

"Oh Nelson, what are you doing to me?" My breaths were heavy. I was completely dumbfounded by the sensations that were flowing through me and my slit sopped in excitement. Lewdly, my backside cocked even higher and that spurred him on even more. Harder and harder, his groin slapped into me and a mist spread from my mouth and onto the cubicle wall. The pressure was building and a huge sense of euphoria was beginning to illuminate underneath my skin.

"Oh my gosh! Don't Stop!" I cried out in joy as my hands scraped the wall. *Where on earth did he find those balls?* My mouth dilated as he continued to blow my mind over and over again. I had never felt like this ever. The sensations he was giving me were running deeper and magnifying more than ever before. Palpitations bolted out of my chest. Our moans echoed around the cube as the delectation began to intensify and my lady lips throbbed in delight.

He was thrashing into me at full force and my head was overflowing with ecstasy. Each hit felt sweeter than the last and my eyes filled with gaiety. But then, he struck again and my mind gushed. He had taken me to a point of no return and my tear ducts immediately flushed with joy. *Wow.* My head repeatedly rose and fell as I tried to process the enormity of erotic opium that was possessing my mind. "Ooooh, Nelson," I called out as I lost all control over my jelly-like limbs and his thrust suddenly deepened.

"Raven…" he breathed as his groin firmly stiffened over my behind and his juices ejected straight into me.

~ Chapter 27 ~

The next morning greeted me with the soothing sounds of water crashing down to the ground and naturally, my spirit began to rise. As I began to resurface, I took a moment to take in all that was bliss. A warm heat caressed my skin through the window and my vagina still tingled from the evening before. A glowing smile grew on my sleeping face as I reminisced on it all. Naturally, my limbs stretched over to Nelson. I felt around for a moment but I couldn't seem to find his body.

Where was he? My eyelids immediately slipped open. Nelson was gone. I rubbed my eyes as my mind tried to make sense of the missing piece in the puzzle. The sound of hitting water still persisted in the background and it wasn't coming from outside. *Nelson?* The lines between dream and wake state were still blurring and a part of me still wanted to embrace the feel of the sheets between my feet. But it was hard to rest easy knowing that I hadn't a clue where Nelson was. A great yawn left my mouth as my tired muscles stretched. Groggily, my feet began to take me towards the root of the sound.

And as I reached the door of the bathroom, my mind was immediately put at ease. "Good morning, early bird," I smiled as I wrapped my dressing gown snugly around me. I hadn't even realised that he had moved. And though the sleep was still encrusted in the corner of my eyes, the sight of the soap bubbles dribbling down his chocolate beauty was more than a wake-up call for me.

"Oh, you're up," his dripping, wet head shot 'round from the shower head, a little startled by my presence. And a pleasurable giggle slipped out between my lips. It was quite refreshing to see Nelson on his toes. "Good morning, my beautiful blackbird." He held a cheeky glint in his eye which I was finding to be infectious.

"What are you doing up so early?" I asked as I voluntarily watched him continue to soap up.

"Oh, I've got to head back to *Montego Bay* quickly. I need to sort something out," he spoke as the sprinkles of water splashed over his face. And my smile slowly dropped.

"Oh," I responded as I internally digested what I really wanted to say. *So you're actually going to leave me here? Alone?* My heart sunk at the thought. I wasn't ready. I'd already been coerced to leave Andrew then Lilah and now Nelson was leaving me alone with my thoughts. *He couldn't.* My chest felt raw but the pride in me didn't want to come across too clingy. I began to smear a plastic smile on my face and searched for something a lot wittier to fire back in his direction. "So I take it there isn't room for one more in the shower, then?" I asked in a light-hearted manner, though the inner me hankered for him to fill my void once more before he left.

"No, I need to be quick, to be honest, but I'll be back by the evening. Will you be alright here by yourself?" he asked though I knew I had no choice in the matter. Whilst my inner me wanted to cry *"No,"* the outer me was more determined to play it cool.

"Well, I suppose I'll have to be," I said as my eyeballs traced my eyelashes momentarily. Though I was slightly peeved that he was leaving me for the day, I wanted to make the most of the time we had left. "I'll tell you what, I'll make us something to eat before you hit the roads while you get yourself ready," I told him as I headed to the kitchen and tried to adjust to the idea of spending the day alone. As Nelson seemed to be in a rush, my eyes scowled the fridge and the cupboards for something quick and easy to make. Intrinsically, I reached for the most basic of ingredients; eggs, beans, bread and plantain; it was the perfect combo for an almost full English. The knock of the pans echoed as I placed them down on the kitchen surfaces and the cans cracked open. And with the sprinkle of some oil and the chop of a knife, the plantain started to sizzle. I watched closely as it transformed from a pale yellow to golden brown.

Ring.
Ring.

Nelson's phone rang from in the living area and my eyes focused in on the sound. *Who on earth was ringing so early?* I wondered as I walked towards his phone and glanced at his illuminating screen. And automatically, my eyes launched back in my head when I realised who it was.

Mara. I headed back to the kitchen. There wasn't an urgent bone in my body that wanted to tell Nelson who had been calling. The right shade of plantain had more of an interest to me than passing on any messages that involved her name so I continued on with the breakfast. The fork whipped 'round the bowl as the egg bound with seasoning and prepared itself for a scramble. Then his phone rang again. The second time, I ignored it. I couldn't bear to see *her* name again. To be honest, whoever was calling him was indeed none of my business although a small bolt of jealousy was beginning to writhe inside of me. *What exactly did he need to sort out in Montego Bay? Why was she calling so much?* I tried my hardest to ignore the filling glaze in my eyelids as I reminded myself that *this* was just a holiday fling. The beans slowly warmed on the stove.

Knock. Knock. Knock.

My head bolted to the front door and my heart launched into my stomach. I was frozen. *Who on earth was that?* My eyes stared at the keyhole from a distance. Nelson was in the shower and I certainly wasn't expecting anybody. *It wasn't Mara, was it? It couldn't have been.* I immediately counteracted my paranoia though I had no idea who had, in fact, knocked on the door. I thought for a moment, toying with the idea of ignoring it and carrying on but my curious nature wouldn't allow me to. *Stop being silly and just check.* My heart pounded as my feet cautiously led me to the door.

AUTHOR'S NOTES

What's to happen next?
Find out how the adventure ends in the third and final instalment
of The Vacation Lodge.
Follow the author to keep up-to-date
with the releases of all forth-coming novels.

CONTACT THE AUTHOR

Website: www.djwalterswriter.com
Instagram: djwalterswriter
Twitter: djwalterswriter
Email: djwalterswriter@gmail.com

ACKNOWLEDGEMENTS

First of all, I would like to thank my mother and father for their ongoing support through my ventures. They have undoubtedly shown patience, loyalty and enthusiasm throughout the entire process and I appreciate them both for all the individual things they have done to allow me to reach this point in my life.

Also, I would like to give thanks to my Sister Shay and my spirit sister Nichole. The Vacation Lodge II wouldn't be complete without these two by my side. Both have provided me with the much-needed feedback that has helped to produce the final product of this novel. Their selflessness incomparable and I will be forever grateful for the input I have received from them. My family are truly my backbone and I appreciate them all.

Additionally, I would like to thank my partner Stefan, who has acted as a mentor and a muse throughout my entire writing journey. Not only has he willingly and unwillingly listened to parts of this novel and given me constructive feedback. But he has acted as a sounding board and inspiration for the creation of both the title and blurb of this book. I am truly grateful for the support both him and his family have offered me.

Furthermore, I would like to thank all those who have supported my journey and shown an ongoing interest in the development of The Vacation Lodge series. I truly appreciate each and every review that I have received and the ongoing love that has been spread through social media. Since publishing, I have been able to network with a variety of people from all walks of life and this has been mainly through the use of the internet. I appreciate the support of every single one of you and I pray that the word continues to spread even further.

And last but not least, I would like to thank all of my employers, both past and present for consciously and subconsciously reminding me daily how important it was for me to complete this novel and share it with the world. For that, I am truly grateful.

ABOUT THE AUTHOR

Dionne Jennene Walters, the author of The Vacation Lodge series, is a captivating erotic novelist who was born and raised in South London, England. Studying at both City University and Goldsmiths University, she has achieved qualifications in Sociology, Criminology and Education. Her studies have helped her develop an intricate understanding of people, behaviour, motives and the way that we learn. As a young child, Walters always showed a strong interest in the performing arts and poetry. And her work as a teacher re-ignited her passion for performances and creative writing that had the ability to capture the audience's attention. Walters holds a strong belief in the power behind words. When they are used wisely, she believes words can excite, inspire and enable anyone to get whatever they desire in life.

Lightning Source UK Ltd.
Milton Keynes UK
UKHW012018191121
394249UK00001B/139